"How 'bout soon? There we're both free."

Ryan was asking her on a date. Expected, she thought, and yet unexpected.

"I don't think that's wise."

"Is there a rule against employees dating? Because your grandmother eloped with your staff minister."

"No, there's no rule. That's not the reason."

"Another man? The doctor at the clinic?"

He had heard Bridget discussing Dr. Hall with her grandmother. "No." *Not yet*, she silently added.

"Then what's stopping you?"

"I don't think we have the same objectives when it comes to relationships."

"It's just dinner." Ryan's voice had dropped to a husky level that made concentrating hard.

"And therein lies the problem." Drawing on her willpower, she straightened. "I'm not interested in just dinner or hanging out or friends with benefits. I'm looking for a guy who's ready now to commit to me and to having a family and who's content making Mustang Valley his home. I don't believe that describes you."

Dear Reader,

Once, sometimes it feels like ages ago, I co-owned and managed a commercial construction company. It actually wasn't that long ago—only four years, in fact—since writing became my only job. But it often seems like decades.

I've always drawn on personal experiences for my books in that I owned and rode horses almost my entire life. I still get to play with horses when I visit my son every week, so it's not as if I've given them up entirely. But I seldom include aspects from my days as a construction company co-owner in my books. That was until *The Cowboy's Perfect Match*. Ryan DeMere is a man of many talents. In addition to being a skilled wrangler, he's not bad with a hammer. He's also ambitious. In order to achieve his goal of owning his own construction company, he flips houses. And he also just happens to be really good-looking!

Bridget O'Malley is the perfect match for Ryan. He knows it and so does she. Except she's not sure she wants to wait until he's achieved his career goals. She's on the fast track to having a family, while he'd like to be more established first. It's a tough situation for both of them, and I hope you enjoy discovering how they reach their happily-ever-after.

Warmest wishes,

Cathy McDavid

HEARTWARMING

The Cowboy's Perfect Match

——

Cathy McDavid

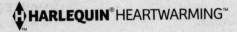

HARLEQUIN® HEARTWARMING™

Recycling programs
for this product may
not exist in your area.

ISBN-13: 978-1-335-51065-5

The Cowboy's Perfect Match

Copyright © 2019 by Cathy McDavid

HARLEQUIN®
www.Harlequin.com

Printed in U.S.A.

Since 2006, *New York Times* bestselling author **Cathy McDavid** has been happily penning contemporary Westerns for Harlequin. Every day, she gets to write about handsome cowboys riding the range or busting a bronc. It's a tough job, but she's willing to make the sacrifice. Cathy shares her Arizona home with her own real-life sweetheart and a trio of odd pets. Her grown twins have left to embark on lives of their own, and she couldn't be prouder of their accomplishments.

Books by Cathy McDavid

Harlequin Western Romance

Mustang Valley

Cowboy for Keeps
Her Holiday Rancher
Come Home, Cowboy
Having the Rancher's Baby
Rescuing the Cowboy
A Baby for the Deputy
The Cowboy's Twin Surprise
The Bull Rider's Valentine

Harlequin Heartwarming

The Sweetheart Ranch

A Cowboy's Christmas Proposal

Visit the Author Profile page
at Harlequin.com for more titles.

To my new Heartwarming sisters who have welcomed me from the start and treated me like a member of the family. Big hug.

CHAPTER ONE

RARELY DID ANYONE beat Bridget O'Malley to the kitchen. Most mornings, she rose by 5:00 a.m. and was elbow-deep in preparing breakfast before her younger sister, Molly, stumbled through the door at six thirty. Grandma Em didn't arrive until seven.

Roll out croissant dough. Soften butter. Slice strawberries and squeeze oranges. Grind coffee beans.

Bridget mentally reviewed the tasks ahead while crossing the spacious parlor, her feet barely making a noise as she expertly avoided the floorboards she knew would creak.

Entering her most sacred of sanctuaries, she drew up short at the sight of both her sister and grandmother sitting at the kitchen table, nonchalantly sipping coffee and eating yogurt parfaits that were intended for Sweetheart Ranch's guests.

"What are you both doing up so early?" Bridget sighed with mild annoyance—she'd have to make more parfaits—and grabbed her apron off the hook. With the practiced ease of someone who'd done this every day of her life since she was fifteen, she slipped the neck loop over her head and knotted the belt.

"I have some things to go over with the two of you before work starts." Grandma Em motioned for Bridget to join them at the table. She didn't live at the ranch, so her early appearance was even more unusual. "This is the only time today all three of us are free."

Bridget put a kettle of water on the stove before sitting. Her brain didn't fully function without the assistance of her ritual morning tea. Steeped, thank you, with boiling water poured slowly over a bag. No instant or those little pods for her.

"Are you wondering about the hayride and cookout tonight?"

"Among other things," Molly answered. "All twelve guests have signed up. Did you finalize the menu?"

"Not quite." Bridget grabbed a stack of guest-meal requests off the table and shuffled the papers like a deck of cards. "Our most recent newlyweds in cabin two want the zucchini, bacon and Gruyère quiche for brunch this morning. Cabin three is gluten-intolerant and cabin five is pescatarian."

"What's that?" Grandma Em asked.

"Eats fish and seafood but no meat."

"Ah. Learn something new every day."

Sweetheart Ranch boasted six cabins in total and construction was scheduled to begin in the fall on another two. Business had been booming since the ranch recently appeared in the Valentine's Day issue of *Southwest Bride* magazine. According to the article, it was one of the top-ten most romantic wedding venues in Arizona.

Additional cabins weren't the only planned expansion. Starting this week they'd added a hayride that ended with a campfire and cookout. Once they hired a full-time wrangler, they'd offer guided trail rides and a monthly "cowboy day." The food part of the operation was also growing. In addition to wedding cakes, continental breakfasts and a specialty honeymoon brunch, light catering was now available.

That last idea had been Bridget's. Grandma Em was owner of the ranch and head wedding coordinator. Molly assisted their grandmother and was in charge of guest relations. Bridget handled the food. Sweetheart Ranch wasn't just a family-run business, it was truly a labor of love. In more ways than one.

I'm thinking of surf and turf," Bridget said. "Grilled shrimp for the pescatarians and anybody else. Steak for the rest. I can easily roast ears of corn on the fire. Then side salad and rolls, both regular and gluten-free."

"Doesn't sound cowboyish enough," Molly mused. "We are a Western-themed wedding ranch."

"I'll add beans."

She shrugged. "I like that."

Not pinto beans, Bridget decided as she shut off the stove and prepared her tea. She couldn't bring herself to serve the unimaginative cowboy standby. Instead, she'd prepare Mexican *charro* beans with just a few poblano peppers for a touch of heat.

Grandma Em went on to talk about their upcoming weddings. April was going to be a busy month for them, as were May and, especially, June. They'd recently set a ranch record on Valentine's Day. Eight ceremonies over a twelve-hour period. They'd be having almost as many ceremonies every Saturday in June.

Several couples had made unusual requests that required extra attention. Everything from a paralyzed groom walking with the aid of a robotic exoskeleton to the ranch's first-ever canine ring bearer to a surprise flash-mob procession down the aisle that would be a huge surprise to the guests.

"The Literary Ladies book club requested

a lunch on the sixteenth." Grandma Em consulted her paper calendar. She was old-school.

Bridget preferred her electronic tablet and was seldom without the device. Not only did she store her recipes and research potential new menu items, but she also kept a detailed calendar and multiple lists without which she'd be a disorganized mess.

"I'm free that day. Do you know what they want?"

"They're thinking along the line of finger sandwiches." Grandma Em passed Bridget a piece of paper. "But I told them you'd call this week and finalize the details. Here's the contact info."

"This is great!" Bridget entered the name and number, her to-do list growing. She'd been considering adding wine tastings and English high teas to the ranch's offerings. The Literary Ladies' lunch would be a good test run.

Molly then brought up their projected reservations and several housekeeping issues, after which she distributed the first-quarter financials.

Giving the reports a cursory glance—the finances were really Molly and Grandma Em's department—Bridget looked at the clock. Six forty-two! At this rate, she'd never get the continental breakfast served in time. Guests started wandering into the main house around seven o'clock, their stomachs growling.

She pushed back from the table and jumped to her feet. "Keep talking. I need to get busy."

While she arranged a mouth-watering selection of homemade croissants and breads on a tray, Grandma Em and Molly continued their discussion. Ranch business soon gave way to the subject of Molly's boyfriend, Owen. He'd asked to bring his three children along on the hayride tonight, if no one minded.

"Of course he can," Grandma Em assured Molly. "He's family."

Both Grandma Em and Molly were deliriously happy. Grandma Em had eloped last November with Homer Foxworthy, a retired minister and Sweetheart Ranch's on-staff wedding officiator. Molly was seriously dating Owen, Homer's great-nephew. Bridget suspected her sister and Owen would one day soon be reserving the chapel for their own nuptials. Unlike their grandmother, Molly would never elope. She was a white-dress, big-splashy-wedding kind of gal.

Bridget remained the sole unattached O'Malley woman. She'd like to say she didn't care. Truthfully, she harbored a tiny bit of jealousy toward her grandmother and younger sister. Happy for them, absolutely. They deserved the wonderful men they'd found. But Bridget also envied them. At thirty-two, her biological clock was ticking. Not fast but faster than it had been. Another birthday looming in the near future and no immediate prospects weren't helping.

Mustang Valley was a cowboy town with a substantial male population. Though Bridget would admit it to no one, that perk was one of the reasons she'd accepted her grandmother's job offer last year. So far, she'd yet to meet anyone with real potential.

Then again, she spent most of her time working, often putting in fifty to sixty hours a week. By the end of the day, she wanted nothing more than to unwind in front of the TV for an hour and rest her aching feet. Most nights she was in bed by nine.

Rushing back and forth between the kitchen and the parlor, Bridget quickly laid out the food. Besides the scrumptious breads and croissants, she'd included fruit salad, homemade jams and almond butter, yogurt parfaits and two choices of fresh-squeezed juices.

There! The room looked beautiful enough to appear in a TV commercial.

Wait a minute. What a great idea! She should tell Molly. Along with everything else she did, the younger O'Malley sister handled the ranch's marketing and advertising.

"Hey," Bridget announced as she entered the kitchen. "What if we do a TV commercial?"

She was met with complete silence. Molly and Grandma Em had left at some point through the back door.

No big deal. She'd tell Molly later. Grabbing her tablet off the counter, Bridget opened up her "idea" file and quickly typed in a note about making a TV commercial. Her eyes fell briefly on yet another of her many lists, this one titled "dating nonnegotiables." Any man she met who failed to meet her criteria wasn't worth pursuing.

Her family teased her about the list, told her she was being ridiculous and limiting her chances. Look at Molly, for example. She'd found a wonderful man who, at first meeting, had seemed completely wrong for her. Bridget didn't care. She wanted a marriage like her mother and late father once had. She'd rather be alone than marry the wrong man, which was the mistake her mother had made with her current husband, Bridget's stepfather.

A few minutes into slicing fresh zucchini for cabin two's quiche, Bridget heard the echo of heavy footsteps in the parlor and assumed the first guests had arrived for breakfast. She wondered if the footsteps belonged to the middle-aged couple who'd been there since Thursday, enjoying a second honeymoon.

"Hello!" a male voice called out. "Anyone here?"

"Help yourself," Bridget answered and wiped her hands on a dish towel. "There's coffee, tea, hot chocolate and juice at the beverage station."

"I can have whatever I want?" he asked, uncertainty in his tone.

"Sure."

She smiled to herself. Must be the groom from cabin five. He and his bride had gotten married two days ago and remained holed up in their cabin since then. When Bridget delivered the couple's specialty brunch yesterday morning, only the bride had come to the door. Bridget guessed the groom had still been in bed and thought "good for them."

Brushing aside a stray lock of hair, she hurried to the parlor and issued a warm greeting to the groom. "Good morning. Nice to see you." She refrained from adding "At last."

He paused, a china plate in one hand and a pair of tongs in the other. His gaze took her in from head to toe, very slowly and very thoroughly. The corners of his wide, handsome mouth turned up into a grin that quickly spread across his entire face. "Nice to see you, too."

There was no mistaking the spark of male interest in his eyes.

"I, um…" Bridget faltered, completely thrown off guard. Grooms didn't respond to her like this. Not that she'd experienced before. She immediately wanted out of this very awkward situation. "If you need anything, just let me know."

"You could join me." His grin widened, and he raised his china plate. "If you haven't eaten yet."

Of all the nerve! He was flirting with her.

When she first glimpsed him, she'd thought how lucky his wife was to marry a tall, good-looking man like him. If not for the fact he was a groom, she'd have mistaken him for one of the local cowboys, what with his well-fitting Wranglers, scuffed boots, Western work shirt and Stetson, which he'd removed and hung on the antique hat rack in the corner.

Now she felt sorry for the bride. They'd been married a mere two days, and her husband was hitting on another woman. Hard as it was for her, Bridget refrained from giving him a piece of her mind.

"Hey, this is good," he said, biting into a croissant.

"Thank you." She pivoted and started for the kitchen.

"Wait. Can't you stay a while?"

She very nearly blurted, "Does your wife have any idea what a jerk you are?" but held her tongue. He was a guest at the ranch, and she wouldn't offend him.

All of a sudden her grandmother glided into the parlor. She barely noticed Bridget and instead addressed the man. "Good, you're here. And getting some breakfast." She patted Bridget's arm as she skirted past her. "Thanks for taking care of him."

"My pleasure," Bridget answered tersely.

"I got distracted and forgot to tell you earlier that Ryan was coming by."

Her grandmother's words caused Bridget to stop short. "Ryan?"

"He's applying for the wrangler job. He bought the old Chandler place. Nora introduced us the other day. She says he's a heck of a worker."

Nora being her grandmother's best friend, a part-time employee of the ranch when they were shorthanded, and neighbor to the Chandlers before they'd moved. She'd talked more than once about the nice, young, single man next door, emphasizing *single*.

"Oh. I didn't know." Bridget felt her cheeks warm. Thank goodness she'd kept her mouth shut. "Nice to meet you, Ryan. Good luck with the interview."

In the kitchen she expelled a long breath, vastly relieved. Meeting Ryan had left her disconcerted. First, because she'd mistaken him for the groom from cabin five. Then, because once she learned he was Nora's neighbor, she'd been briefly intrigued by him.

Remembering he'd purchased the Chandler place put an end to that. To call the old house, with its ramshackle outbuildings, a fixer-upper was being kind. In truth, it was a dump, and owning a decent home ranked number eight on Bridget's dating nonnegotiable list.

"BRING THAT WITH you and let's head to the kitchen."

"Thank you, ma'am." Ryan DeMere followed Mrs. Foxworthy, owner of Sweetheart Ranch. He carried his loaded plate of food in one hand and a glass of orange juice in the other.

Had he overindulged? The way the older woman looked at his plate had him wondering. Ryan did possess a healthy appetite, brought on by working long, hard hours. Plus, the food here was incredible. He generally preferred a hearty country breakfast. Eggs, biscuits, sausages, gravy and hash browns. Fancy breads and fruit were for folks a lot daintier than him.

But these rolls—he'd never tasted anything like them. Darn things just melted in his mouth, and he couldn't stop at one. Or two.

Okay, he'd taken four, having quickly polished off the first one. The rest were stacked on his plate along with three heaping spoonfuls of strawberry jam and a pile of fruit. He supposed that deserved a look. Of concern, if nothing else. Then again, she didn't know about the first croissant, unless her granddaughter tattled on him.

Bridget. He'd caught her name when Mrs. Foxworthy called her by it. She was obviously the cook. No, that wasn't right. His neighbor had referred to Bridget as a chef of some kind. Pastry, maybe? Sous? The other granddaughter helped with the business side and was dating the feed-store owner. He'd met the man several times while buying supplies for his horse but hadn't made the connection until recently, when his neighbor told him about the job opening at the ranch.

Mustang Valley wasn't large by any means. According to the welcome sign at the center of town, there were two thousand residents, give or take. Ryan was probably the newest one, having moved here less than two months ago, when he'd purchased the Chandler place. A run-down, sorry piece of horse property by anyone's standards with a house that most would consider uninhabitable.

It was also perfect for his purposes. In a year to eighteen months, depending on how much the renovations wound up costing, he intended to sell the property for a nice profit.

He'd do it, too. Ryan was no rookie when it came to flipping horse properties. This was his fourth project in eight years. He'd done very well with his first three. If all went as planned, in a few years he'd make enough money to buy his dream ranch. Only then would he settle down in one place.

"Have a seat." Mrs. Foxworthy motioned to the table. "We can talk here, if you don't mind Bridget hovering nearby."

"No, ma'am. I don't."

Not at all. For starters, she was easy on the eyes. Bouncy reddish-blond hair framing the face of an angel, when she wasn't scowling. Nice figure, from what he could tell. That apron did her no favors. Dancing green eyes, his particular weakness. And a great cook.

Could be a little friendlier. Then again, she might not have appreciated his...exuberance. Ryan couldn't help himself. She was an attractive woman. His neighbor, Nora, had said as much, but Ryan took that with a grain of salt.

Then he'd seen Bridget, and his brain turned to mush.

But if he wanted this job—and he did want it—he needed to rein in his enthusiasm. Ryan was the owner of a healthy bank account. But all that money was earmarked for remodeling the house, and he'd need every penny, if not more.

When it came to covering his day-to-day living expenses, he relied entirely on money he earned from side jobs. Those funds were running dangerously low. This past week, he'd begun subsiding on boxed macaroni-and-cheese and bologna sandwiches. Another reason he was currently making a pig of himself.

"Our part-time wrangler wants to retire," Mrs. Foxworthy explained. She'd helped herself to a cup of coffee after offering one to Ryan. "With trail rides starting soon and the addition of three more horses to our stables, we need someone full-time. I forgot to ask, do you have much experience with driving a carriage and hay wagon?"

"Yes, ma'am, I do."

"Call me Emily, please."

"Thank you, Emily." Ryan pushed aside his plate of food. Cramming his face wouldn't look good during an interview. He could finish later.

"I grew up on a working farm outside of Austin. Fourth generation."

"I thought I recognized your drawl. I have relatives from that part of Texas. What kind of farm?"

"Wheat, mostly. Raised some cattle. 'Course, our horses pulled farm wagons. Not fancy carriages. But I'm thinking the mechanics are pretty much the same."

"Bridget and her sister are fifth generation here in Mustang Valley."

She smiled at her granddaughter, who was busy at the counter beating eggs in a bowl. He could see the love Emily had for her granddaughter, and his respect for the older woman increased. Ryan was close to his family, too.

"I'm the youngest of eight," he said. "My parents had a lot of mouths to feed and shoes to buy. We all had to pitch in from an early age. I was harnessing a team by the time I was ten. Driving a tractor when I was eight. Riding horses since, well, I honestly don't remember how old I was when I started riding."

He noticed Bridget sneaking discreet peeks at him as if trying to hide her curiosity. It went both ways. He was curious about her, too, and sneaking peeks.

"Are your parents still in Texas?" Emily asked.

"They are. I'm trying to talk them into moving here after Dad retires. Not sure when that'll be. He's darn near seventy, and still putting in eight-hour days, every day of the week."

"Sounds like you have an excellent work ethic that you come by honestly."

"Yes, ma'am, I do, if I say so myself. I'm also right handy. There isn't much I can't fix or build or cobble together. If you're needing some repairs done, I'm your man."

"That's generous of you to offer." She sipped her coffee. "I'm afraid the hours aren't regular. We perform weddings on any given day, including holidays. Most are on weekends, which means you'd probably work Friday through Sunday."

"Not a problem." Ryan finished off his fruit, remembering to take smaller bites. "My schedule's flexible. And I have no place special to be on weekends."

He caught Bridget casting him another quick glance. How had she interpreted his remark? That he was currently unattached? Well, he was. What about her?

Ryan hadn't been in a serious relationship for some time and didn't see it happening now or in the immediate future. Flipping horse properties didn't allow him to remain in one place very long and most women he met wanted to put down roots. He occasionally dated when the right woman came along—one who was okay with a casual, hanging-out kind of relationship.

Unfortunately, Bridget struck him as a woman with deep, deep roots, being fifth generation and all. Yet another reason to rein in his enthusiasm. Plus, if he got the job she'd be his boss's granddaughter. Darn if those "keep away" signs weren't springing up one after the other.

"Starting tonight, we're having regular hayrides," Emily said. "In the evenings when the weather's warm and in the afternoons during winter months. Right now, we're limiting the hayrides to guests. If they go well, we might open them up to the public. There's a cookout at the end of each ride."

"Sounds great." Ryan glanced at Bridget. She was probably responsible for the food.

"Perhaps you'd like to come along tonight," Emily suggested.

He returned his attention to her. "I'd like that very much." Was she offering him the job? He hesitated because he didn't want to jump to the wrong conclusion.

"You can ride with Big Jim. He's our part-time wrangler. Maybe come early and watch him harness the team."

Ryan finished off his remaining croissant,

using the last piece to mop up his strawberry jam. Emily didn't seem to find him ill-mannered. If anything, she liked his enjoyment of her granddaughter's food.

"How many horses do you have?" he asked.

"Five. Two for driving and three for trail rides. We're planning on offering either sixty- or ninety-minute trail rides. Up to twice a day, one couple each ride."

During their entire conversation, the sound of guests entering the parlor through the front door and helping themselves to the breakfast could be heard. Twice, Bridget carried out a tray or pitcher to replenish the food. In between, she sliced and chopped and mixed and diced.

"I suppose you'd like to know the pay," Emily said.

The amount she named was fair. The perks were better. Besides breakfast every day, Ryan would get dinner at the cookouts and during any other function when a meal was served. Emily was hoping the ranch could eventually host nonwedding events, like family reunions and corporate parties.

There was also double time on holidays as well as paid sick and vacation days after six months. Altogether, considerably more than Ryan had expected.

If he had an inkling to stay past the sale of his latest ranch-flipping project, a job like this one—with growth potential—would be right up his alley. In the meantime, he'd work hard for the O'Malleys. Everything about the job appealed to him, including his coworkers. One in particular.

"I don't like to assume, Emily, but are you officially offering me the job?"

She laughed. "Sorry. I should have been clearer. Yes, I am. Nora's recommendation carries a lot of weight with me. As does Owen's."

"You talk to him?"

"Right before you got here. He thinks you're a straight shooter."

"I try to be."

"Am I to assume you're considering accepting the job?" she asked. "Please take some time to think about it. We're in a rush but not so much we can't wait a day or two."

"I don't need any time to think about it." He reached across the table toward Emily. "I accept."

She shook his hand. "Welcome to Sweetheart Ranch, Ryan. Glad to have you with us."

He couldn't stop his gaze from cutting quickly to Bridget. She was openly staring at him.

"There's some paperwork to sign. Molly will

see to that. She's busy at the moment, though. Meeting with a potential client. She should be free in about an hour." Emily checked the clock on the wall. "Speaking of which, I have an appointment myself at the bank. Otherwise, I'd take you on a tour of the ranch. You can meet Big Jim and, if you're not busy, go with him on the honeymoon carriage ride later this morning."

"I can do that." Ryan waited for Emily to rise first before pushing to his feet. "What time? I'll come back."

"Nonsense. You're here now. No need to make a second trip." She turned to her granddaughter. "Bridget, you'll be finished shortly, won't you?"

"I still have to deliver brunch to cabin two."

"Ryan can go with you," Emily announced. "Then you can take him to the stables and introduce him to Big Jim."

"I need to clean up the parlor."

"It'll keep for a while."

"An unattended buffet won't look good. Molly will be showing the potential client around."

"Molly may want to offer them breakfast. Could be just the ticket to close the sale."

"The food here is good," Ryan concurred.

"Grandma... I—" Bridget blew out an expansive breath. "Fine. I'll do it."

"Great." The older woman swiped her hands together, clearly pleased with this latest turn of events. "I'll see you tonight at the hayride, Ryan, if not sooner."

"Thank you again, Emily, for the opportunity."

"I have a good feeling about this."

"Me, too."

"You can wait here for Bridget."

He sat down after Emily left through the back door.

From across the kitchen Bridget uttered a sound of distress. It might have been because of whatever she was cooking. She did have the oven door cracked open and was staring inside. It also might have been because of her grandmother forcing Ryan on her.

Unable to help himself, he chuckled softly. Working at Sweetheart Ranch was shaping up to be far better than he'd ever imagined.

CHAPTER TWO

"SWEET!" RYAN STOPPED to admire the trim, sleek, fire-engine-red vehicle parked behind the ranch house. "Top speed, how fast can this baby fly?"

Bridget was securing the insulated food container holding brunch for cabin two in the vehicle's rear bed. She then straightened to give him an exasperated look. "You're kidding."

"Not at all." Ryan continued his inspection, circling the front of the vehicle and pausing at the passenger side. "Forty-eight-volt motor, right? I bet you can do eighteen easy. Twenty on the downhill."

"It's a golf cart."

"And a beauty at that. Electric. Eco-friendly." He gave a low whistle of appreciation. "Top-of-the-line and brand-spanking-new."

"Let's go," she told him and slid behind the steering wheel.

He hopped in beside her. "No seat belts?"

"What's the matter?" She turned the key, and the motor purred softly. "Afraid I'm going to push you out?"

He laughed, glad to see she had a sense of humor.

"Hold on to your hat." She released the brake, pressed down with her foot and away they went—at about fifteen miles per hour by Ryan's calculations.

"You have a nice home." He looked back over his shoulder as they pulled away. "Don't see many like it in these parts."

"My great-great-grandparents built the original house in the late 1800s. They were one of the first families to settle in Mustang Valley. Every generation since has remodeled to some degree. Grandma doubled the size of the kitchen when she decided to convert the ranch into a wedding venue and bed-and-breakfast. Made enough room for a walk-in pantry and four-door refrigerator."

"The cabins are new." Ryan studied the row of cozy, identical pine structures with redbrick chimneys and green gable roofs.

"As of last summer. Grandma designed them to resemble the house, with my sister Molly's input. Each one caters to honeymooning couples. Spa tubs. Enclosed courtyards. Privacy windows."

"Maybe you'll give me a tour one of these days, seeing as I can't look inside."

His remark earned him another pained expression from Bridget. "Are you ever serious?"

"No fun in that. Besides, I'm interested strictly from a design standpoint. I'm renovating the Chandler place." He supposed he should start calling it the DeMere place, seeing as he was the owner and not the Chandlers. Then again, since he wouldn't be owning the property for long, sticking to the original name might prove a good idea. It had history, something potentially appealing to a buyer.

"Oh. I didn't realize." Bridget turned right, taking them past the pool and clubhouse. "Though I should have. No offense, but the property needs a ton of work."

"I'm not offended. It does. The run-down condition is the only reason I could afford it." Ryan prided himself on buying smart and selling smarter. "Are the clubhouse and pool also new?"

They puttered past a long narrow building and wrought-iron railing through which Ryan could see sunlight reflecting off sparkling blue water.

"No, but Grandma had everything completely refurbished and modernized. In its former life, the clubhouse was an equipment shed."

Ryan's interest was piqued. "Is there by chance a pool table in there?"

"Nope. Sorry. Just a Ping-Pong table and dartboard."

"Too bad."

"You'll have to go to the Poco Dinero Bar and Grill in town to play pool."

"Why, Miss O'Malley. Are you asking me out on a date?"

She shook her head and rolled her eyes. "Are you always like this?"

"Endearing? Charismatic? 'Fraid so."

"I was thinking annoying and irritating and very full of yourself."

"Give me time. I have a tendency to grow on people."

Bridget sighed and aimed the golf cart toward the second-to-last cabin in the line of six. "I can see why Nora likes you. You're her type."

Ryan held on to the side handle when Bridget pulled to a stop, braking a bit harder than was necessary. Perhaps she really was trying to eject him.

"She's my type, too," he said. "Or she would be if she was younger." His neighbor had to be in her midseventies, possibly older. "Then again, I'm a hip guy and might be able to see past the forty-five-year age difference."

"Wait here," Bridget instructed and turned off the golf cart.

Ryan started to get out. "Need help?"

"No, thanks. I can manage." With a quick flip of her fingers, she unfastened the insulated container and carried it up the short walk to the cabin's front steps.

Ryan watched her, his attention riveted. All the time he kept thinking, *too bad*. Too bad she was his new boss's granddaughter. Too bad she was a settling-down kind of gal. Too bad he needed to behave himself, though she'd probably argue he'd been anything but behaving himself on their short drive.

She marched more than walked to the cabin's front door. Independent, he thought. Feisty. Smart. Talented. Capable. Pretty. Very, very pretty. Those reddish-blond curls of hers were an invitation shouting "Touch me." He'd discover for himself if her hair felt as silky as it appeared, except she'd no doubt slap away his hand.

At her sharp knock, a young man opened the cabin door. A few words were exchanged, and he took the insulated container. Bridget bade him goodbye and marched back to the golf cart with the same purpose as before, her arms swinging at her sides this time.

Did she realize she still wore her apron? Perhaps the garment was so second nature to her, she forgot she had it on.

The moment she climbed back into the golf cart, a musical chime sounded. Reaching into the pocket on her apron bib, she extracted her cell phone and read a text.

"Grandma says Big Jim's going to be a few minutes late."

"Should we go back to the house?" Ryan asked. "If your sister's free, I can fill out my employment paperwork."

"Big Jim won't be long. I'll drop you off at the stables. You can wait for him there."

Yet another *too bad*. In this case, too bad their time together was at an end.

The stables were located farther up the road, a quarter mile past the last cabin. Even at fifteen miles per hour, they made good time. Ryan took in the structure and uttered a low "Wow!"

"We recently expanded the stables as well," Bridget said. "Four more stalls and we increased the size of the paddock out back."

Ryan had built covered stalls at the last two properties he'd flipped. Neither were as nice as these stables, which, while not large, were on par with professional horse ranches. Then again, the stalls he'd built were for private use and not to impress paying guests or appear in magazines.

Bridget parked beside the hitching rail. He expected to be dropped off and left to his own devices while he waited on the soon-to-retire wrangler. To Ryan's vast delight, she shut off the golf cart and hopped out.

"Come on. I'll show you around." Pride tinged her voice. She didn't just work for her grandmother, she loved the ranch.

"I'd like that," he said.

The stables' main door stood open, and Bridget went inside first. Ryan crossed the threshold behind her and stopped to stare.

Windows allowed ample natural illumination, eliminating the need for electric lights during bright sunny days like this one. Nickers filled the air as heads immediately popped over stall doors, eager to investigate the newcomers. The scents of hay and leather and grain filled the air.

"I'm impressed." He went over to the far wall, where the harnesses hung in neat order. Running his hand down the length of a large collar, he noted the fine craftsmanship and pristine condition. Much better than anything his family had ever owned.

"Riding gear's over there." Bridget pointed to the other wall, where a variety of saddles sat perched on racks and bridles dangled from wooden pegs.

Every piece looked recently cleaned and recently polished. Also much better than anything his family owned.

Feeling a little like a fish out of water, he meandered over to the nearest horse. Happy for the attention, the large blond gelding nuzzled Ryan's palm when he extended it.

"Haflinger," he said, then noticed the other horse in the next stall over. They were a perfect match, like twin bookends. "Your driving team, I assume."

"That's Amos." Bridget joined Ryan. "The other is Moses. They're brothers."

"I figured as much."

"These are our recent purchases." She indicated the three quarter horses in the adjoining stalls. "For trail rides. We bought them from a horse rental outfit in Apache Junction."

"They appear tame enough." Ryan estimated the trio were in their late teens and seasoned veterans.

"A lot of our clients have little or no experience riding. We don't want to put them on anything that isn't one-hundred-percent trustworthy. These three are perfect lambs."

"You ride much?"

She moved to pat the nearest broad face and received a contented snort in return. "When I can get away from work. Which isn't often enough. We've been going like gangbusters since we opened last November."

She enjoyed riding. Yet another reason for Ryan to like this woman, who was fascinating him more and more with each new tidbit she revealed.

"Pleasure riding?" he guessed. "No, competitive."

"Both. I grew up active in 4-H and competed in Western horsemanship classes. Later, I took up team roping for a while. Semiprofessionally."

Ryan broke into a wide grin. "We have a lot in common. I team-roped, too." He'd used the money from his winnings as a down payment on his first property. "Why'd you quit?"

"Culinary school. Le Cordon Bleu College." More pride tinged her voice. "It's one of the top schools in the southwest."

No question about it, Bridget O'Malley was so far out of Ryan's league, she might as well reside in outer space.

A horn sounded from outside, accompanied by the crunch of tires on gravel.

Bridget started for the door. "Must be Big Jim."

After introductions were exchanged—Ryan liked the older gentleman right away—Bridget excused herself, claiming she had a lot of work waiting for her.

Her remark reminded Ryan of the hayride and cookout. "See you tonight," he said.

She paused halfway into the golf cart, a puzzled expression on her face. The next instant, realization dawned. "Yeah. Right. See you."

He watched her go before accompanying Big Jim into the stables, his ego suffering a mighty blow.

Clearly, she'd made a far greater impression on him than he had on her.

THE FIRST THING Bridget did when she got back to the ranch house was head to the parlor, where she checked the breakfast sign-in sheet. All the couples had come and gone, the exception being cabin two, whose brunch Bridget had delivered before taking Ryan to the stables.

He was an interesting sort, she thought as she carted trays of food and dirty dishware to the kitchen. An outrageous flirt with enough charm to win over the shyest of wallflowers. Despite seeing right through him, Bridget had not been unaffected and responded more times than she cared to admit.

She'd liked the timbre of his voice when he spoke about his family and heard the fondness he had for them. Having close family ties was a quality she admired in a person. She'd also been quite taken with the expression on his face when he first glimpsed the stables. He'd been genuinely impressed.

And, yes, he was handsome. Not to mention sexy in a rugged, cowboy way. She estimated him to be roughly her age. Maybe a couple years younger. Could she sneak a look at his paperwork without drawing her sister's attention? No, that would be silly and immature.

What did she care how old Ryan was? Other than his age being near hers, she doubted he checked off any other boxes on her list of dating nonnegotiables.

All right, two boxes if she included his looks. No, make that three. On the tall side herself, she appreciated his six-foot-plus height. Dark brown hair the color of chocolate truffles was in direct contrast to a pair of blue-grey eyes that drew her in. His two-day beard, which she should have regarded as scruffy, instead elicited the kind of thrill she shouldn't be feeling.

But that was as far as it went. Even though he was gainfully employed, he didn't strike her as career-driven—another box on her list—and, thus, he was completely wrong for her.

Bridget was ambitious, and also convinced she'd fare better with a guy similar to herself. Her parents had been well-suited in that regard—equal partners rather than one carrying the other. She frequently witnessed her mother's struggles for that equal partnership with her current husband and vowed to avoid winding up in similar circumstances.

Being a realist, Bridget knew men like her late father were rare. That didn't stop her from holding out. Neither did the pressure from her loudly ticking biological clock.

Finishing her tasks one by one, she was engrossed with peeling shrimp for tonight's cookout when her grandmother came up behind her and gave her a peck on the cheek.

"Hey there. How'd it go with our new wrangler?"

"Okay, I guess. I left him with Big Jim."

Grandma Em ducked into the pantry, where Bridget knew she'd leave her purse out of sight on a lower shelf. She emerged a moment later and went straight for the refrigerator, selecting an egg-and-cheese burrito for lunch.

"You want one?" she asked.

"No, I ate earlier." Bridget refused to serve their guests food that wasn't at the peak of freshness. As a result, the O'Malleys dined well on leftovers.

"I just saw them." Grandma sat at the table. "Big Jim and Ryan. They were returning from taking cabin two on their carriage ride through town. Ryan was doing the driving."

"That was quick. Harnessing usually takes a while."

"Not with two people."

"True." Bridget finished with the shrimp and, after a last rinse, she sealed them in a container.

"What do you think of him?"

"Ryan? Hard to say. I just met him." No way would she admit she'd been smitten and responded to his flirtations. Her grandmother would have a field day with that. "He seems nice. And friendly. Maybe a little too friendly."

"That's the way people are in the part of Texas where he's from." Grandma Em added a healthy dollop of hot sauce to her burrito before taking another bite. "They tend to lay it on a mite thick."

"The guests will like him." Putting the shrimp in the refrigerator, Bridget grabbed a bottle of water and sat with her grandmother at the table.

"He was checking you out. I saw him."

"What! No."

"You were checking him out, too."

"I was not." Bridget's protest was met with a laugh. An alarming thought occurred to her. Grandma Em had attempted more than once to play matchmaker with her granddaughters.

"Tell me you didn't hire him simply because he's single and attractive."

"Aha! So you admit it."

"I have eyes. I noticed. There, are you satisfied?"

"A little." Grandma Em smiled brightly. "I hired him because he's qualified, highly recommended by Nora and personable. But if you two were to go out—"

"We're not going out."

"Don't bring up your list." She feigned exasperation. "I'd burn it if I could."

Bridget swallowed a large gulp of water, her throat dry for no apparent reason. "Fine. I won't."

"Honey."

"Grandma, please. I'm not interested in Ryan."

"All the good-looking young men in this town and not one of them appeals to you. How can that be?" her grandmother lamented. "At this rate, I'm never going to have any great-grandchildren."

"Molly will give you some. I bet Owen pops the question in the next few months. In the meantime, you can amuse yourself with his three children."

"They are adorable." She sighed wistfully,

only to promptly sober. "I hate to think of you depriving yourself."

"Of children?" Bridget asked.

"Yes, and a decent man. Like Ryan—"

"Don't say it. You only just met him. No way can you tell if he's decent or totally without morals."

"I can tell. Even though his parents didn't have a lot to go around, they raised him right."

"That, or he's proficient at conning people."

Grandma Em made a sound of disgust. "You don't believe that."

No, Bridget didn't. She was inclined to agree with her grandmother. Ryan had nice manners and an appealing openness about him. A what-you-see-is-what-you-get kind of man.

"Working with him every day, I bet you'll change your mind."

Meaning her grandmother would refuse to quit matchmaking no matter what. If Bridget didn't do something, she'd soon find herself in an awkward situation. But how to deter her grandmother?

The answer was easy. Throw her off track with a carefully calculated distraction.

"There is one man in town who kind of interests me," Bridget said.

"Who's that?"

The more she considered the idea, crazy

though it was, the more she warmed to it. "Dr. Gregory Hall."

Her grandmother's eyebrows rose in surprise only to come together in a pronounced *V.* "Word around town is he's married."

"He's not. He's divorced. Molly told me the other day. She heard it from Nora."

Dr. Hall was a relative newcomer to Mustang Valley. He'd been working at the urgent-care clinic these past seven months. In his later thirties, with clean-cut features, a pleasant bedside manner and short-cropped hair, more pepper than salt, he'd initially created quite a stir. Many of the single women in town had flocked to the clinic with invented complaints just to meet him. Not Bridget. But she had noticed him out and about on several occasions and concurred with the other women. Dr. Hall was hot.

The nonsense had stopped a few weeks after his arrival when he mentioned being married. Now, it had started up again with the news of his divorce.

"Must be recent," Grandma Em observed.

"Pretty recent, apparently. He and his wife… ex-wife," Bridget said, correcting herself, "have been separated a while. That's why he took the position at the clinic."

"Doesn't he have children?"

"A boy and a girl. Ages ten and twelve."

"Bridget, honey. Are you sure you want to get involved with a man who's barely divorced and a father to two preteens?"

"We can go slow at first."

"That's a lot to take on."

"Molly's dating a man with three young children."

"It's different with her and Owen. He's been divorced a while."

Owen was also related to Grandma Em's new husband, but Bridget didn't bring that up.

The more arguments her grandmother made, the more determined she was to potentially pursue Dr. Hall. Gregory. She should start thinking of him by his first name.

"He's exactly the kind of man I'm looking for and meets every requirement on my list."

"I'd hate to see you get hurt," Grandma Em said. "He seems nice and all, but there's a reason his marriage failed."

"He could have married for the wrong reasons. Like Mom and Doug."

Grandma Em frowned, and Bridget realized she'd crossed a line. Her grandmother was very protective of Bridget's mother.

"He's certainly no worse than Ryan," she said, "who lives in a run-down, falling-apart house and drives a beat-up old truck." Owning a decent vehicle was number five on Bridget's list. "I doubt he has two nickels to rub together."

"Don't judge a person by appearances."

"No offense, Grandma, but I can say the same thing to you. You're judging Dr. Hall by *his* appearances. Assuming that he isn't a good person or a great catch because his first marriage ended in divorce."

"Has he asked you out?"

Bridget stood. "Not yet, but he will." She tugged on her apron, then ran her fingers through her hair. "I just need to get my game on."

Granted, it had been a while since Bridget successfully set her sights on a man. She was confident, however, that her long dormant skills would come rushing back. And then her grandmother would stop trying to set her up with Ryan.

She turned and nearly choked. Ryan stood in the doorway, one shoulder propped against the jamb and a mischievous twinkle in his too-arresting eyes. How long had he been standing there, and what, if anything, had he heard?

Bridget squared her shoulders. She didn't care. Let him think what he would. It didn't matter.

"I finished signing the paperwork with Molly." He pushed off the doorjamb. "She sent me here to see if there's anything else you need done before the hayride."

"Actually—" Grandma Em rose from the table "—there's a light burned out in the chapel. We'll need the stepladder to reach it."

The wink Ryan gave her when he left confirmed what Bridget had already surmised. He'd caught some of what she said to her grandmother and found it amusing.

Really? Did he not think her capable of attracting a man? Rather than be dissuaded, her determination to wrangle a date with the hot Dr. Hall grew by leaps and bounds.

CHAPTER THREE

RYAN HELPED THE last guest climb into the hay wagon. The middle-aged woman—Ryan had heard it was a second marriage for both her and her groom—gripped his hand as she stepped from the overturned crate into the wagon's long flatbed. Her husband, who was already in the wagon, hauled her up to join him.

Slightly unsteady and flushed with both excitement and nervousness, she let out a small gasp. "My goodness!"

"I've got you, darling." Her husband anchored her against him.

"Yes, you do." She stood on tiptoes and gave him a peck on the lips.

He guided her to the only empty bale of straw, where they sat down, their hands still joined. Their obvious love for each other reminded Ryan of his own parents. All these years later, the DeMeres still sometimes acted like the pair of teenagers they'd been when they first met.

Ryan hoped to have a marriage like theirs one day. He'd have to wait, though, until he'd made enough to buy that dream ranch. He wasn't about to ask a woman to live amid crumbling walls, even if those walls would be rebuilt and unrecognizable in a year. His nomadic lifestyle and frequent hand-to-mouth survival also didn't make him the best candidate for marriage.

"Everyone ready?" Big Jim called over his shoulder.

He was answered by a chorus of loud cheers from the group of almost twenty, which included two young girls in matching outfits who were impossible for Ryan to tell apart. He picked up the overturned crate and moved it out of the way. They'd need it again when they returned from the hayride.

He hadn't required much instruction from Big Jim. Ryan had gone on plenty of hayrides during his life. His father used to hitch up the horses every Halloween and take the De-Mere kids and their many friends from house to house. He still did, only now the kids were Ryan's many nieces and nephews. Grandpa De-Mere was a favorite relative with them.

Besides Halloween, there'd been church outings and parades and birthday parties. Ryan had also driven the wagon at his cousin's wedding. He'd forgotten to mention that to Emily during their interview.

She hadn't come on the ride. Neither had Bridget, not that Ryan expected her to. He assumed she was busy with the cookout preparations. Nonetheless, he'd suffered a small stab of disappointment.

Ryan had caught only the tail end of Bridget's conversation with her grandmother earlier. Enough to know she was going out with the local doctor or wanted to go out with him. Ryan wasn't sure which. Her remarks had caused a different sort of stab—one of envy. Whoever this doctor was, Ryan didn't like him. He didn't care if the man discovered a cure for cancer, he wasn't right for Bridget.

Neither was Ryan, but that hadn't stopped the giant fist from squeezing his insides. To mask his reaction, he'd smiled and winked at Bridget when leaving with her grandmother. She hadn't responded, and Ryan had been forced to put aside thoughts of her while he handled Emily's various chores and then went home to change clothes for the hayride.

While the horses walked sedately down the long dirt road leading away from the ranch, the sun inched slowly toward the horizon. A wet spring had caused an abundance of blossoms to sprout, turning the normally dry and prickly cacti into striking displays of color that drew a variety of birds and flying insects.

Big Jim pointed out various spots of interest to their passengers. Ryan paid close attention, as he would soon be doing the same thing when he was in charge of the hayrides.

"Over there are the McDowell Mountains, home to the largest urban preserve in the continental United States," Big Jim said. "If you go on a trail ride, and I highly recommend you do, you'll travel through the northern tip of the preserve."

Two couples were already signed up for trail rides on Wednesday and two more on Friday. Ryan figured he'd be going along with Big Jim in order to learn the different routes. Too bad Bridget couldn't come with them. He'd enjoy seeing her in the saddle and away from the kitchen.

The hayride lasted a little over an hour. By then their passengers were in good spirits, hungry from an abundance of fresh air and ready to relax around the campfire.

While everyone strolled to the ranch house, where the fire pit was located, Ryan helped Big Jim unharness and brush down the horses. Ryan had been impressed with the team's performance and mentioned as much to Big Jim.

The older man patted Moses's neck before closing the door on the big gelding's stall.

"They're good boys. I'll miss working with them."

Both horses went straight for their water troughs, then examined their feed bins, which Ryan had filled right before departing on the hayride. The other three horses showed considerable interest in the goings-on only to grow bored when more food wasn't forthcoming.

"What time is the first trail ride on Wednesday?" Ryan asked. "I can bring my own horse if we need an extra one."

"Here's the problem." Big Jim closed and locked the stable door behind them. "Doris is having some tests done over the next few days." He'd mentioned his wife's heart condition earlier. While not life-threatening, it was concerning enough that she was under the care of a cardiologist. Her health issues were the main reason Big Jim wanted to retire. "Maybe Owen can go with you. He's familiar with the mountains."

"I'll ask him."

"Have yourself a good evening." Big Jim headed for his truck.

"Aren't you coming to the cookout?"

"Naw." He yanked open the driver's side door. "Doris gets nervous when she's home alone for too long."

"Good night, then."

Ryan ambled down the road leading to the ranch house. Well before he arrived at the fire pit, he smelled the delicious aroma of food cooking over hot embers. He knew this meal would far surpass the breakfast Bridget had prepared and make returning to his regular diet of bologna sandwiches hard.

She was there, bent over the fire pit and turning foil-wrapped ears of corn on a metal rack. Streaks of soot marred her cheeks and loose hair tumbled into her eyes. She brushed away the strands with the back of her hand.

Ryan was immediately captivated, not that he hadn't been from the moment they'd met.

He passed the ranch guests he'd recently driven on the hayride. Most were sitting at the picnic table or in lawn chairs and sipping adult beverages. They returned his hellos, some thanking him again for the hayride. The two girls insisted on venturing too close to the fire pit and had to be warned away repeatedly by their parents.

Bridget worked quickly, expertly flipping steaks and skewers of shrimp and stirring a cast-iron pot of beans. She fussed and fretted as if creating a masterpiece.

Coming up behind her, he asked, "Need any help?"

She cranked her head around. "I'm good, thanks."

He stayed nearby, anyway, mostly to watch her.

Owen wandered over, two longneck beer bottles in his hands. He'd arrived a short while ago to join the family for the cookout. "Have a seat." He indicated a pair of vacant lawn chairs.

Ryan gladly accepted the offer—of the chair and the beer. "Don't mind if I do."

"How'd your first day go?" Owen asked.

"I think I'm going to like it here." Ryan's gaze strayed to Bridget.

Owen obviously noticed. "She's something else. Works like a fiend with seven arms."

"I don't know how she does it."

"She and Molly grew up in the hospitality business. Emily and her first husband owned and operated the Morning Side Inn in town for over thirty years. The girls spent their summers here, learning the ropes from a young age."

"Runs in the family then."

"This ranch means everything to them."

Ryan couldn't decide if Owen was simply making small talk or issuing a warning. "It's an incredible place."

"Emily's idea. She sold the inn after her first husband died and sunk her entire savings into Sweetheart Ranch."

Definitely a warning, Ryan decided. He wasn't mad. If he had a vested interest in both the ranch and the O'Malley family, like Owen did, he'd be sure the new employee knew the score.

"I appreciate the job," Ryan said, "and I fully plan to give the O'Malleys my best while I'm here."

"Thinking of leaving soon?"

Too late, Ryan realized his mistake. "Are you kidding? That money pit I bought is going to keep me in Mustang Valley for a while."

"You've taken on a big project," Owen agreed. "You doing all the work yourself?"

"As much as I can. The house and outbuildings have good bones, sound electrical and decent plumbing. I know it looks bad but fortunately most of the work is cosmetic. Patch the drywall, a fresh coat of paint, repair the fencing and replace the rotted floorboards on the front porch, and you won't recognize the place."

He then asked Owen about leading the trail rides on Wednesday.

"Wish I could, but I've got no one to cover for me at the store."

"It's okay." Ryan would think of something.

Hearing Molly call his name from the front porch, Owen rose. "Seems I'm needed. If you'll excuse me." He left, reminding the more inquisitive of the two little girls to stay away from the fire.

Ryan got up as well and sought out Bridget to see if she'd changed her mind about requiring his help. The guests were mingling, and he caught bits and pieces of conversations. Most were the couples comparing notes on their weddings and honeymoon stay at the ranch.

A folding table with a red-and-white checkered tablecloth had been set up not far from the picnic table. Emily and an older gentleman who hadn't been on the hayride were arranging paper plates, plasticware and trays of food. Ryan pegged the man as Emily's new husband from the way he leaned in close to when she talked.

He came up behind Bridget. She'd returned to the fire pit and was poking the glowing embers with a metal rod.

"There you are," she said, as if expecting him. "Can you please check on the coffee? The urn is in the kitchen. If it's done, the light on the front will be green. Pour the coffee into the thermos and bring it out here."

"Can do."

When Ryan returned with the thermos, Bridget was delivering platters of steaks and shrimp to the table. He set down the thermos where she indicated.

"Dinner's served," she called and promptly cleared out of the way. The table was instantly mobbed by hungry guests. "Get yourself some dinner," she told Ryan.

"I will when the rush dies down." He nodded at the generous spread. "What about you? Aren't you hungry?"

"I generally wait until later."

"You've been going hard all day. You deserve a break."

"Today's especially busy with the cookout. I actually have some time off tomorrow." Her eyes never veered from the guests, her tense posture indicating she was ready to spring into action if necessary.

What, he wondered, would she be like relaxed and unhurried? He suddenly wanted to know.

"Big Jim's busy with his wife this week and can't lead the trail rides. I asked Owen if he could take me, but he's working." He flashed what he hoped was an enticing smile. "Any possibility you can go with me? I'd hate to get lost in those mountains."

"I..." She hesitated.

"Come on. I promise I'm good company."

She glanced away. "That's what worries me."

He laughed, liking her honest admission.

"Ryan." She turned back to him. "I don't think—"

Suddenly, a high-pitched shriek filled the air, cutting off Bridget's reply. Ryan whirled and saw that one of the girls had fallen against the low block wall surrounding the fire pit, likely pushed there by her sister. A wildly flung arm had hit the grill, knocking it askew.

Ryan didn't think. He dove for the fire pit, his hands already outstretched. Bridget was right behind him.

He grabbed the little girl by the waist and hauled her to safety. Fear and possibly pain contorted her cherub face and tears streamed down her cheeks.

"Mommy!" Her scream filled Ryan's ears. "Mommy!"

"I'm right here, baby." The distraught woman shouldered between two people. "Oh, my gosh. Are you okay?"

Ryan passed the little girl to her mother. "Had yourself a scare, did you? But you're safe now, and you have a good story to tell your friends."

"Thank you so much." The mother immediately began inspecting her daughter for injuries and found nothing worse than a small red mark on the inside of her wrist. With a kiss to the spot and some cooing, the girl's sobs quieted. "This was my fault. I should have been watching her."

Bridget reached out and stroked the little girl's hair. "How about a pink lemonade? If your mom says yes."

The girl nodded.

Her sister beamed a smile at Bridget. "Me, too, please."

"After you apologize to your sister," the mother admonished. She took hold of both girls' hands. "No more playing near the fire, you hear me?"

Emily came over after the mother and girls left. "I see the crisis was averted. Good job, Ryan."

"Just glad I was there."

Dinner resumed. By then, Ryan was ready to eat. He paused while helping himself to both steak and shrimp, and listened to Emily and Bridget's conversation a few feet away, their backs to him.

"Why can't you show him the trails?" Emily asked.

"Grandma…"

"Bridget, he needs a guide. You're the only one available."

They walked away, their voices too low for Ryan to catch more than a random word. Halfway through his meal, Bridget approached. His fork came to a stop midway to his mouth.

"I changed my mind," she said. "I'll go riding with you tomorrow. Meet me at ten sharp."

BRIDGET WENT ON foot to the stables rather than take the golf cart. She figured she could use the few extra minutes before meeting Ryan to clear her head.

She wasn't exactly regretting her decision to go riding with him. Grandma Em was right: he did need to learn the surrounding area before the ranch's first official trail ride tomorrow, and she was the only person available.

Okay, not entirely true. Grandma Em could show him, but with her bad hip she didn't ride much these days. And Molly was occupied with a last-minute midweek wedding tonight, making her unavailable. The couple was requiring very little from Bridget. They'd met at a weight-loss center and were providing their own low-cal cake and refreshments. They were, however, making innumerable requests that Molly and Grandma Em were scrambling to accommodate.

Fortunately, the wedding was a small one. Twenty-five guests, give or take. Though the ranch could accommodate considerably more, their average number hovered in the thirty to forty range. Surprisingly, or maybe not surprisingly, smaller, more intimate weddings were very popular. Especially when the couple could then stay at a Western-themed bed-and-breakfast.

Friday was a different story. That wedding would be Bridget's first attempt at providing light catering. She wasn't nervous. Or so she told herself. She was well prepared and experienced, having practiced the dishes multiple times.

Last week, the bride, her groom and her mother had visited the ranch in order to taste-test a variety of menu options. They'd chosen mini sliders, fried mac-and-cheese lollipops and fruit kebabs. The fried mac-and-cheese lollipops were something new for Bridget and a little tricky to prepare. They were also delicious and an entertaining novelty.

After her ride with Ryan, she was making a trip to the giant membership box store for everything she needed. Other than the fruit, of course, which she'd buy fresh on Friday morning at the farmers' market.

All was going as planned. Every list had been checked and double-checked and every detail scrutinized. No cause to worry, she assured herself.

Ryan's pickup truck came into view as she

crested the small rise. She recognized it from yesterday. Hooked to the rear of the truck was an equally road-weary trailer with two unfamiliar horses tied to the side. His, she presumed.

The large bald-faced paint was saddled and bridled. A smaller bay mare wore only a halter and carried a canvas pack saddle, which had empty pouches hanging from each side of the wooden frame. The three mounts belonging to the ranch were tethered to the hitching post outside the stables. All were saddled but only one was bridled. The remaining two wore halters.

Ryan had yet to see Bridget. As she approached, he untied one of the ranch horses and walked it over to the small mare wearing the pack saddle. Bridget watched as he expertly tied the ranch horse's lead rope to a metal ring on the side of the pack saddle. Both horses stood quietly as if this was old hat to them, tails swishing in matching rhythm to chase away pesky flies.

Curious what he was up to, Bridget asked, "Who else is coming with us?"

He turned at the sound of her voice, his expression lighting up. "No one. Just you and me."

"Why so many horses?"

"I figured they could use some exercise and a little practice." He gestured toward the palomino standing at the hitching rail alongside her stablemate. "She's for you, unless you want a different horse. I guessed at which saddle was yours."

He was correct on both counts. The palomino was her preferred mount and the saddle hers.

"Did my initials burned into the pommel give it away?"

"They might have." He chuckled, a warm, appealing sound.

She went over to the horse and inspected the job he'd done. Cinch tight. Stirrups the right length. She usually used a different bridle but this one would suffice for today.

"Her name is Goldie." Bridget finger-combed the horse's tangled forelock into a semblance of order. "Not very original, I know. She's a sweetie, though."

"You have a farrier?" Ryan went about tying a third horse to the second one, forming a long line.

"He's due next Monday."

"You might want to call him. Goldie's lost a shoe. Right front."

Bridget glanced down, dismayed to see the shoe was indeed missing. "There's a hoof boot in the stables. I'll get it."

"I was hoping you'd say that. I haven't had a chance yet to look around."

Bridget entered the stables and located the hoof boot in a storage cabinet. Back outside, she slipped the rubber boot onto Goldie's un-shod hoof and adjusted the different buckles and straps to ensure a snug fit. It was strictly a temporary measure—the boot would protect the vulnerable underside of Goldie's hoof from the hard, rocky ground until the farrier arrived.

Before long, she and Ryan were on their way. Bridget went ahead, because she knew the trails and Ryan was ponying three horses behind him—his mare and the ranch's two geldings.

Their small parade must have made quite a sight as they left the ranch behind. At the gate, Bridget leaned down and opened the latch one-handed. Once Ryan and the rest of the horses went through, she pushed the gate closed and secured the latch in much the same manner.

"Nicely done," Ryan commented.

"A hangover from years of competing in trail classes."

"But can you jump a ditch and cross a bridge?"

"Please." She pretended to be insulted. "Piece of cake."

"A woman of many talents."

Maybe so, but no way could she have man-aged four horses at the same time. Ryan contin-ued to impress her and she couldn't help asking him about his expertise. "Where'd you learn

CATHY McDAVID 65

to lead a pack string? Surely not on your family's farm."

He grinned again. Maybe she'd impressed him a little by knowing what a pack string was.

"I worked for an outfitter in the Colorado Rockies shortly after high school. One of the best years of my life. Also one of the hardest. We took groups of people on three-, seven- or ten-day trips and were in the saddle from sunup to sundown. A lot of packing and rough terrain and a lot of scary situations. The wranglers were required to carry knives in case we had to cut a horse loose when they fell and got tangled in their gear."

"Any of the people ever fall?"

"Oh, yeah. Once, a woman had to be airlifted out by helicopter when she went down the side of a cliff and broke both her legs."

"Did her horse throw her?"

Ryan shook his head. "She was taking pictures and didn't watch where she was going."

They quickly reached the trailhead, which was clearly identified by the marker attached to a post.

"This is the easiest trail to start with," Bridget said. "A nice hour-long ride with easy hills. I can show you more trails another day."

"A second outing." He'd donned sunglasses,

which hid the spark she knew must be dancing in his blue eyes. "I'm looking forward to it."

"*Show* you on a map," she clarified. "Competent as you are, I'm sure you'll be able to explore on your own."

"You think I'm competent?"

"Is that what I said? I meant egotistical." She ignored him for a full five minutes before finally breaking the silence. "A farm in Texas. An outfitter in Colorado. Team penning somewhere in there. How did you wind up in Arizona and buying the Chandler place?"

"There wasn't much to keep me in Texas. Two of my sisters still lived at home while they were going to college. My folks were also helping to raise my brother's three kids. Tough situation there—his wife left him. I figured one less person to feed and clothe would be a lot easier for everyone."

"I can't imagine being brave enough to strike out on my own at eighteen."

"I won't lie, it wasn't always easy. I learned a lot along the way. Met a bunch of nice folks and made some good friends. I scraped together what money I could when I could. Tried a few things that paid off, like team penning."

"How'd you come to buy the Chandler place, if you don't mind me asking?"

"I passed through Mustang Valley last winter while delivering horses for a buddy of mine."

"Really?"

"I saw the property and thought it had a lot of potential so I called the real-estate agent. The seller was willing to lower his price and, as the saying goes, the rest is history."

Bridget couldn't help feeling there were large chunks missing from Ryan's story. The Chandler place may be run-down, but he hadn't gotten it for free. His salary from Sweetheart Ranch couldn't possibly cover the monthly mortgage payments and pay for expensive renovations. Not to mention annual taxes and insurance.

What little Ryan had revealed about himself, however, was telling. The man didn't stay in one place long and went from job to job. Perhaps that had changed, seeing as he was now a homeowner. More than likely, he craved adventure and excitement and would soon grow bored with a small, quiet town like Mustang Valley.

"Why did you agree to go riding with me today? Was it because your grandmother twisted your arm?"

His question roused Bridget from her musings. She glanced briefly over her shoulder at him, debating if she should answer honestly or not. She decided on the former.

"Partly, yes. I did have the most free time today and am the logical person."

"Tell me about the other part."

"If I said I feel it's my duty to get to know employees better, would you buy that?"

"I would if you dropped the it's-your-duty part."

Bridget held back a laugh. He was what Grandma Em would call a smooth talker. "I liked how you were with that little girl last night at the campfire. She was scared, and you were gentle with her and reassuring. I'm curious how a single man gets to be good with children."

"So much for me thinking I'd impressed you with my manly wagon-driving skills."

He had impressed her. In Bridget's opinion, it took a real man to be comfortable and relaxed with children, though she didn't admit that to Ryan. For all his outward charm and good-old-boy mannerisms, she suspected there was a lot of depth to him. A peek at that depth was why she'd ultimately agreed to show him the trails.

"Most guys I know without kids don't have the first clue what to say to a distraught two-year-old." She could feel his smile without having to look.

"I'm the youngest of eight, remember? I have

a lot of nieces and nephews and have done my share of babysitting."

That, or he was a natural. An intriguing idea, considering his roving lifestyle.

They spent the next hour talking mostly about his job duties at the ranch, with Ryan quizzing her on the daily routine and what to expect. Eventually, they moved to the subject of town. He was very familiar with the small market, as he did most of his shopping there. The auto-parts store was a regular stop—his truck was in constant need of replacement parts. He liked the specials at the Cowboy Up Café, but the hardware store left a lot to be desired. He bought the majority of his building supplies in north Scottsdale at the home-improvement store.

Again, she pondered where he got his money.

"I can unsaddle and put the horses away," he said when they reached the stables. "You've got things to do."

Bridget found she wasn't quite ready to leave. "You sure? I don't mind staying."

"Go on." He swung down from the saddle and tied his horses to the trailer before leading the other two to the hitching post.

She marveled at how they docilely followed Ryan, one after the other. It had been like that on the trail. Not a single hiccup or moment of panic the entire time. She couldn't imagine riding a horse while leading three others. They'd likely start bucking and kicking, and Ryan would have to cut them loose, like when he'd worked for the outfitter.

"He's not Superman," she mumbled under her breath.

"What's that?"

"Oh!" She hadn't heard him come up behind her and gave a quick jerk. Composing herself, she said, "You're, um, going to do just fine leading the trail rides."

"Bridget."

He was suddenly close. Very close. He'd removed his sunglasses and his cowboy hat, and she could see the tiny crinkles at the corners of his eyes. Smell the brisk scent of sunshine and outdoors on him.

Alarm bells started clanging inside her head. "Ryan, I—"

"How 'bout you and I have dinner soon? There has to be an evening we're both free."

He was asking her on a date. Expected, she thought, and yet unexpected.

"I don't think that's wise."

"Is there a rule against employees dating? Because your grandmother eloped with your staff minister."

"No, there's no rule. That's not the reason."

"Another man? The doctor at the clinic?"

He *had* heard Bridget discussing Dr. Hall with her grandmother. "No." Not yet, she silently added.

"Then what's stopping you?"

"I don't think we have the same objectives when it comes to relationships."

"It's just dinner." Ryan's voice had dropped to a husky level that made concentrating hard.

"And therein lies the problem." Drawing on her willpower, she straightened. "I'm not interested in just dinner or hanging out or friends with benefits. I'm looking for a guy who's ready now to commit to me and to having a family and who's content making Mustang Valley his home. I don't believe that describes you."

"I understand." He shrugged, seemingly unfazed by her rejection. "Let me know if you change your mind."

With that, he returned to the horses, leaving Bridget in a state of mild shock and annoyed rather than relieved.

CHAPTER FOUR

RYAN FELT A trifle guilty rummaging through the pantry shelves, but Emily had insisted he make himself at home in the ranch kitchen and to avail himself of anything he needed or wanted. In this case, it was the first-aid kit she'd mentioned was stowed there should an emergency arise.

One had, although it wasn't work-related—which triggered a second stab of guilt. Ryan shouldn't be misusing his employer's resources.

Except if he didn't apply a dressing to the angry red puncture wound on the heel of his right palm, he'd have difficulty saddling the horses for the ranch's first trail ride and holding the reins of his horse.

"Aha!" he exclaimed, spotting a white plastic box with a large red cross tucked away in the far corner of a shelf.

Taking the box with him, he returned to the still-empty kitchen. He'd called out when he first entered through the back door and briefly surveyed the parlor when his greeting wasn't returned. He went no farther, feeling peculiar about traipsing through the house's first-floor rooms by himself even though he'd been told they were open to the public.

He stood at the counter to tend his injury rather than sit at the table. Naturally, he couldn't help thinking about Bridget as he picked through the contents of the first-aid kit and selected the items he'd need.

"You're an idiot," he mumbled to himself, recalling how he'd asked her to have dinner with him the previous morning.

She'd turned him down. No surprise there. The invitation had been spontaneous, which was no excuse. He'd known better but had been caught up in the moment. Bright sunlight reflecting off her hair and the slight scent of cinnamon clinging to her skin had temporarily short-circuited his brain function.

The lapse was compounded by him liking her. She was fun and easy to be with and he'd enjoyed those quick glimpses of the more interesting and complex side of her personality.

Recalling her reaction, he wanted to kick himself. What if Bridget complained to her grandmother that Ryan had behaved inappropriately and Emily got mad? Even though Bridget hadn't appeared offended or insulted, he shouldn't assume.

From this moment on, he vowed to be on

his best behavior. Joking around was acceptable. Flirting, completely off-limits. Any next move—and he doubted there'd be one after her not-happening warning—would have to come from Bridget. He wasn't holding his breath. The odds of them going on a date were pretty much zero.

As if his thoughts had magically conjured her, she suddenly appeared in the doorway. Coming to a stop, she straightened and said, "What are you doing here?" a bit more abruptly than he would have preferred.

Great. Now he'd gone and made things uncomfortable between them. Way to go, numbskull.

"Borrowing the first-aid kit." He flashed what he hoped was the friendly smile of a coworker and held up a bandage. "Hope that's okay."

"Are you hurt?" Concern replaced wariness in her eyes, and her entire demeanor softened as she hurried toward him. "What happened?"

"I wasn't looking where I put my hand and accidently leaned on a nail."

"Let me see."

"I'm fine. Nothing a little antiseptic ointment won't fix."

"Puncture wounds are serious. They can easily become infected." When he didn't move, she held out her hands and insisted, "Come on. Don't be a baby. Let me see."

Baby? Him? Hardly. The reason for his reluctance had to do with proximity. Hers to his. It was hard being mere inches apart. Her touching him would send him into...

"Ryan."

He slowly revealed his palm.

"That looks awful." She cradled his hand in both of hers, inspecting the wound. "When was your last tetanus shot?"

"I have no idea."

"More than ten years ago?"

He shrugged. "I was a kid."

"You need another one. And possibly antibiotics."

He didn't know what he liked more, the warmth in her voice or the warmth of her skin brushing against his as she fussed and fretted.

Cementing his teeth together, he willed himself to remain still while she continued examining his wound. With her head bent low like that, her hair fell forward and formed a curtain of red and gold that concealed her face.

"Where did you do this? Are there exposed nails in the stables?"

He couldn't lie to her. Not with her smooth fingertips tenderly prodding the inflamed and sensitive flesh on his palm.

"In the attic at my house. I was clearing away debris in order to install new insulation."

"You're lucky you only got a puncture wound. It's probably a death trap up there, considering how long that house has sat vacant."

He didn't mention the various animal droppings he'd found, the black-widow spiders and the wasps' nest hanging from a beam near the broken window.

"Sorry. That wasn't nice of me." She peered up at him, and the curtain of her hair parted to reveal a smattering of freckles across her nose.

Ryan was captivated and had to literally shake himself to regain focus.

"You're right," he said. "The attic is a death trap. But if I don't install decent insulation soon, the whole place will become a furnace by next month."

Temperatures in central Arizona regularly reached the high nineties by May. Before long, the ranch would start restricting trail rides and hayrides to early mornings or evenings after the sun went down. They couldn't take the risk. Heatstroke and related conditions were a serious problem in the desert and mountains, for people and animals alike.

Bridget tsked as a mother would to an errant child. "You should be careful."

He'd endure all the scolding she dished out

as long as she continued to hold his hand. "I should have gone to the market and bought my own first-aid supplies. I have no business using yours for something that happened on my own time."

"Nonsense." Without asking him, she moved his hand to the sink, where she turned on the water. "You can't possibly take couples on trail rides without first treating this. In fact, I think you should visit the urgent-care clinic in town."

What better care could a doctor provide than what he was already getting from Bridget? His pain had vanished, and he felt like a million bucks. "That's not necessary."

Fiddling with the faucets, she adjusted the water flow until she was satisfied. Picking up a pump bottle of liquid soap, she instructed him to wash his hands thoroughly.

He inhaled sharply when the water hit his palm. Not because it was hot but because she'd pressed up right next to him. So close, their hips bumped and their arms brushed.

She didn't seem to notice or didn't feel the sparks. Though how she could remain indifferent was beyond him. He was about to spontaneously combust.

Drying his hands on the clean white dish towel she'd retrieved from a drawer, he watched her open the tube of antiseptic cream. When he finished, he obediently showed her his palm. She liberally applied the antibiotic ointment, then covered the wound with a gauze pad and medical tape, which she wrapped around several times.

"You need to get a proper dressing," she announced, inspecting her work with the same attention to detail he imagined she gave each dish she prepared. "This won't hold long."

"It'll do for now."

He took a step back. The next second she looked at him and *bam*! Not just sparks. A whole entire light show erupted.

"I'd—" She quickly averted her head.

Not fast enough, however. Ryan saw realization dawn on her face and heard her stifle a soft gasp. This wild attraction he had for her wasn't one-sided.

Great! Wait, not great. Probably bad. Bridget was right about them having different relationship goals. And, unlike Ryan, she was level-headed enough not to act impulsively or give in to temptations.

She promptly turned away, establishing boundaries. "You need to see the doctor."

"I'll be all right. Besides, the first trail ride starts in less than an hour. I have horses to saddle."

"We'll postpone it."

"I don't want to cause a problem. Your guests are expecting a ride. I'll go to the clinic later, when I'm off work."

"By then you could have blood poisoning." Refusing to take no for an answer, she walked over to the wall phone, which Ryan had learned was connected to the cabins as well as having an outside line. Pressing a series of three numbers, she waited, then said brightly, "Hi, this is Bridget O'Malley. Am I speaking with David? Oh, good. How are you and your bride enjoying your stay?"

She conversed for another minute before rescheduling the trail ride for five that evening. "Yes, you'll get to see another gorgeous sunset. This time on horseback." After saying goodbye, she hung up and addressed Ryan. "The other ride's at noon. That gives us plenty of time to visit the urgent-care clinic."

"Us?"

"I'm taking you, of course."

She was? "I can drive myself," he insisted.

Her exasperated expression conveyed better than words how much she doubted he'd go if left on his own. Two days in her company and she'd already figured him out.

He tried another approach. "I'm sure you have much better things to do."

"We can't have our brand-new wrangler unable to perform his job duties, regardless how you hurt yourself and whether or not the accident occurred on ranch property. We're depending on you."

Ah. Her concern for him was less personal and more business-related. He shouldn't be disappointed.

"You worry too much, Bridget."

"I have a chef friend who spent a week in the hospital after she ignored a knife cut and it lead to sepsis." She quickly gathered up the first-aid-kit contents, returned them to their proper place in the box and closed the lid. "Sit tight. I'll be right back."

She disappeared into the pantry and returned a minute later, without the first-aid kit and carrying her purse.

"I'll drive," she announced.

"If I promise to go to the clinic, will you—"

She cut him off. "I have a stop to make, anyway."

Ultimately, Ryan relented. Bridget was persistent, and he doubted she'd leave him in peace until he was seen by a medical professional.

Just as well. He had no wish to be sidelined from work during his first week simply because he'd refused to get treatment or share confined spaces with Bridget.

Jobs like this one, with flexible hours and

benefits and decent pay, were few and far between. He'd be wise to do whatever was required of him to keep it.

BRIDGET'S STOMACH FLUTTERED in anticipation as she swung her SUV into the medical clinic's parking lot. This wasn't one of her better ideas. Not having Ryan's wound treated—it did look awful and needed tending by a professional. But insisting she accompany him on the slim chance she accidentally-on-purpose ran into Dr. Hall—that rated right up there on the stupid meter.

And why? To prove to her grandmother and herself she wasn't interested in Ryan.

The stunt was something a sixteen-year-old might pull, not a grown woman. Unfortunately, she couldn't back out now. They were here, sitting in a visitor space, with Ryan waiting for her to shut off the engine.

She glanced around the lot. Was Dr. Hall even here? She had no idea what make and model vehicle he drove.

"You okay?"

Ryan's question startled Bridget, and she involuntarily jerked. "Yeah."

"You look nervous."

"Do I?" Mustering a smile, she shifted to

face him. "Just distracted. I thought I saw someone I knew."

What a pathetic excuse. Other than her and Ryan, the parking lot was empty of people.

"You ready?" She opened her door.

"Ready as I'll ever be."

They walked side by side toward the clinic. Bridget let Ryan open the door for her only because he used his uninjured hand. Grandma Em would be pleased; she'd recently commented on his good manners.

Inside, Bridget plunked down in a chair while he signed in at the counter and described his problem to the young woman on duty. A middle-aged couple Bridget knew had recently moved to Mustang Valley, but whom she hadn't officially met, sat across from her. She offered a friendly hello, which they returned.

The woman's nose was beet-red and she dabbed at it with a tissue. The man patted her knee affectionately. "She's got a bad cold," he said, his tone apologetic.

"It's going around," Bridget replied, her attention wandering. There was no sign of Dr. Hall through the reception-counter window.

Ryan finished signing in and sat beside her, balancing a clipboard on his knees. He said, "Howdy" to the couple, and, after answering their question about how he'd injured his hand, tackled the paperwork.

The door leading to the exam rooms opened and a bearded man in scrubs called a name. The woman with a cold and her husband simultaneously stood, wished Ryan good luck and disappeared with the nurse's aide.

Ryan completed the paperwork, more than once exhaling in frustration and muttering remarks about useless information. Eventually, he returned the clipboard to the woman behind the counter and grabbed a magazine from the rack on his way back. He flipped the pages, hardly glancing at them.

It was Bridget's turn to comment. "You're the one who looks nervous now."

"I don't like needles."

Bridget chuckled, only to stop when she realized from Ryan's pinched expression that he was completely serious. "Really? A big, strong man like you?"

"I'm not proud of it."

"Are we talking the fainting kind of needle phobia?"

"That only happened once." He cleared his throat. "Okay, twice."

"Do you faint at the sight of blood, too?"

"I'm not that much of a wimp."

"You drove a nail thirty times the size of any

needle into your hand, and that didn't bother you."

"Not on purpose," he grumbled, as if that made a difference.

"You'll be fine. And a tiny needle is nothing compared to what you'd have to endure if the wound became infected."

"Thanks for coming with me. And for caring," he added.

The sincerity in his voice touched her. "You're welcome, Ryan."

She snuck a sideways peek at him when he resumed flipping magazine pages. He really was a handsome man. She liked how one stubborn lock of dark brown hair insisted on falling over his left eye. And speaking of eyes, his were the most compelling shade. Blue in bright sunlight and grey indoors. Whenever he looked at her, she always got the feeling he could see more than the parts of her she chose to reveal. It was disconcerting. And...intriguing.

Even though he didn't check off enough boxes on her dating nonnegotiable list, she might have gone out with him, anyway, if things were different. Just for kicks and to see what it'd be like.

One date. As much as she liked Ryan, she wasn't settling for less than her ideal life partner. She'd seen both extremes with her mother—a wonderful marriage with Bridget's father and a less-than-satisfying one with her stepdad. For Bridget, there was only one choice. Hold out for the right man.

The fact that she and Ryan worked together was another deterrent. What if they started dating and the relationship suddenly soured? Sweetheart Ranch wasn't large enough for them to avoid each other indefinitely. The situation could become awkward, potentially forcing him to leave and the ranch to lose a valuable employee.

Nope, the family business was too important to risk affecting its smooth and profitable operation over a doomed-from-the-start romance. Important to Grandma Em, who'd invested her entire savings, and to Molly and Bridget.

They didn't just depend on the ranch for their livelihood, they planned to take over for Grandma Em whenever she chose to retire. Bridget hoped to eventually open a pastry shop on the premises, and Molly had recently proposed they convert the downstairs library into a wedding boutique.

Bridget and Ryan simultaneously lifted their heads when the door opened and the nurse's aide reappeared, calling Ryan's name.

He stood slowly and then didn't move. "Don't

suppose I could convince you to come with me and hold my hand?"

"I think you'll do fine on your own."

"It was worth a try."

"Close your eyes and imagine your happy place. I'll be here when you're done."

He followed the nurse's aid, leaving Bridget alone in the waiting room. She glanced at the reception-counter window again. No sign of Dr. Hall. She was half-glad. A calculated bumping-into-him was a stupid idea to begin with.

Ten minutes later, Bridget was reading emails on her phone and starting to get bored when an elderly man, accompanied by his uniformed caregiver, arrived. They went straight for the reception window, and a loud conversation commenced. The elderly man was hard of hearing, his caregiver explained.

"I want to see Dr. Hall," the man insisted.

Bridget couldn't make out the reply.

"What?"

"Dr. Hall isn't here," the caregiver repeated. "The nurse practitioner will see you."

"Well, why didn't you say so?"

Bridget didn't hear the rest of what was said, as her mind whirled. Dr. Hall wasn't in? Whew! She'd come *this close* to embarrassing herself over nothing.

At least Ryan was receiving the medical

treatment he needed. That was the important thing.

Several more minutes passed, with Bridget's boredom increasing. The elderly man and his caregiver had joined her in the waiting area and were discussing his chronic stomach-flu symptoms in raised voices and with unnecessary graphic details. Staring at her phone's clock, Bridget tapped her foot impatiently.

When the front door opened, she assumed a new patient had entered the clinic.

"Hello, Dr. Hall," the woman behind the counter said cheerily. "Glad you're back."

Bridget immediately went on high alert. He was here! Returning from wherever he'd been.

What should she do? What should she say? She hadn't thought far enough ahead.

"Any calls?" He stopped briefly at the window to converse before continuing to the exam rooms, nodding curtly to the people in the waiting room.

Bridget began to panic. In another three seconds he'd be gone, and she'd miss her one and only chance. *Get up*, she told herself. *Say something*.

"Hi, um, Dr. Hall." Bridget jumped to her feet.

He paused, his eyebrows raised.

She approached him. "We, uh, met last November. At Sweetheart Ranch. During the open house. I'm Bridget O'Malley. Emily O'Malley's granddaughter. I'm the resident chef and head of catering."

She was babbling. And acting like an idiot.

"Yes," he finally said, though there was no real recognition on his face. "Nice to see you again."

They shook hands. Bridget's was clammy, she was sure of it. How humiliating. His was softer than she'd expected. Or maybe it was just softer than Ryan's, which she'd held this morning. His had the calluses of someone who worked outdoors and at hard manual labor.

Hands like her father, Bridget suddenly remembered and had no idea where that thought sprang from. But in her mind, she could see a child version of herself clasping her father's big, rough hand and feeling utterly safe.

"If you'll excuse me." Dr. Hall withdrew. "I have patients waiting."

"Yes. Of course. Wait," she said after he'd taken a step. "I wanted to invite you—you and your children—out to the ranch. We're having weekly hayrides and cookouts. Open to the public. Starting this Saturday."

He smiled, less formally this time. "They might enjoy that. Thank you, um…" He paused as if searching his memory.

"Bridget."

"Yes. Sorry."

Swell. She'd made such a minuscule impression her name had slipped his mind after one minute.

"See you soon, I hope. Gregory."

A frown materialized for the briefest of seconds before his features relaxed. "Me, too."

Yikes! Was she wrong to call him by his first name at the clinic? Too personal? Good grief, she was no better than those other women from town who'd thrown themselves at him right and left.

To cover her blunder, she forced a laugh and wiggled her fingers in the air. "'Bye."

It was at that moment she caught sight of Ryan emerging from the exam-room door. He took one look at her waving and grinning and drew up short.

Gregory—Dr. Hall—said, "Excuse me," and stepped around Ryan.

Bridget wished she could shrink to the size of a mouse and scurry away unnoticed. "Done already?" she asked in an attempt to sidetrack Ryan. It didn't work.

"What was that all about?" His blue-grey eyes assessed her.

She noticed only then that his hand was professionally bandaged and he carried a small white paper bag. A prescription, she guessed, filled at the on-site pharmacy.

"Come on." She started walking. "We don't want to be late for the afternoon trail ride. What did the nurse practitioner say, by the way?" She was babbling, not unlike she had with Gregory—er, Dr. Hall.

"That I was smart to listen to you and come in."

"See? What did I tell you?"

"You'll be happy to hear I didn't faint when she gave me a tetanus shot."

"Good for you. What's the prognosis?"

"I'll live. I'm supposed to return in a week for a follow-up visit. And avoid protruding nails."

He was still casting odd glances her way when they reached the parking lot. Bridget ignored them as best she could.

"Didn't you have a stop to make?" Ryan asked once they were on the road.

"What? No. It's all right." She'd forgotten about the excuse she'd given him before. "I can go another day."

His odd glances intensified, making her acutely uncomfortable. It was those blue-grey eyes. They bored right through her.

"Can I ask a personal question?"

"You can ask," she said, not sure what was coming. "I may or may not answer."

"Are you by chance dating the doctor?"

Not yet. Possibly not ever after today. Ryan didn't need to know any of that. Nor would she tell him.

"I'm not going to discuss my private life with you."

"Fair enough." He sat back in his seat and stared out the windshield, his expression inscrutable.

Bridget swallowed a groan.

They passed the remainder of the trip mostly in silence. She couldn't shake the certainty he'd seen right through her ploy to gain Dr. Hall's attention and was too polite to laugh.

CHAPTER FIVE

RYAN WAS NO expert at flirting. He was, however, experienced at it and recognized when a woman was attempting to engage him. Or, like today, attempting to engage another man.

No doubt about it, Bridget had been flirting with the doctor. And doing a rather poor job from what Ryan had witnessed. The doctor had hardly paid her any attention while she laughed and tossed her hair and— Did her fingers cramp or had that been a wave?

Ryan shouldn't find her antics amusing, he thought, as they drove to the ranch. But he did and was trying his hardest not to let Bridget see. He'd rather not crush her hopes. Then again, maybe he would. Different relationship goals aside, he wasn't entirely thrilled with her interest in the local doc. Perhaps he was even a tad jealous of the man. What would it be like to have Bridget attempting to engage him?

Not something he was likely to discover any time soon. Especially as, at the moment, she was barely speaking to him. Sulking or feeling stupid? Both?

They were nearing the ranch when Ryan's cell phone buzzed. He wrestled it from his front shirt pocket, instantly recognizing the number on the display.

"Hi, Nora," he said, answering. "How you doing?"

He sensed Bridget's curiosity and her struggle not to look at him. She, too, was probably wondering why his neighbor and the ranch's part-time employee had called him.

"Thought you should know," Nora said, "there's a pair of what looks like teenage boys roaming your property."

"Hmm. Are you able to see what they're up to?"

"No. They disappeared into the storage shed."

"Nothing much in there."

"You can bet whatever they're up to it starts with the word *trouble*."

Nora was a good neighbor, and if a little nosy it was only to Ryan's benefit. She kept an eye on his place while he was gone and in return he helped her out with the occasional repair. Most mornings he went over to her house for coffee. And he owed her for recommending him to her best friend, Emily O'Malley, when the wrangler position opened up at Sweetheart Ranch.

Ryan pushed back his hat and scratched his

forehead, debating what to do. "I'm not in my truck at the moment."

"I can phone the sheriff's office for you," Nora said.

"They have to be tired of hearing from me."

"What's wrong?" Bridget interrupted.

Ryan moved the phone away from his mouth. "Seems like I have two unwelcome visitors. Possibly getting into mischief."

"You want to stop by? We have time."

"You mind?"

"Not in the least."

"We'll be there in a few minutes," Ryan informed Nora.

"Is that Bridget I hear in the background?" she asked.

"Yeah. We just came from the medical clinic. She insisted I have that puncture wound treated."

"She can be a force when she makes up her mind."

"I'm learning."

Nora chuckled. "My oldest granddaughter, Gianna, is here visiting. Tell Bridget we're coming by the ranch in a little bit."

"If you want, I can stop by when I get off work to check on that leaky bathroom faucet."

"Then you might as well stay for dinner."

"A home-cooked meal? How can I refuse?"

Bridget didn't need directions to Ryan's house. She'd been acquainted with the Chandlers before they moved away. "You have much trouble with trespassers?" she asked.

"Apparently not every neighborhood teenager has figured out the place is no longer vacant. It must have been a party hangout the last few years. There was a lot of damage and vandalism in the garage and outbuildings. Lucky for me they left the main house mostly alone and haven't stolen or destroyed anything of real value."

"Still, that's a shame."

"Yeah. Then again, the damage was another reason I was able to afford the property. I suspect most buyers were put off by the rough condition."

They entered the private drive leading to Ryan's property. In this part of the valley, houses were spaced farther apart than those in town, which was why Nora's view of the teenagers had been limited.

"You removed the fence," Bridget commented as they parked out front.

"It was rotted and an eyesore. I'm planning on replacing it with a split pine fence once I reexcavate the wash and line it with river rock."

"That's a big project."

"But it'll look nice and divert rainwater away

from the house. There's seepage damage on the west side."

Ryan was convinced potential buyers would love a picturesque river-rock wash. He might even add a small footbridge in the middle. But, then, Bridget had a point about it being a costly project requiring months to complete. In hindsight, he might have bitten off more than he could chew with this newest flip.

They circled the house to the backyard, taking a worn dirt path. Another someday-maybe project was laying decorative pavers, so he could convert the path to an attractive walkway that would be even more attractive once he cut back the thorny thatch of overgrown rose bushes.

He studied Bridget as she surveyed their surroundings. Did she notice the faded exterior paint on the house and the missing roof shingles? They were hard to miss, as were the weathered shutters and overgrown landscaping. Ryan had been concentrating the majority of his efforts on the house's interior, with the exception of removing the fence.

An inspection of the shaded horse stalls and outbuildings yielded no errant teenagers in hiding and no fresh evidence of vandalism.

"They must have taken off when they heard us pull in," Ryan said.

"Have you tried posting Keep Out or No Trespassing signs?" Bridget stood at the stalls petting Ryan's two horses. They nickered contentedly, enjoying the attention.

"I could. I have some leftover particleboard and red paint in the workshop. Not convinced how much good it'll do."

"What about a security system?"

"Not in my budget. I might get some of those motion-activated security lights." Except those were only helpful at night. This incident had occurred in broad daylight.

Leaving the horses, they strolled together to the house, Bridget saying nothing. Ryan continued seeing the property through her eyes. Worse than a fixer-upper, it was a wreck.

To his credit, he'd accomplished a great deal since he'd bought the place and was proud of his efforts. She might change her opinion of him if she saw how far he'd come rather than how much work remained.

"Would you like a quick tour of the inside?" he asked. "I've just about finished the living room."

"Lead the way."

They entered the house through the back door. "Oh, my" were Bridget's first words. He supposed he should have warned her that he'd demoed the entire kitchen. In addition to tear-ing out the old floor, he'd removed all the cabinets and countertops. The only appliances left were a ready-for-the-junkyard refrigerator and a microwave sitting atop a rickety table and chairs. Ryan stored his nonperishable food in a crate pushed against the wall.

"I don't cook much," he explained.

"No, you wouldn't." She offered a weak smile. "This way."

They entered the living-room-and-dining-room-combo area. Ryan had laid the ceramic tile himself and spent an entire day scrubbing and resealing the brick fireplace. He'd also painted the walls and taken down the wrought-iron grills over the windows, allowing sunshine to pour in and brighten the formerly dingy room.

"This is pretty," Bridget remarked. "I love the tile."

"Me, too. I drove all the way to south Phoenix to buy it."

"Did you install it yourself?"

"One of my many talents."

"Don't tell me. You spent a summer working for a tile installer."

"Not exactly. I'm self-taught."

"No kidding!"

"I made a lot of mistakes and had to start over more than once."

"Impressive."

Finally. The positive response he'd been waiting for and wanting to hear. She might only like this one thing about his house, but he did have that.

"What's the old saying? Necessity is the mother of invention. For me, it's lack of money. I can't afford to hire professional contractors for every job."

"The going is slow, I imagine."

"That's the downside."

"You'll get there." She met his gaze. "You're a determined man."

Was that admiration he detected? "I've gotten there three times before."

"This isn't your first house?"

He took her arm and guided her between a pair of sawhorses situated at odd angles, being sure to release her the instant any danger of tripping had passed.

"Actually, it's my fourth. In eight years."

"Are you serious?" Bridget's jaw went slack. "You must have been young when you started."

Ryan locked the door behind them, thinking he should do more to secure his outbuildings.

"Early twenties. An opportunity presented itself, and I had a modest bankroll from a recent win at team penning. Believe me when I say the house was a dump. Worse than this one. A tiny cracker box on a tiny lot. Which was good. Not as much time or money needed to remodel it."

"I'm guessing you sold the house and bought another one."

He slid into the front passenger seat. "My plan is to always buy low, remodel economically and then sell at a profit."

"Is your plan succeeding? Well, it must be, seeing as you bought this place."

"I've been averaging about a twenty-percent return on my investments. Not counting my labor."

She shot him a surprised look. "Ryan, that's great. You're making a living at this."

"Hardly," he scoffed. "Every dime of profit I've earned has gone into buying and remodeling the next property, which is always bigger than the last one and with more land. I still need a regular job to feed my face and keep the lights turned on. Eventually, when I've made enough, I'm going to find myself a small ranch. One that doesn't require renovations and where I can run a few head of cattle and build an apartment for my folks to stay when they visit or, if they prefer, live permanently. The farm has gotten to be too much for my dad. I wish he'd sell it so that he and my mom can start taking things easy."

She seemed to like that he was concerned

about his parents and how they'd get along in their retirement years.

"Eventually," he continued, "I'd like to get a regular job or even start my own construction business."

"Good for you." That also seemed to impress Bridget.

She stopped at an intersection and let a pair of women on horseback pass. In Mustang Valley, so Ryan had learned, equine had the right of way.

"Won't happen overnight."

"But you have ambition," Bridget said. "And a direction, even if you have a long road ahead of you. That's more than a lot of people can say."

He liked hearing her praise. He'd have liked it more if she hadn't seen the need to add "a long road." She'd made him feel like he hadn't accomplished enough. Or was that his self-doubt talking?

"What, if I may ask, made you decide to buy that first house? It's a rather ambitious undertaking for someone so young."

Ryan started to give his usual reply, how he saw an opportunity and seized it. Which was true, though not entirely accurate. Instead, he told her the whole story. Why he felt the need eluded him.

"I'm from a big family. You know that."

She nodded.

"We didn't have a lot to go around. I mentioned that, too, when your grandmother interviewed me." He paused, choosing his words. How to be honest without sounding shallow? "I want more than what I had growing up, which wasn't much. I think anyone can look at where I come from and understand that."

"Of course."

"Not because I was deprived. What my siblings and I lacked in material possessions my parents more than made up for with love and dedication. But when I have my own kids—and I do want them one day—they won't grow up with a father who struggles simply to put food on the table and shoes on their feet. Don't get me wrong, I respect the heck out of my dad. He went above and beyond. But I'm going to do my best to have the struggling part out of the way before I bring any kids into this world. I don't need to be rich, but I won't be constantly scraping by, either."

Bridget's expression softened. "That's very commendable."

"I want more for my wife, too. Mom is an incredible woman. She sacrificed everything for my dad and us kids. Who knows what she could have been if she'd been free to pursue an interest other than how to stretch one meal into two or help with homework. My wife will be an equal partner, with her own career if she chooses and my full support. To accomplish that, I have to contribute my share. For me, my share is a decent home. I can do that. I'm good at it."

"You're an interesting man, Ryan DeMere. Part old-fashioned and part forward-thinking." Bridget's gaze searched his face. He wished he knew what she was seeking and if she found it. Unfortunately, all she said was "We should get back to the ranch."

When they arrived, they spotted not just Nora's car in the parking area but Homer's, too.

Bridget hit the garage-door opener. "I wonder what Homer's doing here. He's only at the ranch when he's officiating a wedding."

Ryan followed her into the house, where they found a small gathering of people in the parlor, chatting excitedly.

"What's this?" Bridget called out. "No one told me there was a party today."

"Come join the celebration." Grandma Em slung an arm around Bridget and walked her to Nora and her granddaughter. "Gianna has news."

"She does?" Bridget smiled brightly. "Tell me."

As Ryan watched the exchange, Homer meandered over to stand beside him. He hitched his chin at the younger woman. "Gianna's about to graduate GCU. Hard to believe. Seems like just yesterday she was a little girl."

Ryan figured Gianna's announcement must have something to do with her finding a job or being accepted into graduate school.

"I'm engaged." Gianna held up her left hand for Bridget's inspection, fingers splayed. "Derrick proposed last night."

Bridget's expression appeared to freeze momentarily, and then she produced a smile. "Congratulations. I'm so happy for you."

"Thanks. We haven't set a date yet," Gianna gushed. "We were thinking in about a year. Of course, we want to have the wedding here."

"We'd love that."

"You'll be next." She spun and wagged a finger at Molly. "I'm surprised Owen hasn't proposed yet."

"We're waiting," Molly answered, a sparkle in her eyes Ryan took to mean she fully expected them to make their own announcement in the near future.

Bridget visibly swallowed.

He glanced around. Was he the only one in the room who noticed the subtle signs of tension and slight strain in her voice?

Apparently, yes, because they were all focused on the bride-to-be and not paying attention to anyone else.

Ryan filed away his curiosity about Bridget's reaction for later contemplation and quietly left, sneaking out through the kitchen door. This was an O'Malley family celebration. He didn't belong. And besides, he had to prepare for the trail ride that started in less than an hour.

"CAKE!" MOLLY EXCLAIMED and turned to Bridget. "Is there any left over from yesterday? We have to celebrate." She yanked open the refrigerator door. "What about champagne?"

"No, no." Grandma Em wagged a finger. "Not in the middle of a workday."

"Lemonade, then. And iced tea." Molly removed two pitchers and handed them to Nora. "Somebody grab the plastic cups and paper plates from the pantry."

Bridget let her sister be the one in charge, content to remain in the background. Once the cake was served and drinks poured, Grandma Em lifted her plastic cup. "To Gianna and Derrick. May the two of you be blessed with a lifetime of joy and love."

"Hear! Hear!" Bridget echoed, along with everyone gathered in the kitchen, though with marginally less enthusiasm.

She wasn't envious of the engagement. It just

reminded her of how far away she was from achieving the same state of engaged bliss.

Looking about, she noticed Ryan was missing. When had he ducked out? She checked the clock on the stove. Noon already? He must be taking the couple on their trail ride.

Of course. He was a responsible individual and would have remembered about the ride. She should be glad that guests weren't left waiting. Only a small part of her had wanted him to stay. Silly. What was she thinking? There was nothing romantic between them.

She'd been thinking how much she enjoyed spending the morning with him, hearing about his family and his remarkable career flipping houses.

Who would've guessed? Ryan, a property entrepreneur.

"We need to have a real engagement party," Grandma Em said and linked an arm with Gianna's. "Pull out all the stops. What do you say? The ranch will foot the bill."

Gianna flushed with excitement. "You'd do that for us?"

"Oh, honey, you're practically family."

"Seriously, Emily," Nora said. "That's too much."

Grandma Em ignored her. "Molly, don't we have a free evening a week from Saturday?"

"Technically," Molly answered. "Though the rest of the day is full. We have the Literary Ladies' luncheon at noon and a wedding at three thirty. Other than that, we'd have to look at June or July."

"Saturday is perfect. We'll make it work." Like a general, Grandma Em assumed command of the situation. "Molly, block out the evening. I don't care if the governor calls and wants us to host a wedding, we're booked. Gianna, you and Derrick are in charge of the guest list and invitations. Molly, Bridget and I will do the rest, won't we, girls? All we require is a head count."

"I insist on helping," Nora interjected. "And paying for the food."

Bridget offered to handle the menu, and Molly volunteered to oversee the decorations. Gianna said she and her teenaged sisters would assist with setting up for the party and serving, and then cleaning up afterward.

The good wishes and party planning continued with Bridget watching and listening more than contributing. Twenty minutes later, the impromptu gathering began winding down. Gianna had an exam the next day to study for, and the rest of them needed to get back to work.

"You doing okay?" Grandma Em asked. She was helping Bridget tidy the kitchen.

"A little tired. I was up early this morning."

"I was more curious how you're taking the news of Gianna's engagement."

"I'm thrilled for her and Derrick. Why wouldn't I be? They've been together since their freshman year."

"You used to babysit her and her sisters."

Bridget avoided her grandmother's stare. She truly was thrilled for Gianna, she hadn't been lying. That didn't change the fact that the news had sent an electric jolt to Bridget's biological clock and started it ticking a tiny bit faster.

At thirty-two, she was hardly past her prime. Many women started families at her age or later. But she'd yet to meet her future husband—or start dating him, anyway, she amended, thinking of Dr. Hall. *Gregory.*

Assuming she and Mr. Right wouldn't wed for a year or more after becoming serious, and assuming they chose to wait another year before starting their family, Bridget could easily be closer to thirty-five. More than ten years older than her mother and Grandma Em, who were married and with babies already by their twenty-fifth birthdays.

Yikes! Even though she considered herself a modern woman, midthirties still sounded old to be starting her family. And what if she couldn't become pregnant right away or suffered the unthinkable and had a miscarriage? There were so many uncertainties to consider.

Moving too fast wasn't the solution, she told herself. Neither was choosing the wrong man like her mother, simply because she was feeling pressure—from herself or by circumstances beyond her control.

But sitting on her butt waiting for Mr. Right to magically appear wasn't the best choice, either. Bridget must be proactive. Lightning didn't strike unless a person stood in the open during a thunderstorm. Dr. Hall felt like the right thunderstorm to be standing out in.

"I think you should give Ryan a chance."

Grandma Em's comment penetrated Bridget's thoughts, returning her to the present. "He's nice," she conceded. "I like him. But he's not a good prospect for me."

"Molly didn't think Owen was a good prospect at first. Look how that turned out."

"It's different for them. Owen has a good job with a future." And Molly was two years younger than Bridget. She could afford to wait a little longer to start her own family.

"But he was unemployed when they first met," Grandma Em insisted.

Bridget recalled Ryan's remark about how he refused to wind up financially overextended like his parents. That he wanted to own not merely a nice home, but a small ranch, free and clear, before settling down. By his own admission, that was going to take a while.

"Ryan's not ready for marriage," Bridget said. "And won't be for a long time."

"How do you know?"

"He told me. In pretty much those exact words. We stopped at his house before coming here." She recounted their conversation to her grandmother.

"Okay, maybe he's not the perfect match for you. But he's easy on the eyes and has a great sense of humor. No reason you two can't go out."

"I repeat, Grandma, he's not in the market for a wife."

"He reminds me of your grandfather."

Bridget could see that, only she'd compared Ryan to her late father.

Closing the dishwasher door, she straightened and steeled her resolve. "I invited Doc—Gregory to the hayride on Saturday. He and his children. I ran into him at the clinic when I took Ryan."

"You did?" Grandma Em considered this. "Are they coming?"

"He's going to let me know."

"Hmm. Are you telling me he didn't jump at your invitation?"

"He said it sounded like fun."

"But he didn't commit."

"He was at work. He probably had to check his calendar or confirm with his ex-wife if the children are free."

"Ah…"

Bridget disliked the myriad innuendos her grandmother had infused in that single syllable. They too strongly resembled the feelings she'd had when she and Ryan left the clinic. Gregory hadn't appeared especially excited by her invitation. Quite the contrary. Still, she defended both him and her actions.

"He was busy and had patients waiting."

"Well, if they do come, they're more than welcome. The hayride is open to the public." At that moment, Molly called to Grandma Em from the foyer. "Be right along," she hollered back. But rather than leave, she said to Bridget, "Nora tells me Ryan's been working day and night on his place and is making amazing progress."

Bridget sighed softly, her hope to avoid further discussion of Ryan dashed. "The living room is certainly nice. And he's done some major cleanup, inside and outside. But it's a slow process. He's doing the majority of the work himself. I am, however, impressed with his goals. And his determination."

"That's a plus, yes?"

"He's someone to be admired."

"I think men who are good with their hands are sexy."

"Grandma!"

"There wasn't anything your grandfather couldn't make or fix. A person of many talents." She winked. "I think Ryan's the same."

"He could be," Bridget conceded, and then countered, "But I'd say Gregory is also a man of many talents. And as a doctor, he most certainly must be good with his hands."

"Are you sure he wants more children? He has two already."

Bridget hadn't thought of that. Rather than be deterred, she said, "I'll just have to find that out. When we go on our date."

"You're pretty confident."

"Why do you keep raining on my parade?" Bridget's tone was more defensive than she'd intended.

"I'm not trying to, sweetie. I only hate seeing you hurt. Whether it's because of the doctor or Ryan or any man you set your sights on. I didn't get this old without acquiring a little wisdom along the way." She pressed a hand to her heart. "What counts is in here. Don't let yourself be dazzled by the outside to the extent you lose sight of the truly important things."

At that moment, Molly stuck her head in the kitchen. "Hey, Grandma. I hate to interrupt but

I could really use your help. This bride has a ton of requests."

"I'm coming." Grandma Em pushed off the counter and patted Bridget's cheek before ambling after Molly.

Bridget went straight to work. She had a long list of tasks ahead of her, including prep work on tomorrow's breakfast. Picking up her electronic tablet, she created two new files, one titled "Engagement Party" and the other "Bridal Shower." She purposely ignored the file containing her list of dating nonnegotiables.

Could her grandmother be right? Was Bridget losing sight of the truly important things? She agreed that Ryan had husband potential for one day down the road.

She'd rather not wait that long if possible. Correction, her biological clock would rather not wait. Alone in the kitchen, the ticking increased in volume, becoming loud enough to muffle every other sound.

CHAPTER SIX

RYAN LISTENED TO the conversation behind him as he tied his horse to the hitching rail and loosened the girth.

"Thanks so much!" the young woman gushed. "We had a great time." She threw her arms around Goldie's neck and hugged the palomino mare as if dreading to be parted from her. "You were a perfect angel," she cooed in baby talk. "The best horsey in the whole wide world."

Goldie tolerated the attention like the experienced pro she was, remaining statue-still and barely blinking. Her mind was no doubt on the thick flake of hay and scoop of cracked corn for dinner coming up as soon as she was returned to her stall. After two lengthy trail rides, she and the other horses were more than deserving.

Not to be outdone, the young woman's new husband of two days patted his horse's neck. "Take 'er easy, Uno."

"Glad you both enjoyed yourselves." Ryan sauntered over to join the couple. Today he'd ridden Redbone, the old gelding that belonged to the ranch, rather than trailering over his own horses.

"That sunset was incredible," the man said. "Everything Bridget promised."

During the last ten minutes of their ride, the sun had disappeared behind the distant mountaintops, turning a brilliant, shimmering orange in the last few seconds. Dusk was only now falling, blanketing the ranch in soft hues of grey and blue.

"Incredible sunsets are part of the service," Ryan joked. "Guaranteed three hundred days a year."

His busy day had gotten even busier when another couple requested a last-minute, late afternoon trail ride.

"Do you need help with—" smiling, the young woman took hold of a stirrup on her saddle and raised it "—this?"

"Nope, I'll unsaddle. You two mosey along and enjoy the rest of your evening."

"We will." The man grinned as he put his arm around his bride and walked her down the road toward the cabins.

Ryan watched them go, hoping they made a success of their marriage. They looked good together and appeared crazy in love. Then again, his sister and her ex-husband had looked good and appeared in love. Except now she and her kids were back home, living with Mom and Dad, and her ex was involved with a coworker—something that may or may not have been going on before the divorce.

Yet another reason why Ryan was in no hurry. Marriage was hard, even when two people were committed. Living on a shoestring made it significantly harder. Add kids to the mix right away and the odds of 'til-death-do-us-part were next to impossible.

Statistics proved his parents were the exception. They hadn't merely stayed together for the sake of their many offspring—they were truly in love, even to this day.

Ryan aspired to have the same kind of relationship with his future spouse. The difference between him and his parents was he planned on doing whatever he could *before* marriage to improve the odds. Like owning a decent home with a low, if not nonexistent, mortgage.

When it came to dating, he had a totally different outlook. As long as the gal was willing to keep things casual for the indeterminable future, they'd get along fine and could have a lot of fun.

A shame Bridget was the dating-with-an-agenda type. Sure, he respected her desire to marry and have a family. In his limited experience, that was the goal of many women.

The goal of many parents, too. His had been constantly nagging him this past year, as if by turning thirty he was suddenly running short of options. Bridget might be going through something similar with her family and feeling the effects. Especially now that Nora's granddaughter was engaged, and the O'Malleys were hosting a party.

Ryan inspected Goldie's hoof before leading her into the stables. The farrier was arriving tomorrow morning to replace the shoe she'd thrown. Once all three trail horses were in their stalls, he fed them and the pair of Haflingers. Lastly, he secured the stables for the night, pocketing the key Emily had entrusted to him.

Ambling down the road to where he'd parked his truck, he heard strains of lively music floating on the breeze and stopped in his tracks. Was there an activity in the clubhouse tonight? If so, he'd missed the announcement. Deciding guests must be making merry, he continued toward his truck.

Glancing one last time at the clubhouse, he noticed people moving about through the lighted windows. One of the people had a slim, attractive figure and a wavy mass of strawberry blond hair.

Bridget.

His curiosity roused, Ryan changed direction. At the fork, he veered right and entered the pool area.

Music poured from the open clubhouse door. Ryan knew the tune well, having been forced to partner many a girl at church events during his middle and high school years. "Turkey in the Straw" was a square-dance standard.

He paused at the door. Tonight, Emily's husband, Homer, was doing the calling to recorded music while she and Bridget do-si-doed. The Ping-Pong table and other furniture had been shoved against the wall to create a makeshift dance floor.

Neither Bridget nor her grandmother were very skilled, but they were having a grand time judging by their frequent and loud laughter. Homer, it turned out, was a passably decent caller.

When the song ended, Emily doubled over and rested her hands on her knees. "Whew!" she huffed. "That took a lot out of these ol' bones of mine."

Bridget reached up and swept back the unruly locks of hair that had fallen in her face, her expressive green eyes alight with mirth. "You were terrific, Grandma. I'm the one who kept stepping on your feet."

Homer turned then and spotted Ryan in the door. "Hello there, young man. Come on in."

"I don't want to interrupt."

"Please." Emily beckoned him with a wave. "Bridget needs a new partner. One who isn't out of breath."

"No, Grandma—" Bridget caught herself. "It's late. He probably wants to go home."

Ryan decided in that instant to stay, if only to be contrary. He entered the clubhouse. "I'm in no rush." His own horses at home might not like waiting an extra few minutes for their dinner but they'd survive. "What's the occasion?"

"We're having square-dance lessons after the hayride and cookout on Saturday night." Emily dropped down into one of the metal folding chairs. "This is our first social event open to the public. The square dancing was Bridget's idea. She's the expert."

"I'm no expert," she insisted, her cheeks coloring.

"I seem to recall a trophy and a big blue ribbon in your room."

"Grandma, I was twelve. They were from 4-H summer camp."

"Which makes you the expert here."

She gave her head a defeated shake.

"I've been watching YouTube videos online," Homer announced with a grin. "To practice calling."

"He's a natural." Emily smiled adoringly at

him. "That's what you get from five decades of preaching and marrying folks. A clever way with words."

"There's room for improvement," he conceded.

Ryan enjoyed the dynamics between the three of them, from Emily and Homer's affectionate teasing to Bridget's embarrassment. They made him miss his own family back home in Texas, and he vowed to call his parents on the drive home.

Maybe if things went well, he could arrange a quick trip to see them this fall or winter. It had been a year ago this past Christmas since he last visited, and no way could his parents afford a trip to Arizona. Not that he had a spare bedroom in which to put them up. Yet.

Perhaps he could work on that after finishing the living room. Though he'd been aiming to start on the master bedroom and adjoining bathroom next.

"You ready to try 'Alabama Jubilee'?" Emily asked.

"Whenever you are." Homer returned to his place at the front of the room and fiddled with the karaoke player.

Bridget didn't move. "What about your hand?"

Ryan flexed his fingers. "Practically good as new."

"Stop your dawdling." Emily made a gesture as if pushing them together. "Get to dancing, you two."

Ryan approached Bridget and bowed at the waist, executing the traditional beginning to many square-dance routines. After a pause, Bridget curtsied, plucking at the sides of her invisible dress.

"Gentlemen, face your lady and join hands," Homer began in time to the music.

Ryan clasped Bridget's hands in his. Following Homer's calling wasn't as difficult as he first thought it would be. Square dancing must be a lot like riding a bike: a person never forgets.

They did the allemande left, taking the arms of imaginary other couples. Next, they went to the center and back again, and Ryan gave Bridget a swing before going round and round. When it came time to promenade on home, he captured her left hand in his and looped his right arm over her shoulders to take her right hand. Then, they circled the open space.

Holding her this close, Ryan couldn't take his eyes off her profile and navigated the room blindly. She fit perfectly into the crook of his arm as if by design, and their steps matched in precise rhythm—his to the beat of his racing heart. When she leaned back her head and laughed, he lost himself in the bright melody.

"You're good," she said.

"I have an excellent partner."

She angled her head and met his gaze, his name falling from her lips on a soft breath.

It was then he missed a step, causing her to trip over his foot. She would have tumbled to the floor if he hadn't caught her.

"You okay?" he asked, worriedly helping her to stand straight.

"No harm done." Her smile remained in place, pulling him in until he thought he might drown.

"My fault. I wasn't looking where I was going." He hadn't been able to help himself. Any red-blooded man would have missed a step.

"Me, either."

Because she'd been staring at him? He wasn't sure, but he liked thinking that was the reason.

"I hate to break up this party…" Emily came over, sending Ryan an exaggerated wink that Bridget missed.

He was instantly aware of how tight he held Bridget and moved away, letting his hands drop. "My two left feet got in the way."

"Nonsense," Emily insisted, "you were momentarily distracted." She sent him another wink.

Busted, Ryan thought. If he couldn't hide his attraction to Bridget from her grandmother, how was he expected to hide it from her?

By now, the music had ended. Homer stopped calling and wandered over.

"You have to come to the lessons on Saturday," he said. "We need you and Bridget to demonstrate for the folks."

Ryan hesitated. "I'm not sure about that. I'm pretty rusty."

"You're better than anyone else who'll be there."

"I have an idea," Emily chimed in. "You and Bridget can practice between now and then. Homer's a little rough around the edges, anyway, and could use another session."

"I am?" He feigned shock.

"By Saturday you'll sound like a pro." She surveyed the room. "Let's all meet here again. When's a good time for you both?" Her gaze traveled from Ryan to Bridget.

"I'm awful busy, Grandma."

"She might have another partner in mind," Ryan said, thinking of the doctor. From the change in Bridget's expression, she knew exactly who he was referring to.

"Oh?" Emily tilted her head quizzically at Bridget. "Do tell."

"I don't have another partner in mind," Bridget mumbled.

"Then what about tomorrow? Or Friday?"

"Friday's better for me," she conceded glumly.

"Me, too," Homer added. He was all smiles.

"You're the last holdout, Ryan." Emily crossed her arms over her middle almost in challenge.

"What time?" he finally asked, convinced he wasn't likely to get out of this without a battle with his new boss.

"Six thirty?"

He nodded. "All right."

After ironing out a few more details, they left together. Parting ways outside the clubhouse, Bridget, Emily and Homer returned to the house while Ryan went to his truck.

During the short walk, he silently questioned his sanity. Had he made a huge mistake by agreeing to square dance with Bridget? Earlier today he'd decided to steer clear of her and any possible emotional—or when it came to square dancing, physical—entanglement. But here he was, agreeing to not only dance with her on Saturday night after the hayride, but also to practice with her again in two days.

He should probably make a return trip to the medical clinic. This time to have his head examined.

BRIDGET ADDED A capful of specially formulated laundry detergent to the washing machine, shut the lid and pressed the button marked Delicate. No regular cycle for her linens, and cold water only. That was a must. The next second, the washing machine emitted a series of loud clicks and began filling the drum with water.

She took excellent care of the tablecloths and napkins used in the parlor for receptions. This load had soaked overnight and, after the wash, would dry on a line outside. She'd iron the tablecloths to perfection while still damp and then rehang them to finish the drying process.

The napkins would be starched to a crisp and laid flat for storing. While in culinary school, Bridget had learned how to fold napkins into the shapes of swans and roses, a skill she now used for table decorations during receptions.

Grandma Em appeared in the laundry room, returning one of the spare cabin keys to the numbered holder on the wall. "Why don't you let Tessa do that? Laundry is her job."

Tessa represented the entirety of the ranch's housekeeping staff and worked three hours each morning.

"I like to wash the linens myself," Bridget said.

Resting her back against the dryer, Grandma Em watched her spray kitchen towels with stain remover. "Molly wants to get together tomorrow morning after breakfast to plan Gianna's engagement party. She figures we can do that video-chatting thing with Gianna and her mom."

"Okay. As long as we're done by ten. I have to start prepping food for the cookout as well as make three dozen wedding cupcakes and a cake."

Their one wedding on Friday was a small afternoon affair. Of their two Saturday weddings, the first was hosting their reception at a local restaurant rather than the ranch and the other was serving only cake and punch. Bridget would be done in plenty of time for the cookout.

"Nora may want to be included in the call with her granddaughter," she suggested.

"Good idea. I'll let her know." Grandma Em didn't budge. "By the way, I spoke to your mom earlier and asked if she can come early on Saturday to help with the engagement party."

"And?"

"She'll call back. She was taking Doug to pick up his new golf clubs."

Couldn't he take himself? Bridget gnawed her lower lip. In her opinion, Doug wasn't needy as much as he was insecure. But her mother didn't see it that way and Bridget long ago stopped commenting. Why bother? Her mother would simply say, "You know men, they're all just big children at heart."

Bridget thought differently.

"Aren't you glad for Gianna?" Grandma Em asked.

"What?" Bridget blinked. "Of course. She's very sweet and Nora dotes on her."

"Ever since she and Nora came over and announced the engagement, you've been out of sorts."

Bridget dumped the pretreated towels in the laundry basket, where they'd sit until the load of linens was done.

"My mind's been elsewhere." Like on how Gianna, twelve years Bridget's junior, had already found her soul mate.

"Has Ryan invited you to dinner again?"

Aha! Here was the real reason for her grandmother's lingering.

Bridget played dumb. "Again? What makes you think he invited me to dinner a first time?"

"It's obvious when a man has been bitten by the love bug, and been bitten hard."

Love bug? Ryan?

"Trust me, Grandma, he hasn't been bitten,

and he didn't invite me to dinner." Not yesterday, anyway.

"Hmm. You said no. I figured as much."

Weary of her grandmother's continued matchmaking efforts, Bridget attempted to redirect the subject. "He gave me a tour of his house after we checked the barn and outbuildings." She explained about the call from Nora regarding the trespassing teenagers.

"What did you think of the place? Nora says he's making progress."

"Slow progress. It'll be a showcase one day, but there's a lot of work to be done. He plans on remodeling the entire property, inside and outside."

"Gotta admire a man with ambition."

Bridget set up the ironing board for later. "Did Nora tell you that he flips houses?"

"What's that?"

"He buys fixer-uppers at a low price and then sells them for a profit after he's done with the remodeling. This is his fourth. He's making money at it, apparently."

Grandma Em drew back in surprise. "Good money?"

"Enough, apparently. From what he said, he rolls the profit from each house into the next and lives entirely on his wages. His goal is to eventually buy a small ranch and maybe start his own construction company."

"He *is* ambitious. And here I thought I couldn't like him any more than I do."

Bridget resisted rolling her eyes and headed out of the laundry room.

Grandmother Em trailed after her. "You have to admit, he has much more potential than you originally credited him with."

"He's not looking for a wife."

"Did he say that?"

"Actually, he did. That ambition of his you so admire includes remaining single until he's bought that ranch."

"How long does he suppose that'll take?"

"Two years at least."

"That's nothing." Grandma Em gave a snort. "A man like Ryan might well be worth waiting for."

Not to Bridget. She'd be thirty-four in two years, as her biological clock kept reminding her.

It was true, these days women were getting married and having children in their later thirties and forties all the time. But Bridget was ready now, and she couldn't help wondering if she'd made a mistake by not giving the more serious-minded men she'd dated in the past a chance.

She mentioned none of that to her grandmother. "I'd rather focus on a relationship with immediate potential."

"And miss out on a lot of fun in the meantime? Take it from me. I wasn't serious about Homer when we first dated. That quickly changed."

"The difference is, Homer was ready for marriage and having children one day wasn't part of the picture." Bridget went to the counter, where she uncovered the mixer and chose the right set of beaters for the cupcake batter.

"Is it because Ryan's younger than you?"

"No." The small gap in their ages made no difference to Bridget. "Though if he were older, he might be closer to buying that ranch, marrying and starting a family."

"I bet he could be persuaded to postpone buying a ranch."

"I'd never ask that of him." She recalled his desire to start out married life with more than his parents had. "He'd eventually come to resent me. We'd both end up miserable and angry and hurt."

"I hate to admit that I see your point." Grandma Em's shoulders sagged. "I don't necessarily agree, however. People in love find a way."

"We're not in love."

"You could be. If you let yourself."

Bridget was tired of the back-and-forth. "When you eloped with Homer after a whirlwind courtship, even missing the opening of Sweetheart Ranch, I supported you. Unconditionally. I'd like you to support my decision to not get involved with a man who isn't ready to commit."

"You're right." Grandma went over and tucked an errant lock of hair behind Bridget's ear. "I just want you to be happy."

Like *she* was happy, Bridget thought. Her grandmother had found a beautiful and satisfying love. It was natural for her to wish the same for Bridget, especially now that Molly had found love with Owen. Not to mention Nora's granddaughter's recent engagement.

"You don't need to worry about me," Bridget said, kissing her grandmother's cheek before breaking away to open the refrigerator door.

"For what it's worth, you're too good for that doctor."

Bridget refused to be dragged into another discussion on Gregory. "Did you read my suggestions for Saturday's menu?"

"Remind me."

"Southwestern grilled chicken with lime butter, cheddar ranch potatoes, shredded zucchini and black-bean salad, and fire-roasted mari-nated tomatoes."

"Sounds delicious. Though we could have had plain old hamburgers and hot dogs. Then you wouldn't have to work so hard."

"Grandma! Watch your mouth," Bridget joked. "This is no ordinary backyard cookout."

"What's for dessert?"

"I haven't decided."

Grandma Em started a fresh pot of coffee. "Will you be able to go on the hayride?"

"I doubt it. I'll be too busy with the food."

Suddenly, Molly burst into the kitchen, an I've-got-news-for-you grin on her face. "You'll never guess who's just called and booked an appointment for Saturday morning." Before anyone could answer, she blurted, "Dr. Hall from the urgent-care clinic!"

"You don't say?" Grandma Em's gaze flew to Bridget, whose heart executed a quick sideways tumble.

"Yeah." Molly grabbed a cookie from the jar Bridget kept constantly filled. "He wants some information for his sister. She's research-ing venues in the area. She and her fiancé live in Vermont but are having their wedding here. A second wedding, actually, for her family. They're also having one next month in Ver-mont for his. Guess they figure two weddings are easier than making one of their families fly across the country. Anyway, he promised her he'd stop by and get some information."

"How very interesting." Grandma Em didn't disguise the curious tone in her voice.

Bridget realized she'd been toying with her hair and forced her hand to her side. Fortunately, Molly had no idea about her designs on Gregory. Neither was she picking up on their grandmother's subtle innuendoes. Thank goodness.

"He also signed up for the hayride and cookout on Saturday," Molly added.

"He did?" Bridget's heart executed another tumble, higher this time.

"Gotta run." Molly headed for the door. "Just had to tell you. He'll be here early, before clinic hours."

Grandma Em cornered Bridget the instant they were alone. "Does this mean you've changed your mind and will be going on the hayride after all?"

CHAPTER SEVEN

EMILY TILTED THE map in order for Ryan to better see and tapped the center with her finger. "If you take the south road instead of the west, you can make a circle here and people will have a nice view of Pinnacle Peak."

They sat at the kitchen table, finishing the last of their pastries and discussing the route for tonight's hayride. Early morning meetings had become a regular habit for them this past week. Emily liked going over the day's business with Ryan and troubleshooting any potential problems. He strongly suspected she simply liked the company.

He didn't mind. He, too, enjoyed their meetings. Not only did they help him do a better job, but he also got to partake of Bridget's many culinary delights and had a front-row view of her at work. Her bustling and fussing and mumbling to herself was nothing short of entertaining.

"The west road's in better condition for a hayride." Ryan bit into a melt-in-your-mouth pastry. "Fewer ruts and holes."

"True," Emily agreed.

He'd ridden both roads yesterday morning before their one scheduled trail ride in order to check conditions and familiarize himself with the routes. He'd rather not encounter any unpleasant surprises during his first solo effort driving the team.

After more discussion, he and Emily decided on the west road. At the long kitchen counter, Bridget flitted about, busily chopping and dicing and slicing and mixing. Food for the cookout tonight, Ryan assumed.

She seemed more agitated than usual, and he wondered what was bothering her. Could it be him sitting in close range? Other than square-dance practice last night, they'd had little contact these past two days. And there'd been no close calls during last night's practice, like the first time.

Two other couples had been recruited. Molly and Owen, along with friends of Homer's, had brought the number to eight. As in typical square-dance fashion, Ryan had traded partners frequently. There'd been no opportunity to lose himself in Bridget's startling green eyes or hold her closer than was necessitated by the dance pattern.

Knowing minimal contact was for the best

hadn't stopped Ryan from missing their previous intense connection.

Watching her at work this morning, he pictured her preparing a romantic dinner for two in his newly remodeled kitchen. Out of the question, of course, but tell that to his vivid imagination.

She clearly wasn't having similar fantasies. When not gnawing on her lower lip, she was wringing her hands or randomly moving objects about. Then, while pouring marinade sauce over the chicken pieces arranged in a pan, she spilled some and made a much bigger deal of it than was warranted, grumbling complaints under her breath.

"There's a total of three carriage rides this weekend," Emily said, shifting gears from the hayride to the ranch's signature amenity. "Amos and Moses are going to have quite a workout."

The Haflinger draft-horse brothers were up to it. Sturdy and strong, they'd been bred to work and loved to pull. "They'll do fine," Ryan assured her. "None of the carriage rides are more than an hour long, and we'll be walking the entire way."

"How are the new trail horses doing? No problems?"

"Not a single complaint from the guests.

The farrier was here on Thursday and replaced Goldie's shoe."

"That's good." Emily consulted a printed-out schedule. "We have one to two trail rides every day for the next two weeks, which, by Molly's calculations, is our break-even point."

"Is that enough?" Ryan asked. "Wouldn't it be better if we were making a profit?" He did worry about job security. The previous wrangler, Big Jim, had been part-time. Ryan had easily logged forty hours his first week and would do so again next week. According to *his* calculations, he was costing the ranch twice what Big Jim had.

"Making a profit is always preferable," Emily said. "For now, trail rides are a popular selling point to potential wedding clients and honeymooning guests. As long as we're breaking even, I'm tickled pink. The ranch is still in its first year of operation. I wake up most days amazed we're doing as well as we are and not on the brink of financial ruin."

They no sooner moved to the next item on Emily's list when the bell over the front door jangled, announcing a visitor.

Bridget gave a small jump and dropped an empty aluminum mixing bowl onto the tile floor. It clattered loudly before spinning in a circle.

"Sorry." Flushing profusely, she bent and grabbed the bowl. "My fingers are slippery."

Ryan leaned back in his chair and studied her. Something definitely had her on edge today. The visitor, perhaps? A strong possibility given the dropped bowl and her sudden obsession with inspecting each and every potato in the bag.

"Must be the doctor." Emily grinned at Bridget. "He's early."

"The same doctor from the clinic?" Ryan pushed aside his suddenly tasteless pastry.

"Yes, indeed." Emily's voice contained an odd lilt Ryan couldn't quite identify. "He's here for his sister. She's researching wedding venues. Isn't that nice?"

Again, Emily appeared to find considerable amusement in Bridget's nervous reaction to her comments. With the force she scrubbed the potatoes, they wouldn't require peeling. The skin would simply flake right off.

Ryan tamped down his twinge of jealousy. Bridget's relationship with the doctor was none of his concern. She'd made that much clear the other day. The same day he'd made it clear to her that he wasn't ready to settle down.

Molly abruptly stuck her head into the kitchen. "Bridget, do you have a second? Dr. Hall would like some information for his sister on wedding cakes and the catering menu. Can you talk to him?"

"Sure, sure." Bridget ripped off her apron and tossed it aside, seemingly not caring that it landed half in the sink. "Be right there. Let me grab my book and price sheet."

Molly left and Bridget flew into a flurry, sweeping a binder and her tablet off the counter in one motion. On her way out, she stopped to study her reflection in the microwave door over the stove. Ryan swore he saw her extract a tube of lipstick from her jeans pocket and uncap it one-handed.

"Don't worry about her."

Emily's voice penetrated his thoughts. He turned to face her, realizing he'd been staring after Bridget. "I'm not."

"She isn't interested in him. Not really. She just keeps telling herself she is. It's a defense mechanism."

"Against what?"

Emily laughed. "Why, you, silly."

"Sorry. I'm confused."

"She's afraid of liking you too much."

"There's nothing between us."

"More's the pity," Emily said sadly.

Ryan decided not to pursue his boss's re-mark. He'd likely get his hopes up only to have them dashed.

He stood, then carried his plate and coffee cup from the table to the sink and, moving Bridget's apron aside, loaded them in the dishwasher. "I'd best get to work. Amos and Moses won't groom themselves."

"Me, too, I suppose."

All at once they heard the rumble of a large vehicle pulling up in front of the house.

"Must be Owen," Emily announced. "He bought a new pony for his children and mentioned stopping by on his way home. Come on, let's take a look at the little fellow."

Ryan accompanied her outside. There, Owen was lowering the rear gate on his horse trailer. A moment later he led out what was quite possibly the cutest pony on the face of the planet. Barely three feet tall at the withers, he was brown with large white patches. Or was he white with large brown patches? Either way, Popeye, as he was named, looked curiously about with large, expressive eyes.

"He's adorable," Emily exclaimed and promptly lavished the pony with scratches between his ears and kisses on his nose. "The children will love him. If they don't I'll take him off your hands."

Molly came outside and made an even bigger fuss over Popeye than her grandmother. Had she finished her appointment with the doctor? Ryan's gaze kept drifting to the house's front door. Neither Bridget nor the doctor had emerged. Were they together?

Owen returned Popeye to the trailer and was about to close the rear gate when Bridget and the doctor finally appeared. Instead of joining everyone else, they remained on the veranda talking, Bridget quite animatedly. Like at the clinic, she tossed her hair and smiled up at him. Once…no, twice, she reached out and touched his upper arm.

Ryan took note of the man's designer cargo pants, the hundred-dollar haircut he sported and his daily workout physique. The BMW in the parking area surely belonged to him. And he was a doctor. An esteemed and respected professional. He probably lived in that cluster of expensive luxury homes in the foothills south of town.

No way could Ryan, a wrangler who drove a nine-year-old pickup and survived paycheck to paycheck, compete with him.

With a "See you all later," Ryan moseyed off toward the stables. Bridget's flirtatious laughter followed him, carried on the breeze.

BONELESS GRILLED CHICKEN had been a good choice for tonight's menu. It wouldn't take long to cook, even over coals. With the side dishes either ready and chilling in the refrigerator or warming in the oven, Bridget was free to go on the hayride.

Only because Gregory will be there.

Yes, she didn't dispute the small, nagging voice inside her. If not for him signing up for the ride, Bridget would have stayed home. But he *had* signed up, giving her another opportunity to drop more subtle hints that she was available and interested.

He'd been affable this morning when he stopped by the ranch. Nothing more. She must, she decided, be doing something wrong. That, or she was really rusty at male-female interaction.

No, impossible. Ryan responded to her even when she wasn't trying, which was always.

Heading out the kitchen door, she cut through the pool area, careful not to let her gaze travel to the clubhouse. Seeing it reminded her of square-dancing practice. That first night when Ryan had held her, and she'd enjoyed the sensation of his arms circling her waist much more than she should have.

Thankfully, three other couples had attended the second practice. Avoiding another brush with unintentional intimate physical contact had been easily accomplished.

You liked him holding you.

Stop it! she demanded of the voice. The only

reason she'd liked it at all, and she wasn't admitting to anything, was because over two years had passed since a man last held her and twirled her and looked at her as if he wanted nothing more than to taste her cherry lip gloss.

Bridget forced her thoughts back to the present. Avoiding Ryan at the post-cookout square dance tonight shouldn't be a problem as at least twenty people were expected. More if Nora and her friends came.

With luck, one of those twenty people would be the handsome Dr. Hall.

She waited for the same tingling sensation to spread through her middle as when Ryan had slipped his arm around her waist and promenaded her across the room. It didn't happen.

Swatting away a pesky gnat, she hurried up the road toward the stables. Too late, she realized she hadn't checked the parking area beside the main house. She'd noticed earlier today that Gregory drove a BMW.

A very nice metallic silver sedan. Item number five on her nonnegotiable dating list most definitely checked off. She could see herself sitting in the front passenger seat, leather upholstery no doubt, and beaming a smile at Gregory, who would be sitting behind the wheel and skillfully navigating them to their first date.

What kind of food did he like? She'd meant

to ask that while they discussed potential catering options for his sister. Only she'd gotten flustered and forgotten. Admittedly, she'd been trying too hard—a direct result of her insecurities.

He'd been at the ranch on business, she reminded herself, and not there to flirt. Same as the other day at the clinic. If anything, she respected him even more for his professionalism. Tonight would be different, however. The hayride and cookout—and square dance, if he went—were purely social.

As she neared the stables, she searched the faces of those gathered outside. None of them were Gregory's. She removed her phone from her jeans pocket and checked the time. Twelve minutes before the hayride was due to leave. He could be on his way.

Saying hello to the guests, she wound her way closer to the wagon.

"Bridget! You're here."

Hearing her name, she turned. "Oh, hi, Grandma. I thought you weren't going on the hayride."

"I'm not. I'm seeing off the guests. But I'm glad you're going."

She was? Had she deduced Bridget's plans?

"You've been working hard the last few days," Grandma Em continued. "Good to see you taking a break. And it doesn't hurt for one of us to mingle a little with the guests."

"O-kay."

Where was Gregory? Bridget strained to see past her grandmother and down the dirt road leading toward the house without appearing obvious.

"Time to load up," Ryan called out.

He'd been making last-minute adjustments to the harnesses and answering questions. He'd also been posing for pictures with the guests. *Lots* of pictures. Apparently he was photogenic.

She couldn't argue with that. He had that sexy cowboy swagger when he walked and rugged good looks. The kind of looks that had women wondering if he was a good guy or a bad guy and hoping for a little of each.

Standing at the foot of the wagon, he said, "Let's load up. One at a time."

People meandered toward the wagon, forming a line. Seeing no sign of Gregory and his children, Bridget tried not to panic. It proved difficult and her glance continually cut to the road in search of them. Should she go on the hayride? Stay behind and wait?

She silently chided herself. Here she was, yet again, acting stupid over the doctor. Obviously, he'd canceled at the last minute. She should go home. Get a head start on the cookout.

Suddenly, he appeared in the door to the stables, his children in tow. Bridget's heart jumped. They must have been inside petting the other horses. Anticipation mingled with relief and coursed through her.

She headed for the stables, her path on a collision course with his. At the last second, she glanced sideways. Huge mistake. Ryan stared at her, emotion flashing in his eyes. Disappointment? Irritation? She ignored him but felt his stare on the back of her neck as she made her way to the stables.

Gregory saw her then, and she produced a smile. The next second, both her mouth and her steps simultaneously froze in place as an attractive woman emerged from the stables. When she reached Gregory, he casually slipped his hand into hers. She said something too soft for Bridget to hear. In response, he cupped her cheek with his free hand.

A date. Gregory had brought a date to the hayride. Not a first date, either, from the looks of it. Bridget swayed slightly as the realization took hold.

In what felt like slow motion, Gregory, the woman and his two children began walking straight for Bridget.

She tried to speak, managing only a wobbly "Hello."

"Hey." He smiled at her, too. It was considerably less bright than the one he'd showered on the woman. "Bridget, this is my friend Celeste." His tone could have melted butter when he spoke the word *friend*. "Celeste, this is Bridget, head chef at the ranch."

"Nice to meet you." Celeste's name couldn't fit her any better. With her pale blond hair and flawless complexion, she was as luminous as a shining star.

Bridget felt drab in comparison.

"Welcome to Sweetheart Ranch." She swallowed against her dry throat. "Enjoy yourself on the hayride."

Convinced acute embarrassment must be written all over her face, she started to leave. No question about it, she was definitely staying home now.

"Will you be at the cookout later?" Celeste asked pleasantly.

"She's the chef. Of course she'll be there." Gregory's laugh was warm and rich. It was the kind of laugh Bridget had hoped to coax from him during their two awkward encounters.

Here was her chance to execute a clean escape. He didn't know she was going on the ride. No one did, other than Grandma Em. And with starry Celeste completely occupying him, neither would notice her exit.

"Have a good evening." Bridget almost got away, but her grandmother stopped her.

"Wait. Where are you going?"

"I've changed my mind about the ride," Bridget muttered.

"Nonsense. Just because that doctor fellow brought a woman along?"

"She has nothing to do with it."

"Then why are you running away like a dog with its tail between its legs."

"Grandma, please."

"There's no reason not to go on the ride. And don't bring up the cookout. I happen to know for a fact you have everything ready, right down to the condiment tray."

Bridget watched as Ryan helped the last guest into the wagon.

"All the seats are taken," she countered. Seats being the bales of straw.

"Sit up front with Ryan."

No way. He knew Gregory had brought a date. He'd helped Celeste into the wagon, for crying out loud.

"I'd rather not." She was in no mood for his teasing.

"Bridget, honey. Don't let that doctor fellow make you feel bad or doubt yourself. You're a beautiful, strong, talented young woman who also happens to be an incredible catch. You'll find the right man, and he'll be darn lucky to have you."

Bridget rubbed her throat where a painful lump had lodged. If her grandmother had made even one tiny remark about her and Ryan dating, she'd have whirled on her heels and left. But her grandmother hadn't. Rather, she'd tapped into the very center of the emotions eating away at her.

"Fine. I'll go."

"That's my girl. Now, come on. I told Ryan I'd untie the horses for him."

They walked to the front of the wagon, where Ryan sat waiting. Gathering the four long reins and weaving them between his fingers, he sent her a quizzical look.

"I'm riding with you," Bridget explained. "If that's all right."

"Climb aboard." He scooted over.

Holding on to the wagon wheel for balance, she placed a foot on the small metal step and hauled herself up. Twisting ungraciously, she plopped down into the seat. The springs creaked beneath the sudden assault.

She glowered at Ryan, silently daring him to comment. He wisely refrained.

Grandma Em went over to the hitching rail and, at Ryan's signal, untied the lead ropes. She then moved to the side and raised her hand in farewell.

"Have a great ride everyone."

She was answered by an enthusiastic chorus of goodbyes.

"Ready?" Ryan pulled back on the reins and called to Amos and Moses. "Haw, haw." Ears pricked forward, the draft horses swung their large heads to the left and shuffled their feet. When Ryan jostled the reins and shouted, "Step up," they began slowly walking, pulling the wagon away from the hitching rail easy as pie.

"What changed your mind about coming on the hayride?" Ryan asked when they were underway.

"The food's ready. No reason I couldn't."

"I meant what changed your mind about going after you found out Dr. What's-His-Name brought his girlfriend?"

"She's his date. She may not be his girlfriend."

"Didn't you see them together? If she's not his girlfriend, he wants her to be."

Ryan was right. Bridget refused to give him the satisfaction, however.

"I haven't been on a hayride since last Christmas," she said. "I thought it might be fun. And it might be if we stop talking about Gregory," she added caustically.

"Okeydokey."

They traveled along in silence, Bridget half listening to the lively chatter of the twenty people behind her in the wagon and enjoying the scenery.

Spring was her favorite time of year. All around them, palo verde trees had exploded with yellow blossoms that layered the ground beneath the trees like a blanket of gold. Here and there, century plants had pushed forth their spindly stalks, some of them thirty feet tall and laden with blossoms at the top.

Before long, they reached a gate, the same one she'd opened while astride her horse the day she and Ryan went riding together.

He reined the horses to a stop with a loud "Whoa." Nodding at the gate, he asked, "Do you mind?"

"Not at all." She climbed down and held the gate open while the wagon passed through.

On the other side, Ryan stopped the horses again and waited for her. When she was once more seated, he clucked to the horses.

"It's a beautiful evening." He offered her a smile. "Sorry you're not here with a different guy."

"I don't mind."

"Ah. I fall into the I-don't-mind category."

"It's not like that," Bridget insisted.

"For the record, I'm glad the doctor has a girlfriend. And before you warn me off for the tenth time, I'm glad because he doesn't deserve you, Bridget. Not if he can't see what a great gal you are."

Her grandmother had said something similar to her before the ride and with the same sincerity in her voice as Ryan's.

"Thank you," she murmured softly, the painful lump reappearing.

"And also, for the record—" he took his eyes off the road ahead of them to gaze at her "—there isn't anyone else I'd rather have sitting next to me."

Bridget tried to convince herself he was only trying to make her feel better. Deep inside, she knew that wasn't true. Everything from the intensity of his stare to the seductive timbre of his voice told her just how much he liked being with her.

For the first time all day, Bridget forgot about Dr. What's-His-Name.

CHAPTER EIGHT

RYAN UPENDED THE bucket and poured grain into Amos's feed trough. The big gelding shoved his arm aside and attempted to gulp bites midair as the grain fell.

"Slow down, will you?" Ryan moved the empty bucket out of range. "There's enough fat on you to feed you till summer."

An exaggeration, certainly, although Amos and his brother, Moses, both carried a spare tire around their middles.

Ryan ran a hand along Amos's back before leaving the stall. The formerly gleaming hide that Ryan had painstakingly brushed had been dulled by dust and sweat. He'd have his work cut out for him in the morning, getting the pair of Haflingers shiny and pretty for the carriage rides around town.

Neither horse was the least bit concerned with appearance as they munched on their dinner.

"Wish *I* had something to eat." Ryan rested an arm on the stall door. "I missed the cookout."

Unharnessing had taken time, almost as much as harnessing, and he'd worked up an appetite. Hearing the passengers talk excitedly about the cookout menu during the hayride and knowing Bridget's culinary skills firsthand had whetted his appetite further.

"The doctor has a girlfriend," he told Moses, who shot him a sideways glance while chewing. "Yeah, that's what I say. Good. He probably snores or has a secret gambling habit or is a picky eater. That would crush Bridget. She loves experimenting with food."

Who was Ryan fooling? He suspected the doctor was a nice guy. The fact that he felt inferior was his problem and no reason to invent flaws where none existed.

"I can't decide if I should go to the square dance or not."

In the stall across from Amos, Goldie emitted a high-pitched squeal and kicked at the wall. Her neighbor had dared to reach his nose between the bars separating them and given her a love nip on the rump, which she neither appreciated nor reciprocated.

"I can relate, buddy," Ryan told the brown gelding. "Women are fickle creatures."

Goldie snorted as if insulted.

He crossed the aisle to her stall. "Do you think I should go to the dance?"

To prove his point about being fickle, Goldie ignored her neighbor in favor of Ryan and placed her head on his shoulder in the equine version of a hug.

He stroked her neck. At least this female liked his attention.

"Should I take that as a yes?"

Goldie sniffed his neck, the noise loud in his ear like a jet engine at takeoff.

"You're right. I did promise Emily I'd help demonstrate the steps."

Beside them, the brown gelding stomped his foot on the ground.

"Easy, boy. No reason to get jealous."

Given the chance, Ryan could easily lose his heart to Bridget. Not just lose, but give it away. That wouldn't happen, though. Not when they were maintaining a safe distance from each other.

Moving out from beneath Goldie's head, he noticed a smudge on his collar left by the horse and brushed at it. "Good thing I brought a clean shirt with me."

He replaced the lid on the grain barrel and shut off all but one security light before leaving the stables. At his truck, which he'd parked alongside the stables, he opened the passenger door and lifted the shirt from where he'd hung it.

Ryan owned exactly two dress Western shirts. This was the better of the two. Laying it on the seat, he undid the snaps of the shirt he wore. They popped open one after the other with a quick *rat-tat-tat*. Stripping off the dirty shirt, he bunched it into a ball and threw it on the floor in front of the passenger seat. His white undershirt gleamed bright in the glow of the moon.

"There you are."

The voice startled him. Seeing a familiar silhouette materialize from around the stables, surprise morphed into delight and then anticipation.

"Hi." He offered Bridget a grin. "What brings you here?"

She stepped closer. The same moonlight that lit his undershirt also illuminated her lovely features. He stood there, dumbstruck and more than a little lovestruck.

"You missed dinner." She held up a covered plate he hadn't seen at first. "I thought you might be hungry."

"I am. A little." For food. For her. For what they couldn't have.

She studied him intently. "Did I catch you at a bad time?"

"Just changing shirts." He didn't dare tell her

the truth, that she'd dazzled him. "Don't want to go to the dance smelling like horses."

Something in her eyes flickered. "You don't smell like horses."

How did she know? They weren't close enough for her to tell.

He could remedy that. Six long strides in her direction should do the trick.

"Folks at the dance may beg to differ," he said, not moving. "In fact, I should wash up a bit." He stuck a hand in the back pocket of his jeans and produced a handkerchief. "Be right back."

The more distance between them, the easier it became for Ryan to focus, and he forced himself to relax.

Without soap, cold water from the spigot on the side of the stables would have to do. Wetting the handkerchief, he scrubbed it over his face and neck, then washed his forearms and hands. Not much, but it would have to suffice.

Sensing he wasn't alone, he turned and spied Bridget retreating. Had she been watching him? Hard to tell, but he thought she had and smiled to himself.

Feeling marginally refreshed, he returned to his truck and donned the clean shirt. Bridget was sitting on the bench and not looking his way. He used the opportunity to tuck in the shirt and adjust his belt before joining her.

"Here." She lifted the plate to him.

"Mind if I sit?"

"Please do."

The bench wasn't much wider than the wagon seat had been. During the ride, they'd inadvertently bumped shoulders and knees while traveling over rocks and potholes in the road. Ryan wished for a pothole now.

He removed the plastic wrap covering the plate. "What have we here?"

"Grilled chicken on ciabatta bread. I was going for ease and efficiency. The square dance starts in fifteen minutes. Not to rush you or anything."

"Thanks." He lifted a long, green slender object from the stack next to the sandwich.

"Pickled asparagus," Bridget said. "Homemade. My grandmother's recipe."

"Emily cooks, too?"

"My other grandmother. She passed away a few years ago. As the story goes, she took first place eighteen years straight at the state fair with her pickled asparagus."

"Is that true?"

Bridget shrugged. "I've seen the ribbons and newspaper articles. And the asparagus are good."

Ryan took a big bite, appreciating the crunch and burst of sour, spicy flavors. "I can see why she won so often." He finished a second asparagus. "Is she the one you inherited your love of cooking from?"

"I'd like to think I did. She was a country cook and not much when it came to gourmet cuisine. But you never had better fried chicken and mashed potatoes in your life."

Ryan finished his sandwich while Bridget shared a fond memory, when her paternal grandmother taught her how to boil, peel and can tomatoes at the tender age of six.

"She sounds like a great lady," Ryan said.

"My dad's death nearly broke her. She wasn't the same afterward. None of us were."

"How did he die?"

"Automobile accident. He lived for five weeks afterward, the last one in a hospice facility. Technically, he died from pneumonia." Her voice cracked. "He just wasn't strong enough to fight it off."

"I'm sorry."

"Me, too. I was fourteen at the time. All these years later, and I still miss him." She turned misty eyes on him. "I must sound like a little girl to you."

"You sound like a daughter who adored her father."

Ryan lifted his arm. To heck with rules and warnings. Bridget needed a hug, and he wanted to give her one.

Before he could accomplish his goal, she planted her palms on her thighs and pushed to her feet. Had she seen the hug coming and wanted to avoid it?

"We should hurry," she said.

"You're right."

"I didn't intend to be so maudlin. Not sure where that came from."

Standing, Ryan disposed of the paper plate and plastic wrap. "Before we go, tell me something." He came over and stood toe-to-toe with her, forcing her to look up at him.

"Should I be worried?" Her teasing tone held a note of concern.

"Why did you bring me supper?"

"You missed the cookout."

"You could've sent someone else or brought it to the clubhouse. Why the personal delivery?"

"No reason."

"I want to know."

She inhaled slowly. "My way of saying thanks, I guess, for helping me not to feel entirely stupid about Gregory—Dr. Hall—bringing a date."

"And here I thought you liked me."

"I do. Like you," she added, as if trying out the words.

"Trust me, Bridget. I like you, too."

He waited for her gaze to connect with his. When it did, the jolt of awareness nearly brought him to his knees. Every fiber of his being urged him to take her in his arms and kiss her, until they were both breathless and until they'd forgotten all the reasons why being together was a bad idea.

He refrained only by drawing on every ounce of his willpower. No way was he starting something he couldn't finish, regardless of how tempting. Instead, he settled for leaning in another fraction of an inch and reveling in the incredible scent of her that always reminded him of deliciously decadent desserts.

"He's the stupid one, Bridget," Ryan said. "Not you. Don't ever think differently."

She shook her head. "I don't know what I was thinking. I'm really not interested in Gregory. I tried to convince myself I was because he checked off so many boxes."

"Boxes?"

She glanced away. "Nothing."

"Tell me."

"I kind of have this list. Qualities I'm looking for in a man. Gregory has a lot of them." She sighed. "Apparently I should have included a reciprocal interest in me as one of those qualities."

Ryan satisfied that requirement and then some. He didn't ask how many of her other desired qualities he possessed, afraid he'd come up short.

"Come on." She swiped her hands together as if being done with something. The doctor perhaps? "Grandma will chew us out if we're late."

Together, they walked to the clubhouse. Loud voices reached their ears well before they got there.

Bridget took Ryan's hand and pulled him along the last thirty feet, half running and half walking. At the gate to the clubhouse, she let go, and disappointment squeezed his chest. Her impulsiveness, innocent though it had been, excited him more than any overt come-on.

They entered the brightly lit, crowded room. In addition to furniture being pushed against the walls, folding chairs had been set up and a linen-covered table held water and other beverages. Square dancing was thirsty work.

"Hurry up!" Emily motioned for Ryan and Bridget to join her and Homer at the front of the room. "Is everyone ready?" she asked the group, who nodded like obedient children. "I know we have some square dancers here. Let's see a show of hands."

To Ryan's surprise, and Bridget's, too, given her slack-jawed expression, the doctor was among those who raised their hands. Celeste giggled and gave his arm a friendly shove.

"Wonderful. You can help Bridget and Ryan demonstrate." Emily beckoned them to the front of the room. "Now, the four of you form a small circle, boy-girl, boy-girl. This first dance is a very simple one," she told the people watching. "When it's your turn, just listen to Homer, and you'll be fine. If you mess up, don't worry. Have yourself a good laugh and keep going."

The doctor's date stood to Ryan's left and Bridget to his right. She shifted uncomfortably, her glance darting frequently to the doctor.

Emily pressed a button on the karaoke machine, and the music started.

"Bow to your partner," Homer called in a singsong voice.

The four dancers executed the bows.

"Now bow to your left."

They bowed again, Ryan to the doctor's girlfriend, and Bridget to the doctor.

"First swing your partner," Homer called. "Then, gentlemen swing the pretty gal to your left. Take her hand and circle around."

Ryan watched as the doctor grabbed hold of

Bridget's hand, the same one Ryan had been holding minutes ago on their walk to the clubhouse, and lean close to whisper in her ear.

Grinding his teeth together, Ryan barely noticed his partner as they executed the steps. If he had known for one second that another man, especially the doctor, would be holding Bridget and whispering in her ear, he would have stolen her away long before they got here.

SHE'D SURVIVED. BRIDGET had danced with Gregory and avoided stumbling or making inane comments or bolting for the door after embarrassment overload. In an odd way, she found relief in his complete disinterest in her. Each time they'd come together according to the call, he'd given her the briefest of glances before peering over his shoulder at Celeste.

Count yourself lucky. If not for tonight, Bridget might have continued carrying on with her ridiculous plan for who knew how long.

Taking another swig from her bottle of water, she watched the square dancers. Everyone appeared to be enjoying themselves. Even Gregory's children had joined in once or twice.

For this song, Ryan was partnering with Nora. At just shy of five feet tall, she was dwarfed by his six-feet-plus height. Regardless, she beamed at him as they met up in the middle of the circle, looking a decade younger than her actual years.

Did Ryan have that effect on Bridget, too? She was quite certain he did. He'd soothed her injured ego, so, of course, she'd smiled up at him. *His* interest in her was genuine, not faked or a figment of her imagination.

Then again, she thought as her eyes followed him circling the dance floor, he was every bit as sweet and attentive to Nora as he'd been to her. Perhaps Bridget was misreading the signals. Sadly, it wouldn't be the first time.

The very next second, he glanced her way and their gazes connected. Bridget's breath stilled. Her first instinct was to look away. She didn't, however, and his mouth widened into a hey-there grin.

The signal couldn't be any clearer. Ryan liked her. Liked her in *that* way. Possibly a lot.

What should she do? Certainly not encourage him. If anything, she should walk away and initiate a conversation with someone else.

Nope. Instead, Bridget smiled back. In response, he winked. She laughed and rolled her eyes. Homer made a call that swept the dancers away in the opposite direction, and Ryan was gone, ending their playful exchange.

"Were you just flirting with Ryan?"

Bridget froze at the sound of Molly's voice. "What? No. We weren't even talking."

"Please. Spare me. Two people don't have to be talking to flirt."

"We're friends. Coworkers," she emphasized.

"Uh-huh."

"We sat together in the wagon during the hayride, and we demonstrated the square dancing."

"That's all it takes."

"Right. To be friends."

"To start something romantic." Molly jostled her arm playfully.

Bridget bit down hard rather than say something she'd regret. Her sister was head over heels in love with Owen. Consequently, she saw romance everywhere and in every person.

"There's nothing between us."

Not unless Bridget counted her and Ryan's undeniable chemistry when she'd tripped during square-dancing practice and their almost-kiss earlier tonight *and* him repeatedly asking her out. Molly being Molly, she'd blow the incidents out of proportion.

"This square-dancing demonstration," Molly said. "Think that will be a permanent gig for you and him?"

"I don't know. Grandma didn't say."

The plan was to have monthly hayrides and

square dances open to the public if this one went well. By all accounts, it was. Grandma Em might indeed ask Bridget and Ryan to demonstrate again. Bridget mulled that notion, trying it on for size.

"The same thing happened with Owen," Molly commented.

"Square dancing?"

"Not that, silly. Quit being intentionally obtuse."

Bridget was being obtuse but played dumb. "What are you talking about?"

"You remember. Owen started out as our temporary wedding officiant. Then he assumed the wrangler duties while Big Jim's wife was having all those medical tests." Molly counted the items on her fingers. "Next there were the campfires. And don't forget the Holly Daze Festival—"

Bridget cut her off. "Get to the point."

"Little by little, Owen became indispensable. To the ranch and eventually to me."

"Demonstrating square dancing is hardly indispensable."

Molly went on as if she hadn't heard Bridget. "Being independent women and all, we tend to think we don't need a man about the place. Somehow, we always do."

"The ranch may need a man, but, personally, I'm doing fine on my own."

Molly abruptly changed the subject. "You're not upset about Gianna's engagement, are you?"

Did everyone think Bridget was emotionally fragile and needed protecting?

"I'm not upset." She enunciated each word. "I'm happy for them."

"She was kidding when she said Owen and I are next. Rest assured, we're content with the status quo."

"For goodness' sake. Promise me you're not postponing getting engaged on my account."

"No."

Molly's monosyllabic answer didn't convince Bridget. "Let me set the record straight. I don't compare myself to you or anyone else. Nor do I have feelings of jealousy or inadequacy. I happen to be very satisfied with my life. I work at the job of my dreams, I live in a beautiful home with my family close by and I have a whole slew of friends."

"If you're so satisfied, why are you talking through clenched teeth?"

Was she? Bridget forced herself to relax.

"Look," Molly said, "I didn't mean to imply your life is lacking."

"Just because I'm not in a relationship at the moment is no reason to pity or coddle me."

"I don't pity you. I may coddle a little," Molly admitted. "You are my big sister, and I love you." She gave Bridget's shoulder a fond squeeze. "The right guy's going to come along. Probably when you least expect him."

Why did people always think empty platitudes were the right thing to say? Bridget felt worse than ever.

"Just look at me and Owen," Molly continued, unaware of Bridget's inner turmoil. "I didn't think he was the one at first and required a fair amount of convincing. But the difference between you and me is I remained open to possibilities."

Possibilities like Ryan. Molly might as well have said his name out loud, she wasn't fooling Bridget.

"I am open. Always."

"Ha-ha-ha." Molly pretended to laugh. "If you were, you wouldn't have that stupid dating list."

It was true. Bridget had never been one to fall fast and hard. Too careful. Too independent. Too picky. The list kept her grounded and helped her make smart choices. A less careful woman would leap at the chance to go out with Ryan, long-term potential or not, and end up hurt. Not Bridget.

She promptly shoved thoughts of him to the

recesses of her mind—where they belonged as long as he wasn't husband and father material.

The next moment, Owen appeared and asked Molly for a dance. Thank goodness! Bridget was fast becoming tired of painful and difficult conversations with her family...and herself.

Molly and Owen took their positions on the dance floor as Grandma Em changed the music on the karaoke player. Bridget supposed she could leave; it wasn't as if the people there needed any more demonstrations.

Waving to her grandmother, she pointed toward the door, conveying her intentions. Grandma Em made a sad face. Bridget pressed her stacked hands to her cheek and tilted her head, indicating she was tired and going to bed, and then started for the door.

She didn't make it as far as the clubhouse gate when she heard someone approaching from behind.

"Wait up," Ryan said. "I'll walk you home."

She had to laugh. "I'll be fine. Thank you, though."

"It's late. Almost ten. And dark." Not taking no for an answer, he fell into step beside her.

"The house is a quarter mile away. What could possibly happen to me?"

"You'd be surprised."

There was a quality to the timbre of his

voice that caused her nerve endings to shoot tiny sparks.

She should thank him for his concern and hurry to the house before she made a giant mistake. But no, she didn't.

Ignoring every warning she'd issued herself earlier, she matched her steps to his, which, while long in stride, were slow. He was obviously taking his time, perhaps prolonging the moment when they'd say good-night. That was her guess. Or was it her hope?

At the kitchen door, they paused beneath the small overhang. She debated inviting him inside for coffee.

"Will I see you at breakfast?" he asked.

Where else would she be at 7:00 a.m.? Even on a Sunday, guests needed to be fed.

"I'll be there," she answered. "The newly-weds in cabin four have requested red velvet pancakes with whipped cream-cheese icing. That's a little too much sugar first thing in the morning for me, but to each their own."

"Is there such a thing as too much sugar?"

She laughed softly. "Not on your first morning as husband and wife, apparently."

"What would you order on your first morning with your new husband?"

"I don't know. I've never thought about it."

"Healthy or decadent?" He moved deliberately closer, and his proximity bombarded her senses.

Wasn't this what she'd secretly wanted all along? Ryan moving closer, and her not resisting? Yes. It was. And Bridget took full advantage.

She inhaled slowly, enjoying his scent, masculine with a trace of tea tree oil that might be from his shampoo. She listened to the sound of his breathing, which increased fraction by fraction along with her heartbeat. She gazed into his handsome face, with its strong lines and penetrating eyes, letting it fill her vision until she saw only him and nothing else.

"I'd, um, probably have a very traditional breakfast."

"Like?"

Thinking coherently was becoming increasingly hard for Bridget. "Eggs Benedict. Except I'd use chorizo instead of Canadian bacon."

"What else?"

She drew back ever so slightly. "Are you really interested in this?"

His voice lowered, and he narrowed the gap between them. "I'm interested in you."

He touched her then, the fingers of his large, work-calloused hands sliding into her hair and cupping the sides of her head. Bridget's limbs went weak, and she melted into his embrace.

"What else?" he repeated.

"Mango salsa."

"Keep going."

She tried, really she did. But his mouth hovered inches above hers, and his fingers were sifting through her hair. Her thoughts scattered like a starburst despite her best attempt to contain them. In another instant, her increasingly heavy eyelids would drift close.

"Tomatoes," she uttered with effort. "Fried with, um, spices and scallions."

"Sounds tasty."

Taste. Yes. It was the only sense remaining that Bridget hadn't experienced with Ryan.

"And French press coffee with fresh cream, a dash of cinnamon and, um, uh, raw sugar."

"We can't forget the sugar. I like my...coffee sweet."

The corners of his incredibly sexy mouth curved into a teasing smile that let her know he wasn't talking about coffee. In response, she rose up on her tiptoes.

"Don't stop there." He angled her head for what could only be easier access.

Bridget didn't and parted her lips.

Ryan groaned like a man defeated and covered her mouth with his. She couldn't get mad at him; she had issued the invitation, after all.

And Bridget was very glad she had. He didn't disappoint.

His lips demanded a response from hers and willingly got one. She let him take what he wanted and then took from him in return, savoring the kiss, which was better and sweeter than any cream-cheese icing or raw sugar.

His other arm circled her waist, pulling her against him until they were impossibly close. Deliciously close. She looped her arms around his shoulders before her liquefied knees buckled.

He broke off the kiss and whispered, "You're so beautiful, Bridget."

She believed him. He made her feel beautiful. And special and cherished. All with a mere kiss. How absolutely extraordinary.

When she thought—no, feared—he might release her, he returned to her mouth for more and more, erasing any lingering uncertainties she had about the extent of his feelings for her.

They stayed like they were, lips fused and heartbeats in sync. Bridget couldn't say for how long. A minute? Ten? That had never happened to her before. With any man. Ever. She didn't lose herself completely.

Eventually, and too soon for her preference, Ryan ended the kiss and set her aside. She uttered a small sound of protest when his hands fell away.

"I'd better leave. Before I…before we…" He didn't finish. There was no need.

"Okay. Right."

"Good night, Bridget. Sleep tight." Briefly caressing her cheek with his palm, he pivoted and walked away in the direction of the stables, where he'd left his truck.

"Good night, Ryan," she called after him and fumbled her way inside.

The kitchen floor seemed to shift beneath her feet, and Bridget grabbed for the counter. She imagined Molly telling her that was what it felt like to be a goner.

CHAPTER NINE

RYAN KISSED ME.

"Yes, ma'am." Bridget blinked, focusing. "We can certainly provide that."

I kissed him back.

"What do they want?" Molly whispered. She sat at the registration counter, staring up at Bridget.

"No problem." Bridget moved the phone away from her mouth and whispered, "Scones."

The Literary Ladies were having their catered luncheon this coming Saturday at noon. Bridget, Molly and Grandma Em would have about an hour after the ladies left to prepare for their three-thirty wedding. Assuming the reception was done by five thirty at the latest, that left a slim ninety minutes before guests began knocking on the door for Gianna and her fiancé's engagement party.

It was going to be quite a day, nonstop from beginning to end, and a busy three days leading up to it. Bridget couldn't afford to be distracted. And, yet, she was.

I should have stopped him.

But then she'd have missed out on the experience of a lifetime.

She hadn't been alone with Ryan since their kiss. Not that she was avoiding him. They interacted frequently during the day for normal ranch business. She did, however, always make sure someone else was there and would do so until her resolve was firmly boosted.

"I'm sorry, what was that?" Chagrined, she asked the caller to repeat herself.

"No raisins," the woman said with a hint of disgust in her voice. "Mildred hates them and will spit them out. You can use those dried cranberries on half the scones, if you want."

"Dried cranberries it is."

They discussed a few more details while Molly sat there and watched Bridget's every move. Thankfully, she managed to finalize the luncheon menu without losing focus again.

Normally, she'd have taken the call in the kitchen and not had to endure her sister's unwavering scrutiny. But Bridget had been refilling crystal bowls in the chapel with potpourri, and Molly had informed her of the call on her way past the registration counter.

Twice. Bridget hadn't heard Molly the first time. She'd been lost in memories of Ryan and the other night.

What was she going to do? She supposed

they needed to talk about the kiss sooner or later.

"Yes, ma'am," she said, "I'm looking forward to the luncheon, too. Call me if you need anything. See you then."

Passing the phone to Molly, she blew out a long breath. "Whew."

"Are you okay?" Molly asked before she could make good her escape.

"Wonderful."

"You sure?"

No, she wasn't. She was filling every waking moment with things like making potpourri from leftover floral arrangements all in an attempt to stop herself from dwelling on Ryan. So far, her success rate was a big fat zero.

"Just excited about the Literary Ladies' luncheon," Bridget fibbed. "It's my first nonwedding catered event at the ranch." Seizing the opportunity to divert the conversation from herself, she asked, "What's the head count for Gianna's party?"

"As of today, seventy-two."

"Wow! That many?"

"There are a few additional plus-ones we weren't expecting. Is that okay?"

"Of course. I'll just make a few extra dozen baked brie bites and smoked trout crostini." More things to keep her busy.

"Don't forget the meatballs."

"As if Grandma would let me."

Their grandmother didn't mind the fancy-schmancy finger foods, as she'd referred to them, as long as there were a few basic offerings that appealed to the menfolk. Bridget had drawn the line at cocktail wieners swimming in barbecue sauce and cheese on crackers, but was okay with the meatballs and pizza rounds. Naturally, she'd dress them up.

While not a full dinner, there would be more than enough offerings to fill the guests' stomachs. Not to mention dessert. Bridget was making a deconstructed Boston cream pie, Gianna's favorite, according to Nora. Well, regular Boston cream pie. Hopefully, Gianna and everyone else would like Bridget's version.

"Did you hear?" Molly asked. "Mom called earlier. She and Doug are arriving Friday morning. He wanted to wait and come Saturday, but Mom put her foot down. I'm glad because we can use her help."

Their mother often lent a hand with weddings and events when she was in town and available, making Sweetheart Ranch a true family business.

What would her mother think of Ryan? She'd like him, Bridget had no doubt. He'd charm her like he had Grandma Em, Nora and, yes, Bridget, too.

Since apparently everything reminded her of Ryan, she decided to retreat to the kitchen, her usual sanctuary when troubled or overwhelmed. "I have a lunch to prepare. Ryan's taking two couples on an extended trail ride today that includes a stop at Juniper Pass along the way."

"How are things between you and Ryan?" Molly asked.

"Fine."

"I just wondered."

"Why?" *Please don't mention Saturday night. Please, please, please.*

"To start with, he went chasing after you at the square dance. And you've been off in another world since."

"I'm not off in another world." Bridget was firmly planted in this one. Specifically, at the kitchen door with her arms wrapped around Ryan and his mouth coaxing the most incredible responses from her.

"Come on," Molly insisted. "What happened? Did you have a fight?"

"No."

Her look of concern vanished, replaced with a smile. "Wait. Not a fight. Something else. Like a close encounter of the intimate kind?"

The phone had been ringing off the hook for the past two hours. Now, when Bridget most needed an interruption, it remained frustratingly quiet.

"I'm not going to quit pestering you until you tell me," Molly said.

She wouldn't. Molly was nothing if not persistent.

"All right." Bridget relented and prayed she wasn't making a mistake. "We kissed."

Molly gasped. "Tell me everything. Was it good? I bet it was. He looks like he'd be a good kisser."

"Not good."

"What? No!" Molly's features fell.

"It was great." Incredible. Mind-shattering.

Another gasp. "I knew it!"

"Also wrong. We made a mistake." Bridget explained about Ryan's house flipping, his goal of starting his own construction business one day and his hope of making his parents' retirement years easier. Mostly she explained about him not being ready for a serious relationship.

"How long are we talking about? A year? Two?"

"At minimum."

"Then wait for him."

"Easy for you to say. You're only thirty and probably marrying Owen soon. I bet you'll be pregnant by your first anniversary. In the meantime, you can satisfy your need for nurturing by being a stepmom to his kids. I, on the other hand, am thirty-two with no prospects."

"Lots of women these days get married and start families later."

Bad enough Bridget felt the need to keep reminding herself of that. Now she had other people saying it to her.

"I don't want to be one of them," she snapped, and instantly regretted her outburst. "Sorry."

Molly looked remorseful. "I'm the one who's sorry. I was being insensitive."

"I think I'd be less touchy if you and Grandma weren't constantly throwing Ryan at me." Bridget pushed her hair back with her hand. "That makes me feel even more like I'm running out of time."

"Can I ask something without you taking it the wrong way?"

"I'll try."

"Do you regret putting your career first all these years?"

Bridget considered the question for a moment before answering. "What I regret is not dating more when I had the chance. I could have done both—work and a personal life aren't mutually exclusive."

"Might your standards be a little high?" Molly inquired gently.

There it was again, the reference to her strict criteria for a man worthy of her attention.

Yeesh. Just thinking of it like that made Bridget want to cringe. When had she become such a snob?

"It's not your fault," Molly said. "Dad set the bar pretty high. Most men can't compare."

Bridget did want to find a man like their father. He'd been the love of their mother's life and the best father two daughters could ever ask for. She was also scared of losing the right man once she found him. Her father's sudden death had left them shell-shocked and devastated.

The dating list gave her a sense of security. She wasn't ready to cast it aside just yet.

"It's easy for me to tell you to quit worrying," Molly said. "But I won't. You being ready now for a husband and family is reasonable. Problem is, the guy hasn't yet materialized and you're wondering if he ever will. Those are perfectly normal feelings."

What Bridget heard, even though Molly didn't say it, was "At your age."

"Obviously, you and Ryan are attracted to each other," Molly continued. "There's no law saying you can't simply date with no end goal."

Bridget had been through this already with Grandma Em. "I would hate to start caring for someone only to become frustrated and angry when their timetable doesn't match mine. We'd both wind up hurt and angry."

"You're right." Molly's shoulders slumped. "He's just so darn cute."

The phone on the registration counter rang. Finally! Molly reached for the receiver.

"There's my cue to get to work."

"Mine, too."

Bridget dragged her feet to the kitchen. It was barely past 11:00 a.m., and she was already exhausted. Ongoing emotional tug-of-wars and deflecting well-intentioned family members did that to a person. As did preoccupation to the point of obsessing over one small kiss.

Since easily portable food worked best for taking on trail rides, sandwiches were Bridget's meal of choice. She'd planned on preparing pulled pork with sweet slaw topping on potato rolls.

After assembling the ingredients on the counter, she got down to business. Twisting off the lid on a jar of mayonnaise she'd made earlier in the week, she paused. Something wasn't right. Holding the jar to her nose, she sniffed.

Bridget prided herself on her sense of smell, a trait vital to any good chef. Today it told her the mayonnaise was on the verge of spoiling.

"Swell," she grumbled under her breath.

What now? There wasn't enough time before the trail ride to prepare a fresh batch of mayonnaise, even if she had all the ingredients. Store-bought wasn't an option; Bridget didn't keep any in the house. Perish the thought.

Weighing her options, she decided on going with a different sandwich. Unfortunately, an inspection of the refrigerator contents yielded few ideas and nothing that excited her.

Seconds stretched into minutes. She needed to walk the packed lunch boxes to the stables soon or risk delaying the trail ride.

Massaging her forehead, she muttered, "Think, Bridget, think."

Her mind refused to cooperate, remaining a jumble. Unbidden tears filled her eyes, and she dashed angrily at them with the heels of her hands. She wasn't normally a crier. She was stronger than that.

Of course, Ryan chose that exact moment to throw open the kitchen door, a big grin on his face, a twinkle in his eyes and a cheerful "Good morning" coming from the lips that were responsible for Bridget's present state of confusion.

RYAN DREW UP SHORT. Was Bridget crying? He couldn't tell for certain. She'd quickly averted her face and had yet to look directly at him. But he swore those had been tears he'd spotted in her eyes.

He stood there, debating if he should ask her what was the matter or leave her in peace. Staying won out. He couldn't walk away, not when she was upset and despite the fact that he might be the cause.

In the three days since they'd kissed, he'd been careful to limit their discussions to work. In large part because he was curious how she'd react to the kiss and if she'd seek him out.

To his great disappointment, she'd said nothing and done nothing. When they were together, she acted as if nothing intimate had transpired between them. Ryan refused to believe that was due to a lack of interest in him. Bridget had kissed him back and then some.

Frustrated with maintaining his distance and frustrated with constantly second-guessing her, he stepped over the threshold and shut the door behind him. Crossing the kitchen toward her, he asked, "Are you okay?"

"Me? Yes."

She sent him a quick sideways glance but avoided direct eye contact. A lower bin in the refrigerator seemed to demand her entire attention, and she rifled through it without making a selection.

"That's okay. You don't have to tell me."

"No. I don't."

She was back in control, the way he knew she liked it, every trace of her earlier tears vanished.

But Ryan had seen her lose control and felt the instant she'd let go when he held her in his arms. Moments like that were rare, and he'd give anything for another one with Bridget.

"It's just that you looked…" He started to say "distraught" but changed his mind. "Preoccupied."

"My mayonnaise is spoiled." She indicated the jar in the sink.

"Does mayonnaise spoil?" With the copious amounts of bologna sandwiches he consumed, there was no chance of his mayonnaise spoiling.

"It does. And homemade mayonnaise spoils faster than store-bought."

"You don't keep any store-bought handy for, like, emergencies?"

"I'm going to pretend you didn't say that."

Ryan poured himself a glass of water from the dispenser in the corner, his original reason for coming to the kitchen. Okay, and to see if she was here. "No offense, but is spoiled mayo a big deal?"

"I was going to prepare sweet slaw topping for the pulled-pork sandwiches."

"I'm sure the pulled pork will be good with nothing on top or plain cheese."

She whirled to face him then, her expression one of horror. "Plain cheese?"

"What about barbecue sauce?"

"Even worse."

Bringing his water with him, he pulled out a chair and sat at the table. "I doubt the guests will care."

"*I* care."

"All right then. What else do you have for the sandwiches?"

"That's the problem." Shoulders sagging, she stuck her nose back inside the open refrigerator. "I'm low on food. I've been using what's on hand rather than making an extra trip to the farmers' market and warehouse store."

"You're creative. Surely you'll come up with something delicious. You always do."

She grumbled under her breath.

"What's in there? Start calling out names. I bet inspiration will strike."

She turned her head and gaped at him as if he'd suggested *he* make lunch.

"Try it. You have nothing to lose."

With a this-is-futile shrug, she did as he said, poking through drawers and shelves.

"Portobello mushrooms, fennel, cayenne and serrano peppers, romaine lettuce—"

"What's wrong with lettuce? It's a sandwich standard."

"Lettuce?" Again, that expression of horror.

"Okay. Nix the leafy greens. Keep going."

She paused momentarily but then continued. "Cabbage, of course, for the slaw, half a honeydew melon, a pear, a pineapple, a slightly puckered zucchini—"

"Wait!" Ryan stopped her once more. "You have a pineapple? A whole one?"

Bridget reached in and withdrew the prickly fruit to show him.

"Fry up some slices and top the pulled pork with them."

She went from gawking at him to gawking at the pineapple, blinking as if she expected it to explode in her hand.

"My mom used to grill pineapple along with ribs and chicken," Ryan said. "I'd put the pineapple on top of my meat and eat it that way. Grossed out my brothers and sisters, but it was good. Might not be bad on a pulled-pork sandwich."

"I don't believe it."

"Yeah. You're right. Stupid idea."

"No. It's an excellent idea." Bridget straightened and sighed. "I'm just mad. At myself," she quickly added. "I should have thought of pineapple. I'm better than that. Much better."

She set the pineapple on the counter and closed the refrigerator door. Next, she opened a cupboard and selected various bottles and jars. Removing a knife from the impressive rack by the stove, she put the pineapple on the cutting board.

"You were right earlier. I am preoccupied."

"With anything in particular?"

She severed the top from the pineapple with one swift slice of the knife. "You have to ask?"

"I wondered."

"Wonder no more."

Several knife strokes later, six perfectly uniform golden slices lay on the cutting board, fanned out like a deck of cards. She then removed a sauté pan from a lower cupboard and set it on a burner.

"Want to talk about it?" he asked.

"Not particularly."

Dropping a generous slab of butter into the pan, she poured and shook and sprinkled various seasonings onto the pineapple slices, finishing with brown-sugar crumbles. By then, the butter had melted, and she carefully arranged the pineapple slices in the pan one by one.

While they sautéed, she prepared the rest of the lunches, which included sides and desserts. Wrapping the finished sandwiches tightly in plastic and placing them in a saddlebag-proof container that would protect them from being bounced around, she transferred everything into a paper bag for transport to the stables.

Ryan drained the last of his water. He had only a few minutes to spare before he needed to head out. The horses were saddled and waiting. All that remained was the lunch, which was now ready.

He stood and accepted the bag from Bridget's outstretched hands, waiting until she met his gaze. "Everything looks delicious."

"Thanks for your help."

"My pleasure."

"I owe you one."

"Ah! Well, in that case—"

"It's a figure of speech, Ryan."

"I beg to differ. A promise is a promise." He'd been kidding initially. The idea, however, was growing on him.

"I'm not kissing you again," she stated.

"I was thinking of dinner."

"Dinner." She crossed her arms over her middle as if weighing the pros and cons. "Okay."

"No fooling?" He hadn't thought she'd agree

that easily. "Tomorrow night then. I'll pick you up at six."

"Uh-uh." She shook her head. "You can come by at six to pick up *your* dinner. And then take it home with you."

"I'd rather we went out to eat."

"You said dinner. No other conditions. Either I fix you a to-go dinner, or the deal's off." She smiled with satisfaction, obviously convinced she'd won this round.

Ryan wasn't giving up. Not without a fight.

"All right. Dinner to go. That works for me."

"Any requests?"

"A picnic. Fried chicken. Potato salad. Rolls. Deviled eggs. Some of your grandmother's pickled asparagus. I'll leave dessert up to you."

She eyes slowly narrowed. "That's a tall order."

"And fix enough for two," he said.

"Ryan."

He softened his voice. "Have dinner with me, Bridget."

"I don't want to encourage you. We're in different places."

"Fear not. You won't break my heart."

"What if you break mine?"

He'd move heaven and earth to prevent that. "I promise, I'll behave. We'll just be two friends sharing a meal together at some nice outdoor location."

She hesitated. He took that as an indication her defenses were weakening and pressed his advantage.

"It's just a picnic. Plus, like you said, you owe me."

"Seems a lot to repay for a simple sandwich-topping suggestion. I would have come up with something on my own."

"Never a doubt."

He flashed a smile. She turned away from him and began clearing the counter.

Ryan accepted defeat. It had been a long shot after all and probably for the best. He hadn't been truthful about her not breaking his heart. He could feel one small crack starting to form even now.

But then she surprised him.

"Tomorrow evening doesn't work for me. Are you free Thursday?"

"As it happens, I am." He'd gladly break his prior date with the master-bathroom light fixture.

"I choose the place."

He nodded. "Wherever you want."

"The park near the center of town. There's an area on the south side with tables beneath gazebos."

The park. Made sense for a picnic, Ryan supposed, though he'd have preferred someplace more secluded and romantic. Then again, anywhere with Bridget could be romantic if he set his mind to it.

"I'll pick you up."

"I'll meet you there."

"Fair enough." He'd compromise if it meant getting her away from the ranch and alone with him.

Tugging on the brim of his cowboy hat with his free hand, he headed out, taking the bag containing lunches for the trail ride with him.

He had a spring to his step the entire walk to the stables. One of the guests waiting on him commented about him being in a good mood.

He was. And if all went well on his picnic with Bridget, his good mood would last indefinitely.

CHAPTER TEN

BRIDGET ARRIVED EARLY at the park on Thursday. Thirty minutes, to be precise, because preparedness was a part of her nature that she seemed to have no control over. Also, because she'd been eager to avoid her grandmother and sister's prying questions.

Both had commented on her frying chicken that afternoon and asked why. Bridget had concocted what she considered a plausible excuse—Owen's children were arriving early for their weekend visit with their dad, and they loved fried chicken. Grandma Em and Molly's skeptical responses let Bridget know they weren't convinced. The timely arrival of a client had saved her from further interrogation and allowed her to finish preparing the picnic dinner undisturbed.

She wasn't hiding anything, she told herself while unpacking food containers and arranging condiments. She was merely avoiding an awkward situation where her grandmother and sister jumped to the wrong conclusion and started needling her about why she was going on a picnic dinner with Ryan. Which they would have most certainly done, leaving her hard-pressed for an answer.

Actually, Bridget did have an answer. She just wasn't willing to admit her reasons to anyone, much less herself. If she did, her defenses against him would crumble and leave her vulnerable.

Mostly Bridget had arrived at the park early because she wanted to have everything ready before he appeared. That way, there'd be less time for them to spend together. They could get right down to the business of eating, and eating meant less talking. Less talking meant fewer probing questions about their recent kiss.

Food often served as her shield in uncomfortable situations or a crutch when her confidence lagged. Tonight was no exception. Being self-aware enough to realize this fact about herself didn't change her behavior. When it came to Ryan and her susceptibility to him, she needed every available means of protection.

Hearing high-pitched laughter, she glanced up from emptying the soft-sided cooler, her eyes searching until she found the source. Not far away was the playground area, where young children happily swung from bars, whooshed down slides and frolicked in the sand. Their parents supervised from conveniently placed benches or, like Bridget, the picnic tables.

Assured all was well, she returned her attention to the dinner. The menu was very traditional, as Ryan had requested. She'd controlled her desire to fancy up the food, other than the chicken. There, she used her own version of secret herbs and spices. The end result was good, if she said so herself.

Checking the lid on the last covered dish, she again scanned the playground area. Seeing her friend Frankie, who was there with her twin daughters, she waved. Frankie gave her the A-OK sign, and Bridget relaxed.

Not for long, however. There was no mistaking the tall male figure strolling toward her along the paved walkway. Broad shoulders, long, casual strides, trademark cowboy hat and self-assured air. Ryan was here.

He drew the attention of every female in the immediate vicinity, Bridget's included. Darn it. Why couldn't she exercise more restraint?

As he neared, she realized he was holding something at his side. A moment later, the object became clear, and she sighed. Partly from frustration and partly from the small thrill coursing through her. When was the last time a man had brought her flowers?

"These are for you," he said and held out the colorful bouquet.

"Thank you." She noted he'd wrapped the cut ends in a damp paper towel to keep them fresh.

"I had a little free time this afternoon," he said, "so I trimmed the rosebushes on the side of the house. These are some of the prettiest blooms."

Indeed, they were lovely. Bridget remembered the rosebushes from when they'd stopped at his house after the clinic to check on the vandals, and he'd given her a tour.

"How's your hand?" she asked. "Should you be doing yard work yet?"

"I wore gloves."

She placed the roses in a paper cup filled with water from one of the bottles she'd brought. They tilted heavily to one side, and she had to lean them against the cooler.

Without thinking, she lowered her head and inhaled. The heady scent was made more so by the fact that these weren't just any roses. Ryan had chosen the blooms especially for her.

She straightened, her glance automatically going to Frankie at the playground. Apparently her friend had spotted Ryan giving Bridget the bouquet, because her broad smile was unmistakable.

Great. Yet another person to make excuses to about Ryan.

"I have my follow-up appointment at the clinic tomorrow," he said matter-of-factly.

"That's good." She returned her attention to him. "Did you finish taking your antibiotics?"

"I did." One corner of his very attractive mouth curved up in a teasing smile. "Any message you'd like me to give the doctor if I see him?"

"Very funny."

"Not that I'm afraid of a little competition—"

"Can we not talk about him anymore or ever again?" She clamped a hand to her forehead.

"You're right. That was a cheap shot." He surveyed the spread laid out on the table, his face lighting up. "This looks incredible. You outdid yourself, as usual."

"The chicken's cold. Hope you don't mind."

"Mind? It's my favorite." He lifted the lid and peeked underneath. "You made enough for a small army."

"That's because I'm feeding a small army."

"I admit to having a healthy appetite. Not sure I can eat *that* much."

Bridget cupped her hands around her mouth and hollered, "Cody. Marisa. Willa. Get a move on. Dinner's ready."

In the playground area, three small heads popped up.

"We're digging a ditch," Cody answered, a pail and shovel in his hand.

"You can go back to playing after we eat. And bring Popeye with you," she added.

Frankie walked to where the children were digging their ditch alongside her twin daughters. She'd been keeping an eye on Bridget's charges as a favor while she readied the picnic dinner.

Cody ran ahead to fetch the pony standing outside the playground area. He'd been tied but at some point his lead rope came undone. He'd wandered all of four feet, to a slightly grassier spot, where he'd stayed, grazing happily.

Even in this section of the equine-friendly town park, horses could be found carrying their young charges from one place to another or standing idly by and munching on the grass. Most riders, however, were using the designated bridle path circling the park. The gorgeous spring evening was ideal for just such an activity. In the riding arena on the other side of the large green belt, hunter-jumpers horses sailed over fences arranged in intricate patterns.

At the boy's approach, the pony raised his head and pricked his ears. A minute later, he was following obediently behind Cody at a slow trot. The girls brought up the rear, holding hands and running on their short legs.

"Let me guess," Ryan said. "Owen's kids?"

"Yes." Bridget indicated for him to sit. "They're off school tomorrow—something about a teacher conference—so Owen has them an extra day this weekend. He and Molly are at the town council meeting. They asked me to babysit, and I said yes. It was their idea to bring Popeye along."

Ryan eyed Bridget suspiciously as he hoisted one long leg over the table's bench seat and sat. "You knew you were babysitting the other day when you agreed to this."

She lifted a shoulder.

"I should be mad," he said.

"Aren't you?"

By then, the children were upon them, redcheeked from exertion and brimming with curiosity about Ryan. Cody had dropped Popeye's reins a few feet away from the table. The pony didn't appear inclined to wander. The grass here was as tasty as the patch by the playground.

"Hi, kids!" Ryan flashed a friendly grin. "What's going on?"

"Who are you?" Cody demanded.

The girls were considerably shier and remained where they were at the end of the table. Willa had recently turned two and Marisa would be four this summer. At almost six, and the oldest, Cody was the self-appointed spokesman for the trio.

"I'm Ryan. I work at Sweetheart Ranch."

"With Molly and me," Bridget added.

Cody was inspecting the food and, like Ryan, lifting lids and covers. Marisa and Willa still hadn't moved and peered at Ryan with avid interest.

"Come over here, pal." Ryan hitched his chin at Cody and patted the empty spot beside him. "Park yourself next to me. Your sisters can sit with Bridget."

"Yeah!" The boy hopped onto the bench seat beside Ryan. "Girls on that side, boys on this side."

"For now." Ryan grinned down at him. "Trust me, one of these days when you're older, you'll change your mind." When Bridget snorted, he chuckled. "I'm not wrong."

His easy, likeable manner eventually won over the girls, too, as easily as it had Bridget. Who'd have guessed he was good with kids? Then again, he did have a lot of nieces and nephews.

She considered herself lucky not to be sitting next to him. Otherwise, she'd surely fall further under his spell.

But the instant she sat, she realized her mistake. Sitting across from him, staring at his face throughout the entire meal, was just as difficult as having his heart-fluttering presence beside her.

Who was she kidding? Staring at Ryan wasn't a hardship. Not at all.

RYAN FOUND A like mind in young Cody. Or, should he say a like *stomach*? As Bridget distributed the plates, both Ryan and Cody filled theirs to overflowing.

The girls were fussy eaters and needed a bit of encouragement. Willa, it turned out, detested baked beans. Her older sister, Marisa, didn't want any potato salad because of the "red stuff" in it, which was actually diced red peppers.

"That's the best part," Ryan exclaimed.

Nobody's fool, she narrowed her gaze at him.

"Haven't you ever heard that peppers make your hair curly? Just look at Bridget's. She got her curly hair from peppers."

He'd heard his sister use this fabrication with her daughters, only the food they didn't want to eat was bread crust.

"And her hair's red 'cause she ate red peppers." Grinning, Cody took a big bite of potato salad, only to stop in midswallow. "Will mine turn red?"

Ryan reached over and patted the boy's head. "Only works on girls."

"Whew!" He shoveled another forkful into his mouth.

Marisa showed that she was considerably smarter than her brother. At least, she was less gullible. "That's not true. You made it up." Turning to Bridget for confirmation, she asked, "Didn't he?"

"Well…even if it's not true, peppers are pretty delicious."

"They're hot."

"These are sweet peppers. Try one."

"Sweet peppers give little girls curls *and* make them sweet," Ryan said. "Everyone knows that."

Marisa frowned, but she tried a bite of the potato salad, anyway. After she swallowed, she held out a strand of her hair for inspection in an apparent attempt to detect any curls or change in color.

Willa was too busy stuffing herself with deviled eggs to contribute to the conversation. Bridget fussed and fretted over her, trying to get the little girl to eat something else. Ryan didn't suppose one meal of nothing more than deviled eggs would hurt Willa but kept his opinion to himself.

He reached for another piece of chicken. "This is really good, Bridget. Hats off to the chef."

He felt Cody's stare on him. "What's up, pal?"

"You didn't take your hat off."

"Got me there." Ryan tsked, removed his hat and set it on the seat beside him.

Copying him, Willa tugged off her cap and dropped it in her lap. She then reached out with her chubby hand and snatched a chicken leg from the platter.

Bridget scrunched her pretty mouth in consternation. "Huh."

"Kids are funny," Ryan said between bites. "You push, they push back."

"I think a lot of adults are like that, too."

Was she referring to him? He could dig his heels in when inclined.

"You learn about children from your nieces and nephews?" she asked.

"I do have a lot of them. Sixteen at last count."

"All in Texas?"

"Most. My oldest brother and his family live in Louisiana. I have a sister who teaches elementary school in Ohio. Other than that, the rest are still fairly close to the folks. No more than a couple hours away."

"Didn't you say one of your sisters and her children live with your parents?"

"Off them is more like it." Ryan softened his tone. "Sorry. That wasn't fair. Her ex is a real piece of work."

"Would she and her children come to Arizona if your parents move here?"

"I doubt it. The terms of the divorce don't allow either of them to relocate the kids out of Texas without the other's consent. Her ex won't give it." Ryan finished the last of his chicken. "That wouldn't be a bad thing, her staying. She needs to stand on her own two feet."

"Would your parents leave her and the rest of your family? You mentioned a lot of nieces and nephews."

"That's a good question, and I don't have the answer. I'd like them to spend at least some of the year here. Like the winters."

"I'm giving this to Popeye." Cody bent down and retrieved the roll he'd dropped on the ground. "It's dirty."

"Ponies don't eat rolls," Bridget said.

"He likes crackers."

Ryan helped the boy scramble out of his seat. "We had a mule when I was growing up that ate bananas."

They all laughed when Popeye bobbed his head comically as he first mouthed and then spit out the roll.

Cody ran back to the table and shouted, "Gross!"

The remainder of the meal progressed comfortably. Ryan enjoyed interacting with Owen's kids. They were cute and precocious. Any disappointment he'd experienced at not being alone with Bridget had quickly faded. He enjoyed seeing her with the kids and found amusement in her failed attempts to supervise them. Not that Ryan was an expert. His laissez-faire approach annoyed his siblings, too, when he babysat their broods.

"Will you take us on a wagon ride?" Cody asked after Ryan had explained in simple terms just what he did at the ranch for Grandma Em, as they called her.

"If you're here for the next one and your dad says it's okay."

"Dad let me drive the carriage once."

"How 'bout that? Pretty exciting."

Finally overcoming their shyness, the girls joined in the conversation. Marisa told Ryan about their pet cat that lived in her father's feed store. Willa, who still didn't talk a whole lot, giggled along with her siblings at Ryan's teasing and jokes.

"Bridget, can we go back to our ditch?" Cody asked the second they were finished with dessert.

Key lime pie. It was incredible.

"I'd rather you didn't," she said. "It's starting to get dark."

Her response was met with a trio of loud groans. Willa dropped her head onto the table in exaggerated disappointment.

"Why don't I take you and your sisters for a ride on Popeye?" Ryan suggested. "Bridget can come, too."

Cody objected. "She's too big to ride a pony."

"I'll walk," she assured him.

Ryan placed all three children on the pony, Cody in front and in charge of the reins, Marisa in the back and little Willa stuffed in the middle. Once everyone was settled, they started out.

"Are you sure they're okay?" Bridget asked Ryan, eyeing the pony and children worriedly.

"Popeye's short. They don't have far to fall. And the grass is soft."

She gawked at him in disbelief. "That's your safety plan?"

"Let's see how they do before getting all worked up."

"Men! You seem to think children are replaceable."

"They aren't?"

"Very funny," she scolded. "If anything happens to these three, Owen will never forgive me."

All of Bridget's concerns came to naught. The kids behaved, no pushing or shoving, and Popeye's speed was no faster than a slow trot, no matter how much Cody nudged him in the sides. After five minutes, Willa wanted down, leaving Cody and Marisa to ride double.

Bridget carried the little girl and before long she laid her head on Bridget's shoulder. If not asleep, she was almost there. Bridget and Ryan's conversation appeared to lull her rather than disturb her.

Ryan had a hard time taking his eyes off the pair. It was easy to see why Bridget wanted to marry and have a family. She was a natural with Willa, and her enjoyment of the children's antics shone in her face like a burst of sunshine.

He found himself thinking it was a shame they couldn't have met two years from now, when he'd be more ready for that marriage and family she so very much wanted, only to change his mind. He may not be the right guy for Bridget, but he wouldn't trade knowing her now for anything. Even with the disappointing reality that friendship was all there'd ever be between them.

"Have you had any more trouble with vandals?" she asked.

"Nope. I think the increase in activity is keeping them away. I'm having insulation for the attic delivered tomorrow morning and a dozen pine four-by-four beams in the afternoon."

"What are those for?"

"The living room and the master bedroom. I want to distress them first before installing them in the ceilings."

"That should look amazing. Give the rooms real dimension."

He nodded. "I agree."

"Hard work, too."

"I'll need to hire help. Installing beams is a two-man job."

"You have anyone in mind?"

"Nora has a grandson. He's going to community college and works construction during the summers. I can probably afford him."

"Scott." Bridget nodded. "I know him. He should do all right."

"Nora has yet to steer anyone wrong with her recommendations."

"You're saying that only because she recommended you for the wrangler job."

"You have to admit, she has an eye for talent."

Bridget huffed. "You're incorrigible."

"Comes from being the baby of the family. I'm also a little spoiled."

"I don't think that."

He was tempted to ask her exactly what she thought of him, but didn't.

They walked for several more moments, enjoying the mild breeze. After a while, he asked, "How did you get into cooking? I know you went to that fancy school in Scottsdale—Emily told me. And I also know your other grandmother influenced you, the pickled-asparagus champion. But why become a chef?"

"I've always like to cook." She stroked Willa's soft curls as she talked, her gaze drifting. "I also used to like to eat. A lot. I guess you could have called me chubby."

"I find that hard to believe." Nearly impossible. Her figure, while curvy in all the right places, was trim.

"I have the pictures to prove it. A therapist might say I ate my feelings after my dad died." Her smile dimmed. "My weight spiraled. I gained twenty pounds that first year. And then another twenty pounds. Being a teenager, I was naturally self-conscious. My classmates weren't kind, and I became a target for their teasing. I hated my senior year."

Ryan heard the pain she must have endured in her sandpaper voice. He imagined a younger version of her, grieving over her father's sudden and tragic death, and being mercilessly teased by her classmates. He not only felt for her, but he also admired her courage in overcoming the bullying incidents and not letting them define her.

"After I graduated," she continued, "and during my gap year, I started making better food choices. And because I liked to eat, I began experimenting with healthier recipes that were also delicious. Eventually, my enjoyment of cooking developed into a passion. It was Grandma Em's idea that I go to cooking school."

"Well, this may be chauvinistic of me to say, but you look fantastic."

"Thank you." She accepted his compliment with grace. "Along the way, I dropped weight. Being on my feet all day helps. I suppose it's kind of ironic that my specialty is pastries."

"I have to say, I admire your dedication."

"Funny." Her smile returned. "I've said the same thing about you."

"Really?" He made a derisive sound. "Out loud?"

"Yes, out loud. You work hard. You're dedicated. You have a goal in sight."

"You do, too. Your grandmother told me

about you wanting to expand the catering side of the business."

Bridget glanced over at Cody and Marisa, who continued to plod along on Popeye. With diminishing interest from his riders, the pony frequently stopped to lower his head and sample some grass. Neither Ryan nor Bridget bothered to stop him.

"I enjoy creating, and not just with food," she said.

"I get it. I like to think taking a house from a falling-down shack to completely renovated is a kind of creativity."

"Absolutely. My late grandfather, Grandma Em's first husband, used to build furniture. He made the buffet in the parlor and the bookshelves in the library."

"Another way we're alike."

"You and my grandfather?" she asked.

"You and me."

"Hmm." She studied him. "You think we're alike?"

What he wanted to tell her was that after kissing her last weekend, they were so much alike it scared him. No two people could set off that many sparks without being completely in-sync.

Instincts told him he wasn't alone with his feelings, though she was probably going to resist more than him. Bridget was like that, pragmatic to a fault. And Ryan didn't fit her ideal version of a long-term prospect.

Taking the long way, they returned to the picnic table and she lowered Willa to the ground. The little girl whimpered at being awakened, then came fully alert when Ryan helped her brother and sister down from the pony. Playtime was resuming.

"Stay close," Bridget warned them.

Ryan helped her pack the leftovers and dispose of the trash. During the process, their hands and fingers frequently brushed. More than once, their gazes connected and held. He wished, like him, she was inclined to take this incredible attraction between them a step further. But she wasn't.

"Thanks again for dinner." He zipped closed the soft-sided cooler. "It was delicious. Maybe we could…" He let her infer the rest, which she did.

"If you're suggesting we do this again sometime, let me stop you there."

So her thoughts *had* been going in the same direction as his. Or was that the opposite direction?

"A guy can dream."

"I'm sorry if kissing you the other night gave you the wrong idea."

"Oh, please don't apologize. You'll spoil the memory."

"Are you ever serious?"

He sidled over to her and dipped his head, bringing his mouth perilously close to hers. "I can be very serious when the moment calls for it."

"Please," she whispered.

"Please go away?" Throwing all caution to the wind, he skimmed his lips over hers. The brief contact was electric. "Or, please kiss you?"

She hesitated, and he felt her resolve weakening.

"At least tell me you're tempted," he said, stealing another quick taste of her.

"I am. Very much."

That was all he needed to hear. Ryan's arm went around her waist, circling it and drawing her hard against him.

"You drive me crazy," he said against the soft skin of her cheek.

"That's not my intention." Her breath quickened.

So did Ryan's. "Don't stop. I like it."

Before he could kiss her until they were both wild with wanting, they were interrupted.

"Daddy's here," Cody hollered.

As if poked with a live wire, Bridget sprang

away from him, retreating from the dangerous ground they'd treaded on for a second time.

Ryan nonchalantly turned, giving Owen and Molly a friendly wave. "Howdy, folks."

Beside him, Bridget began fussing with the already organized ice chests. Ryan wasn't worried. What could Owen and Molly possibly have seen? Nothing more than Ryan "this close" to covering Bridget's lips with his. Oh, and the roses in the paper cup. Let them draw their own conclusion.

The kids rushed to greet their dad and his girlfriend, as Cody had called Molly. Hugs and kisses were exchanged.

"Thanks again for babysitting," Owen said when they were within conversing distance.

"How was the meeting?" Bridget asked, her voice a little too high and thin.

"Good. Informative," Owen said at the same time Molly answered, "Long and tedious."

"You hungry?" Bridget pointed to the coolers. "There's plenty."

"No, thanks." Molly began corralling the kids while Owen retrieved Popeye. "We ate before the meeting."

Ryan slung the strap of one cooler over his shoulder and was just reaching for the second one when Molly startled him with an unexpected question.

"Will we see you at Gianna's engagement party on Saturday?"

"Um… I wasn't planning on going." He hadn't been invited.

"Please come. You're more than welcome."

"I don't know Gianna."

"But you're Nora's neighbor and friend. I'm sure she'd love to have you."

He glanced at Bridget, whose eyes were downcast as she swept crumbs off the table with a paper napkin. Avoiding him? He thought yes.

"I'll think about it," he answered. "Thanks for the invite."

"And feel free to bring a plus-one," Molly added with a mischievous smile. "If you want."

Bridget's head snapped up, and she divided her stare between her sister and Ryan.

He grinned. He couldn't have asked for a better reaction from her.

CHAPTER ELEVEN

RYAN WENT AROUND the back of his truck to the passenger side, where he opened the door. Tonight, for Gianna's engagement party, he'd parked in the designated area by the ranch house rather than the stables. He wouldn't have minded walking, but he didn't want to cause his date needless difficulty traversing the uneven dirt road in her fancy dress shoes.

His original intention had been to ignore Molly's offer for him to bring a plus-one. Then, an opportunity presented itself, and Ryan took advantage.

"You look nice tonight," he said, taking his date's elbow and assisting her from the truck. "That's a very pretty dress."

"I suppose I should say 'what, this old thing?'" She dismissed him with a wave.

He could tell from her broad smile that she was genuinely touched by his compliment.

Accepting the arm he offered, they strolled past vehicles belonging to earlier arrivals.

"The house looks nice," Ryan commented as they neared.

"Indeed it does."

He'd seen the effort the O'Malleys and Gianna's family had put into preparing for the party during these last two days and had pitched in to help when asked. In addition to yard work, when he wasn't giving trail or carriage rides, Ryan had carted various loads from here to there and gone on two runs to town for supplies. The end result of the intensive labor was even more impressive in the dark of evening.

Multicolored lanterns had been strung along the eaves and emitted a welcoming rainbow glow. Gold and silver pinwheels, resembling those children played with, were stuck in the potted plants lining the walkway and spun gaily, propelled by the gentle breeze. Voices peppered with laughter and soft music carried from inside the brightly lit house.

"Looks like there's quite a crowd already," Ryan observed.

They weren't late. Neither were they early.

"Emily has a lot of friends in the valley," his date commented. "That's what happens when you own and operate a local business for over three decades."

They climbed the few steps leading to the veranda and approached the front door. It was partially ajar, and a sign taped beneath the antique knocker invited guests to come in.

Once inside, they were immediately approached by a teenaged girl who occasionally worked at the ranch. At the moment, she was taking the guests' outerwear for temporary holding. Those who'd brought gifts were shown a table just around the corner to the left.

"Thank you, my dear." Ryan's date patted the teenager's cheek. "You're doing an excellent job."

She smiled at the praise and pointed toward the parlor. "Everyone's in there."

Ryan placed a hand on his date's back and gently guided her ahead of him. Once in the parlor, they were instantly approached by their hosts, Emily and Homer, who stood sentry near the arched entryway.

"You came together!" Emily exclaimed. "How nice."

"Made sense," Nora answered, "seeing as we're neighbors. Why drive two vehicles when one will do?" She kissed both Emily and Homer on their cheeks. "Besides, I'd be crazy to turn down a lift from a handsome young man."

Ryan gave Emily a brief hug and shook Homer's hand. "Don't let her fool you. She played hard to get."

Nora cackled, and they all joined in.

"There's food and a bar in the library," Emily said. "Help yourself. Bridget's prepared a veritable feast. 'Course, you know that. You helped set up."

"Are Gianna and Derrick here?" Nora asked, searching the room.

"Somewhere." Emily also looked around. "I just saw them."

In the next instant, her and Homer's attention was diverted by new guests heading in their direction.

"Would you like a drink?" Ryan led Nora deeper into the parlor.

"A small glass of white wine."

"You mingle. I'll be right back."

Ryan left her to locate the bar in the library. A glance over his shoulder assured him that Nora had wasted no time striking up a conversation with a couple he didn't know.

A quick scan of the room revealed few familiar faces. Not surprising, since Ryan hadn't been in town very long and generally stuck close to his house and Sweetheart Ranch. On the other hand, he and the clerks at the home-improvement store in north Scottsdale were on a first-name basis.

After ordering drinks from the bartender—Nora's wine and a beer for himself—he nodded and issued a hello to the people forming a line behind him. Ryan wasn't entirely sure what he was doing at the engagement party. He was merely an employee at the ranch and a recent one at that.

Actually, he did know why. Nora disliked driving at night, and she hadn't wanted to inconvenience her already busy son and daughter-in-law for a lift. If not for that, Ryan might have politely begged off.

Without consciously directing it, his gaze sought Bridget. She was nowhere in sight, and he assumed she was in the kitchen overseeing the food.

During the past several days, he'd looked for any small sign from Emily that she suspected he'd kissed Bridget after the square dance and again at the park on Thursday and detected none. Nor, for that matter, had Bridget given any indication they'd kissed. She was either doing an excellent job pretending neither kiss had happened or she didn't care.

Could she be hiding from him in the kitchen and not necessarily seeing to the food? Ryan ground his teeth together. This warm-one-minute-and-cool-the-next routine was frustrating him. It was also keeping his interest in Bridget at peak level.

A thought occurred to him. Was she purposely playing him?

He decided no. She wasn't the relationship-game type. The mixed signals she was giving more likely stemmed from her uncertainties about her feelings.

Accepting the wineglass and bottle of beer from the bartender, Ryan navigated a path back to Nora through the increasing crowd. She'd moved in the short time he was gone and was now chatting with Bridget's mother and step-dad, whom Ryan had met earlier today while helping to prepare for the party.

Nora spotted him and gestured him over. Ryan hesitated. Not that he didn't like Bridget's parents—her mom seemed to be an especially nice lady. But standing beside her and making small talk might prove awkward when all he could think about was getting alone with her daughter and picking up right where that last interrupted kiss had left off.

"Thank you," Nora said, accepting the wine-glass he held out. "You know Caroline, of course, and her husband, Doug."

"How are you doing tonight?" Ryan flashed a smile at Caroline and shook Doug's hand.

The other man's attention immediately wandered. He wore the pained expression of someone who would rather be somewhere—*anywhere*—else. Ryan recalled that Bridget wasn't thrilled with her mother's choice of a second husband. While not wanting to jump to conclusions, his initial impression of Doug wasn't great.

"I've been hearing all about you," Caroline said, her tone like honey. "You have a real fan."

"Nora's prejudiced." Ryan grinned fondly at his date. "Comes from her being my neighbor and a good friend."

"Oh, not Nora," Caroline corrected him. "My mother. She's quite fond of you and singing your praises."

"The feeling's entirely mutual."

"I'd venture to say my daughters are fond of you, too. Bridget especially."

Ryan chuckled. "I can't imagine her mentioning my name, much less talking about me."

"She doesn't. Not a single peep." A look of amusement lit Caroline's face. The resemblance between her and her daughters was striking. "Which tells me a great deal. When Bridget's smitten with a fellow, she clams up. I think she's afraid of jinxing a good thing."

"Not sure I agree with you." From everything Bridget had told Ryan, she didn't consider him a good thing.

The subject of their discussion suddenly emerged from the doorway leading from the kitchen. Cheeks flushed and movements hurried, she carried a large platter, which she placed on the table. Those standing in the immediate vicinity let out exclamations of approval.

"Oh, my!"

"Those look scrumptious."

Ryan had yet to sample any of the food but harbored no doubt whatsoever that it was delicious. The finger-food fare couldn't be called hors d'oeuvres and was instead more along the lines of mini entrées. The elaborate cake on display could have been served at a five-star restaurant.

"Does that girl ever stop working?" Caroline's expression softened as she watched her oldest daughter. "She gets that from my mother, you know. Mom's a workaholic, too."

"I wish she'd take a break," Nora said, "and enjoy the party."

Doug abruptly excused himself. "Be right back."

Ryan noticed that no one responded to or appeared even the least bit distressed at Doug's exit.

Seeing Bridget's mother and stepdad together made Ryan appreciate her determination not to marry just anyone and instead wait for the right person. He also better understood why she wouldn't want to waste time with someone like him, a guy intent on waiting until he was in a better position financially before taking the plunge.

The revelation gave him pause. He'd been wrong to kiss her and wrong to want to try again. Better he back off now before making a mistake they both regretted.

At the same moment he came to that conclusion, Bridget broke away from the trio of young women she'd been speaking with and made straight for Ryan. His heart forgot about the warning he'd given himself moments earlier and started beating with the force of a bass drum.

No, not him. She was heading for her mother. As the haze surrounding Ryan cleared, he realized Caroline had hailed Bridget.

"Stop worrying so much about the food." She put an arm around Bridget and hugged her tight. "You're missing out on all the fun."

"I think everything's under control. For the moment," Bridget added, unwilling to fully relinquish her catering duties.

"Ryan cleaned up rather nicely, wouldn't you say?" Nora tilted her head at him.

Bridget hesitated, then admitted, "Yes. He did."

"You, too." Those two words were the most his turned-to-mush brain could manage. Bridget was absolutely gorgeous.

No apron tonight, she wore a flowing pale

cocktail dress, cinched at the waist to flatter her figure and short enough to reveal a pair of shapely legs. Already, he was rethinking his resolve not to kiss her again. Should the chance present itself, he'd spirit her away to a hidden corner and keep her entirely to himself.

"Your food is a hit." Nora turned toward Bridget. "I'd get something to eat except the table is mobbed."

"This party's important to Gianna. I just want everyone to enjoy themselves."

Owen's kids chose that moment to round the corner and burst into the parlor. With Cody in the lead, they "crashed" the party.

"Uh-oh." Caroline's smile widened. "Seems we have some escapees in our midst."

High on excitement, the kids ran straight for Bridget and her mother.

Cody ground to a halt. "Can we have some cake, Bridget?"

His sisters hugged Bridget's legs, their exuberant giggles sounding like chipmunk chatter.

"Hey, you three." She relaxed for the first time since joining them. "Where's your babysitter?"

"On her phone," Cody announced.

Bridget reached down and stroked Cody's hair. "Well, the cake hasn't been served yet. You'll have to wait."

"Daddy's going to make us go back upstairs."

"I promise to personally bring you each a piece."

"I know you." Marisa extracted herself from Bridget in order to point at Ryan and accuse with four-year-old candidness.

"I know you, too." He grinned. "I saw you at the park the other day."

"Are you Bridget's boyfriend?"

All eyes zeroed in on Bridget, including Ryan's.

"No," she replied after an awkward pause. "He came to the party. With Ms. Nora."

"Oh." Marisa's shoulders slumped.

She wasn't the only one who wished things were different.

No, wait, Ryan reminded himself. *Bridget's off-limits.* Why did he keep forgetting?

Easy, he thought, letting his gaze linger on her lovely face. She had that effect on him.

"I agree, little one." Caroline bent and addressed Marisa. "I don't think him being Bridget's boyfriend is such a bad idea."

"Mom!" Bridget groaned with embarrassment.

Ryan couldn't help grinning. She was cute when flustered.

"There you are." Owen appeared at the same time the babysitter rounded the corner.

"S-sorry, Mr. Caufield," the teenaged girl

stammered, rushing forward. "I swear I looked away for just a minute, and they were gone."

While Owen and the sitter collected his kids, Bridget used the opportunity to sneak away. Ryan didn't go after her. That would only give credence to the boyfriend remark.

After that, Nora took Ryan around the party, introducing him to various guests. She was a wealth of information, whispering tidbits of interest about each person as they approached and adding how knowing them might benefit Ryan.

Eventually, she asked him to fetch her a second glass of wine. Gianna's dad was planning on making a toast soon. Ryan did as she asked, skipping a second beer for himself. One was his limit when driving. He didn't hurry back; his vantage point at the bar gave him an unobstructed view of Bridget. She was talking with the same friend who'd watched the kids at the playground the other night.

Perhaps sensing his stare, she looked up. He gave her a small shrug, his way of apologizing for the uncomfortable comment earlier. She shrugged in return, a small smile tugging at her mouth. At least she wasn't mad.

When she angled her head appealingly, his throat went completely dry. A condition repeated swallowing didn't alleviate. This steering clear of personal involvement sure wasn't easy.

"Hi, aren't you Ryan DeMere?"

He pivoted to discover a smartly dressed middle-aged woman standing next to him. "Howdy. Have we met?" He'd been introduced to so many people tonight, his memory was cloudy.

"Not formally. I'm Cheryl-Anne Nivens." She shook his hand. "I know Emily and Owen from the local business owners' association and the town meetings." She smiled coyly. "Of all the people here, you're the most interesting one. I've been trying to wrangle a moment alone with you all evening."

He laughed and shook his head. "You must be mistaken. I'm the least interesting person here."

"Aren't you remodeling the old Chandler place?"

"Yes." He wondered how she knew that and where this conversation was going.

"I had my eye on that property as an investment for a client. You beat me to the punch."

"Sorry?"

"I should explain. I co-own and manage a real-estate-and-commercial-brokerage company. My partner in crime—" she pointed to a woman across the room "—was the broker who handled Owen's purchase of the feed store."

"I see."

With practiced ease, she reached into her

evening bag and extracted a business card, which she then handed to Ryan.

"My client still has an interest in the property, if you're in the market to sell."

"There's a lot of work still to be done."

Cheryl-Anne didn't miss a beat. "Like I said, my client's looking for investment properties. He might be willing to hire you on to finish the work. I won't lie, Ryan. That property has a lot of potential, and Mustang Valley is a growing community."

He was admittedly intrigued, though cautious. "I'm not sure—"

"Let me ask you this." She tapped a long, pink nail against her chin. "Would you be willing to show me the place? Just for kicks."

Ryan pondered that offer for a moment. He liked the idea of obtaining a real-estate professional's opinion of his property's value, even if he wasn't yet willing to sell.

"I might."

She beamed. "Wonderful."

They exchanged information, deciding on a day and time during the upcoming week to meet. That accomplished, they parted ways, Ryan to deliver Nora's wine. While he searched for her, he thought about his upcoming meeting with Cheryl-Anne.

Up until this moment, he'd never considered

selling his house before the remodeling was complete. But if he could get a decent price, one where he made sufficient profit, he'd be that much further along in his plan to buy a ranch. And be a more suitable romantic interest for Bridget.

What would she think of that? What did he?

He found Nora just as someone clinked a glass with a spoon to silence the room. Gianna's dad was preparing to make his toast.

"What took you so long?" Nora whispered.

"Sorry. I was talking to someone."

"Must have been one heck of a conversation. You look like a dog who stumbled upon a big old bone for the taking."

Ryan cautioned himself to relax. Nothing had happened yet and might never.

Nonetheless, the encounter with Cheryl-Anne had his spirits soaring and his mind conjuring endless possibilities.

"WILL ONE OF you steady the ladder for me?" Ryan stared down from his shaky perch atop the six-foot ladder. "Seriously, I could use a little help here."

Two inquisitive faces stared up at him. Neither one made a move, other than to flick an ear.

"Come on, guys. The whole point of this

light is so that I can ride you at night. It's getting too hot during the day."

His large paint gelding snorted in disinterest and ambled off to investigate the old yoga ball Ryan had put in the half-acre paddock to amuse the horses and hopefully get them to do more than stand in the shade, swishing flies away with their tails and pawing the dusty ground.

Meteorologists were predicting the southern half of Arizona would reach triple-digit temperatures by month's end. The same hot weather had already affected carriage and trail rides at Sweetheart Ranch. Before long, there would be no outings between the hours of nine in the morning and six in the evening. Since the monthly Saturday hayrides and cookouts were traditionally an evening event, they wouldn't change.

Ryan's latest idea had been to install a single flood light on the pole at the south end of the paddock. That way, he could at least exercise his horses on the evenings he wasn't working. He'd been neglecting them a little since starting at Sweetheart Ranch and was beginning to feel guilty.

With one hand holding the new light fixture in place and his other one wielding a cordless drill, he said, "Not one of you willing to help?"

The mare bumped the fourth step on the ladder with her nose, causing it to wobble precariously.

"Wrong kind of help." With his hands full, all Ryan could do was lean against the pole, hold his breath and hope for the best. Eventually, the ladder steadied.

In hindsight, he realized he should have tackled this task before letting the horses out of their stalls and into the paddock. But he'd wanted to clean the stalls and get this floodlight installed prior to his one-o'clock appointment with Cheryl-Anne, the real-estate agent he'd met at the engagement party.

As a result, he was rushed, drenched in sweat and growing increasingly irritated. At this rate, he wouldn't have time to shower and change clothes before she arrived.

Tucking the cordless drill between his arm and his rib cage, he realigned the screw with his thumb and forefinger while steadying the light fixture with his remaining fingers. It wasn't easy. Feeling the threads on the screw catch, he again attempted to drill the screw into place before his fingers cramped or he lost his balance and face-planted in the dirt.

This time, the screw went in smoothly, and he grunted with relief. Five more to go and he was done. Climbing down the ladder, he was met by the mare, who sniffed his back and hat with avid interest, as if something might have changed in the short span of time he'd been installing the light.

"Cross your hooves," he said and flipped the switch on the pole. The light illuminated, dimly at first and then with increasing brightness. "Happy day. We're in business."

Ryan collapsed the ladder, then carried it and the drill with him across the paddock. The gelding joined up with them, and both horses lumbered after Ryan like a pair of loyal dogs. At the gate, he left them behind. If it was possible for horses to show disappointment, they did, as their expressions fell.

"I'll be back. Be on your best behavior for the real-estate agent."

In response, the gelding sniffed the mare, getting a little too personal. She gave him a swift but harmless kick in return, missing him by several inches.

"Great. I ask one thing of you and already you're fighting."

Not for the first time he wondered if he'd been wrong to make this appointment today. Selling the property ahead of schedule, possibly clearing the way for him and Bridget to date, could well be no more than a pipe dream. Heck, he hadn't even talked to her about it.

There was no reason to, not unless something actually came of this appointment. And he had his doubts.

With no carriage rides scheduled, Ryan was free until late afternoon, when he'd return to the ranch for an evening trail ride and the horses' regular feeding. Thanks to the increasing heat, his work schedule was wacky. He was going to have to get used to it, though, until fall, when the days finally cooled down.

Coming out of the shed after storing the ladder and drill, he heard a woman calling. "Hello, there you are."

Cheryl-Anne appeared from around the side of the house. Forty-five minutes ahead of schedule.

"Shoot," he muttered under his breath before mustering a smile and striding toward her.

"I hope you don't mind me showing up early," she said when they were near enough to converse. "My previous appointment finished early."

"No problem."

"I tried calling but you didn't answer."

Ryan patted his shirt pocket. It was empty. Then he remembered. "I must have left my phone inside."

"Can you still show me around or should I come back?"

"Stay. By all means." He removed his cowboy

hat and, after combing fingers through his damp hair, replaced it. "As long as you don't mind a little dirt. I haven't had a chance to clean up."

"I don't mind." She beamed. "I'm a real-estate agent. I've met people in every state imaginable, from a tuxedo to a swimsuit."

Ryan had to laugh at that. "Where do you want to start?"

"We're here." Her gesture encompassed the entire outside. "Might as well walk the grounds."

"Bear in mind, this entire place is a work-in-progress."

"Remember, I looked at it last winter before you bought it. I can already see the improvements you've made."

They started the tour at the paddock. "Watch your step," Ryan warned her.

"I came prepared." She lifted one of her feet. The athletic shoes she wore were in contrast to her professional attire of dress slacks and a blouse. "I carry a pair in the car for just such occasions as this one."

They inspected each of the outbuildings and the covered stalls. Ryan's horses followed, intrigued by this new visitor. Though clearly not a horse person, Cheryl-Anne didn't mind.

Finishing with the outside, they went into the house. Whereas Bridget's reaction had been one of surprise and mild horror when she saw the bare kitchen, Cheryl-Anne wanted to know what kind of cabinets Ryan intended on installing and offered enthusiastic encouragement. Not only that, but she also made several good suggestions for some of the other rooms.

"The master bathroom is huge. Have you considered an eco-friendly shower? They're popular right now."

He hadn't.

"You could easily tear down that ugly wooden stoop off the kitchen door—sorry, but it is ugly—and lay pavers to make a patio. I'd recommend adding a built-in barbecue and a lattice roof."

He could.

"You might want to consider an under-the-counter wine refrigerator in the kitchen. You'll have room with that island you're adding."

He might.

By the end of the tour, he realized he liked the real-estate agent. She was smart and personable, as well as knowledgeable and experienced. She was also frustratingly noncommittal when it came to discussing money and any potential buyers.

Unable to wait, Ryan asked, "What do you think I could get for the place?"

"As of today or when you're done with the remodeling?"

"Both?"

She smiled. "Let's sit down."

The only chairs available were in the kitchen. Ryan was embarrassed by the sorry condition of his dining set but Cheryl-Anne claimed to have seen worse.

"What are you looking to get?" she asked once they were seated.

Ryan had anticipated this question and named an amount based on what he'd paid for the property, the cost of improvements to date and a reasonable profit. "That's the lowest I'd take," he said. "I'd start out higher."

Cheryl-Anne nodded thoughtfully. "Not unreasonable. And in line with the current market. Would you be willing to stay on and complete the remodeling? Just looking at all our options."

Our options. Real-estate agents tended to talk like that, those he'd dealt with, anyway. He supposed they were trying to make the other person feel like the two of them were on the same team.

"I'd be willing. In fact, that would be preferable." He wasn't ready to leave Sweetheart Ranch or move from Mustang Valley. "I'd have to be paid for my services."

"Naturally."

"If I were to list the property with you, would you recommend I stop remodeling?" he asked. "I don't want to continue investing money and energy, not without raising the sales price accordingly."

"Good question." She sent him an approving look. "You're no dummy."

"This isn't my first rodeo."

"That's right. You've bought and sold properties before." Her smile grew. "We could have an interesting partnership."

Ryan just wanted to get through *this* sale, if he even agreed to list the property with her. He still had more questions.

"I recommend you absolutely continue with the landscaping for now. As I always say, an attractive outside will bring people inside. We can figure your landscaping budget into the listing price. Do you have an amount?"

He told her. "That includes reexcavating the wash in the front yard and laying river rock."

"It'll be eye-catching when you're done."

They talked for another forty minutes, covering everything from Cheryl-Anne's commission to Ryan having a home inspection. At one point, he grabbed a piece of scrap paper and jotted down some notes to himself.

"I have a listing agreement here," Cheryl-Anne said, reaching for her messenger bag and obviously hoping to close the deal.

"Can I have some time to think about it?"

And review the agreement, he silently added.

He'd signed three previous ones and had some idea of the terms he wanted, those he'd reject and which ones he'd negotiate. He'd also like to chat with his dad and possibly his brother.

"Don't take too long," Cheryl-Anne cautioned. "My investor is definitely interested, but we're also looking at other properties."

She was nudging Ryan to sign with her. He got that. But he wasn't giving in that quickly.

"If I sell to your buyer, you'd be agent for both parties."

Her eyebrows rose. In surprise or appreciation, Ryan wasn't sure.

"You are correct," she said.

"Can we negotiate your rate under those circumstances?"

"My, my. Your mama didn't raise no fool."

They covered several more of Ryan's concerns. To her credit, Cheryl-Anne appeared to be up front with him.

"I'll call you tomorrow," he said. "The day after at the latest."

He walked her to her car, where they shook hands.

"I'm not sorry you beat me to the punch on this property," she told him. "You're going to turn it into something special."

"I hope so."

She studied him with a critical eye. "I'd like

to do business with you, Ryan. I think I can sell this place and make us both some money. With luck, a lot of money."

"Thanks for coming out today."

He waited in the driveway and watched while she drove away, his emotions a jumble. The main reason he'd asked for time to review the listing agreement was so that he could replay their meeting in his mind. Half of what Cheryl-Anne had said was an attempt to sell him on her services. He needed to separate that from the truly important stuff.

Mostly he needed to decide if he wanted to make a little return on his investment now or complete the remodeling and make potentially much more two years down the road.

There were pros and cons to both, Bridget being one of the biggest pros for selling now. He knew he shouldn't consider her in any decision he made. Technically, they didn't have a relationship beyond being coworkers.

But it was hard not to consider her when, with each passing day, he wanted her in his life more and more. Perhaps even permanently.

CHAPTER TWELVE

"THESE ORCHIDS ARE EXQUISITE." Grandma Em stepped back from the table to stare admiringly.

"Thanks." Bridget didn't disagree with her grandmother. This wedding cake was one of her best efforts to date.

"They look so real. Did you take a picture?"

"Yeah. Right before you came in."

With her cell phone. And while the device did well enough, Bridget was starting to think more professional photographs were in order. There were so many things they could do with them. Their website and brochure, to name two. The catering catalog she'd been slowly putting together, for another.

This particular cake would make an incredible cover. Bridget had labored for hours over the delicate and nearly flawless petals and leaves. No simple icing for her—she'd incorporated a variety of edible components including candy pieces, fruit, chocolate shavings and spun sugar. It would be delicious.

Although, how anyone could think of eating her gorgeous creation was beyond her.

The mere thought of a knife slicing through the flowers physically pained her. She would have to get over it, she chided herself, if she intended to continue baking wedding cakes like this one.

"Have you ever thought of hiring our own staff photographer, Grandma?" she asked. "One with experience shooting food."

The two women stepped away from what Bridget referred to as the cake table—today it had been moved from the corner to beneath the window, where the silver and gold adornments on the cake glittered in the afternoon sunlight.

"Most of our clients hire their own," Grandma Em answered. "Or recruit a family member."

"They hire their own because we don't offer that service."

When requested, Grandma Em supplied a list of recommended photographers and videographers, along with musicians and florists. They also enjoyed reciprocal agreements with several local businesses, passing out each other's brochures when appropriate.

"I suppose it wouldn't hurt to explore the possibility," she said. "See what it entails."

"Molly still thinks we should turn the library into a wedding-accessories boutique." Bridget added another folded linen napkin swan to the "flock" sitting on the end of the table.

"Where is she, anyway?"

"Readying the dressing rooms. The bride is supposed to be here any minute and the groom not long after that."

"You're both full of such good ideas."

Bridget and her grandmother next took turns fiddling with the centerpiece and arranging silver flatware. Nothing plastic or paper for this reception, per the couple's request.

This was by far Sweetheart Ranch's most elaborate and expensive wedding to date. Besides the extensive catering menu and five-tier cake, a string quartet had been hired to perform both before the wedding and during the reception. A standing floral arch had been placed at the chapel altar for the bride and groom and their officiant to stand beneath during the ceremony, silk ribbons with tails that reached the floor adorned the pews and each guest would receive a gift bag filled with wedding mementoes.

The reception was merely the start of the celebration. After the customary pictures were taken, the bride and groom would be driven through town in the carriage wearing their full wedding garb. This, rather than waiting until the next morning, as usual. The ride, along with

the ceremony and reception, would be captured
for posterity by the videographer.

Ryan was at that moment readying the carriage and horses. Bridget knew this because
she'd caught a glimpse of him earlier giving
baths to Moses and Amos.

They hadn't talked much this past week, not
since the engagement party for Nora's granddaughter. Her choice, Bridget reminded herself.
She'd been thrown by little Marisa's remark
about Ryan being Bridget's boyfriend and her
mother's adamant endorsement. It hit too close
to home as Bridget had been entertaining similar notions herself.

Funny, though. Ryan hadn't been seeking
her out like usual. At first, she hadn't noticed,
and when she finally did, she attributed it to
their hectic schedules. The cabins were at one-
hundred-percent occupancy, and they'd had
three midweek weddings. After a while, she'd
begun to suspect he was purposely keeping his
distance from her. It was mildly annoying, as
much as she was keeping her distance from
him.

"Do you really think we could make money
with an in-house wedding boutique?" Grandma
asked, rousing Bridget from her too-frequent
thoughts of Ryan. "People seem to order online more and more these days. And there are

those we're-getting-married websites that are all the rage."

"You're right. But I think people tend to book their venue and even their honeymoon long before they purchase invitations or printed napkins or guest books with matching feather pens. We might be able to cash in on impulse buying when they come here to view the ranch and book their wedding."

"Maybe." Grandma Em rubbed the small of her back and sighed wearily. "More than a photographer, one of these days soon, we're going to have to hire part-time help for you and Molly. I'm not sure how much longer I can continue."

Her grandmother's declaration caused Bridget to stop in the middle of straightening the bow on the cake cutter. "What are you talking about?"

"I'm thinking of retiring."

"Grandma, no!"

"I'll be seventy-nine on my next birthday. Long past retirement age. This ranch was my last hurrah. I've always intended for you and your sister to take over one day and for me to live off my investments." She leveled a finger at Bridget. "Naturally, I expect to remain on call."

"Forget it. You retiring is a long way off."

"Not that long. Homer and I want to travel

in his RV while we still can. We've got a few more destinations on our bucket lists."

"We can't manage without you." Bridget didn't like thinking of her grandmother getting older. Or of leaving. She'd miss her terribly.

"Nonsense. Just look at what you've done this week alone. You landed a brunch for the Valley Community Church mothers' group."

"Only because two of their members also belong to the Literary Ladies."

"And if you hadn't done such a wonderful job with *their* luncheon, the mothers' group would have found another venue for their brunch." Grandma Em faced Bridget and planted her hands on her pudgy hips. "And another reason we need to think about hiring more help, you and your sister are working way too hard. Neither of you has time for a personal life. And by personal life, I mean dating."

"I beg to differ," Bridget said. "Molly has found plenty of time for her and Owen."

"Attending town-council meetings and the children's activities isn't the same as dating."

"Well… I don't know. They seem to enjoy it."

"If they don't spend some quality time together *alone*, how's she going to get the man to propose? Look at Gianna. She's not even graduated ASU and she's already engaged."

Bridget knew her grandmother hadn't intended for her remark to sting, yet it did. Everyone else around Bridget was finding love and moving toward a happily-ever-after future. Everyone but her.

Was her family right? Was she being too particular and were her standards too high? She didn't want to be one of those people who looked back on their lives years from now and counted the regrets.

Ryan strolled into the parlor at that moment. Bridget didn't want to think it was in response to the direction her thoughts had taken.

"Aren't you handsome?" Grandma Em sent Bridget an arch look. "Better-looking even than last weekend at Gianna's party."

Bridget stopped herself from searching for a hiding spot. Her grandmother couldn't be more obvious.

"I wasn't being filmed then." Ryan tugged on the brim of what appeared to be a brand-new Stetson.

His bright turquoise Western dress shirt was also new or had been laboriously ironed until the creases were razor-sharp. Paired with his black jeans, the color popped.

"Not that it matters," Grandma Em said, "but I approve."

His glance cut to Bridget, who was suddenly

very aware of the soiled apron she wore over a T-shirt and shorts. She'd yet to change into her customary event uniform of a chef jacket and slacks.

"You do look handsome," she finally mumbled.

He grinned, and the zing she'd been trying to avoid all week coursed through her at lightning speed, leaving her simultaneously weak and exhilarated.

"I'd, um, better check on the spinach puffs."

It was a lame excuse. None of the hors d'oeuvres required her attention, Bridget had everything perfectly in hand. Except, apparently, her persistent attraction to Ryan.

Retreating to the kitchen, she came to a halt in front of the counter, her breath catching.

"Need any help?"

Hearing Ryan's voice, Bridget went still. He'd followed her to the kitchen and now stood directly behind her.

WHEN BRIDGET INSISTED she didn't need any help, Ryan instead grabbed a chilled water bottle from the refrigerator. He should probably return to the stables and wait for a better opportunity to talk with her. But he was *this* close to listing his property with Cheryl-Anne and wanted Bridget's response before actually signing on the dotted line.

If she was enthused, and he hoped she would be, he'd take that as an indicator that she, too, was willing to advance their relationship to the next level.

Then what? They'd start dating? If he didn't have honorable intentions, as his grandfather used to say, Ryan should mosey on down the road. Anything else would be unfair to Bridget.

"Is something wrong?"

Her question startled him, a reaction he tried to mask by taking a long swig of water.

Recapping the bottle, he said, "Nothing."

"You look nervous."

Yes, he was. Scared witless at the prospect of having a discussion with Bridget that could potentially change the course of his life.

"Don't let the videographer get to you," she said.

He didn't correct her assumption. "I've never been filmed before. Not by a professional."

"Other than a few quick shots of you and the scenery, I'm pretty sure the camera will be pointed at the couple. They're the center of attention and what people will want to watch in the finished film. Not the carriage driver. Even one who looks as good as you do," she added shyly.

"Thanks."

Here, he thought, was his opportunity. But he got no further than clearing his throat when Emily breezed into the kitchen.

"Ryan, there you are. The photographer and video person, whatever they call her, would like to meet you outside in about twenty minutes. They want some before-the-carriage-ride shots."

"Can do," he said.

She paused to study him. "Are you okay?"

"Fine."

"He's nervous," Bridget informed her grandmother.

Emily dismissed the remark with a wave and repeated Bridget's earlier assurances. "Don't worry about a thing."

Easy for her to say. She wasn't on the brink of a huge decision that could potentially backfire.

What was the matter with him, anyway? If selling early and moving forward with Bridget was the right course, shouldn't he have more confidence? He might if he knew for certain how Bridget felt. There was a big difference between wanting a serious relationship and wanting a serious relationship *with him*.

Ryan tugged on his suddenly too-tight shirt

collar. When did they start making these so small?

"Did you hear the story about how our bride and groom met?" Emily grabbed a towel and began polishing the champagne glasses Bridget had set out for the reception. "It's so cute." She didn't wait for either Ryan or Bridget to respond. "Apparently the groom never noticed the bride. They worked at the same large manufacturing company. She's quiet and…what's that word people use for someone who's smart and who likes science and technology?"

"A nerd?" Bridget supplied.

"That's it. She's a nerd. The groom normally likes, and this was her description, more outgoing and sexy women even though they, and, again, her description, always wound up breaking his heart. Then one rainy day he had a flat tire in the company parking lot. She spotted him on her way to her car and came to his rescue." Emily pressed a hand to her heart.

"She did?" Bridget asked, pausing work to listen.

"Yes." Emily set down one glass and picked up another. "While he was waiting for roadside assistance, she changed his flat tire. Didn't care that she got soaked to the skin. As you'd expect, he noticed her after that." Emily ended the recounting on a wistful smile. "Just think, they'd have missed out on marrying the love of their lives if that one circumstance hadn't caused them to open up to possibilities."

Was there a message in there for Ryan?

"That is a cute story," Bridget said and submerged a bottle of champagne in a silver bucket of ice.

"I should write a book." Emily straightened. "I hear so many great things from people." Evidently not expecting any comments, she set down the towel. "I'd better head out there. The groom and his party should be arriving any minute, and you know how frantic Molly gets when we're on countdown to the ceremony." She stopped at the door leading to the parlor. "Ryan, don't forget to meet the folks outside for pictures."

"No, ma'am." When he and Bridget were alone, he again offered to help. "Put me to work."

"Trying to vent your nervous energy?"

"Something like that."

"Here." She handed him the towel. "You can finish polishing the champagne glasses."

Not the perfect chore for Ryan and his big, clumsy fingers. But he did his best and waited for the right moment to mention listing his property.

"You adjusting to the new split schedule?"

she asked. "I know it must be hard having a chunk of time off in the middle of the day."

"Actually, it's working out well for me. I'm getting more done on the house." Seeing a chance, Ryan took it. "I, um, met with a real-estate agent the other day."

"Are you buying another property?"

"No, I'm thinking of listing mine."

He'd discussed his options with his parents during a long phone call yesterday and been forthcoming with his reasons. His mother couldn't have been more tickled at the prospect of him dating.

Bridget stopped what she was doing and turned to face him, her eyes wide in surprise. "I didn't realize you were considering selling."

"I wasn't. Not until the engagement party, which is where the real-estate agent and I met. She and the business broker Owen used to buy the feed store are partners."

"I think she belongs to the same business owners' association as Grandma."

"She mentioned that."

"Did you research her any? Check her references?"

"I read the testimonials listed on her company's website and the reviews posted on Yelp. They're pretty good. Owen speaks well of her partner, if that's any indication."

"Wouldn't you be better off selling when the renovations are complete? Not that I know the first thing about the real-estate market."

"I probably would."

Ryan couldn't decide if she was discouraging him from selling or examining the situation from all angles like he'd done. Only one way to know—lay it all out there.

"On the other hand," he continued, "if I sold now, I could make some money and be that much closer to buying the ranch."

"Wow."

Hmm. Was that wow like, "What a great idea and potentially good for us," or wow like, "I can't believe you'd be that foolish." He wished he knew.

"Cheryl-Anne, that's the real-estate agent's name, she has a client who buys investment properties and is very interested in my place. She thinks I can contract with him after the sale to finish the renovations." He explained more of Cheryl-Anne's idea.

"Is that what you want?"

"Again, pros and cons. I'd be paid for my services, which, besides the money, would be good experience if I'm serious about eventually starting my own construction company."

"There's a lot to consider," Bridget mused.

"No kidding."

"What does your gut tell you?"

"That there's no harm in signing the listing agreement. I don't have to take any offer." That was the advice his dad had given him. "I can always say no."

"True."

She stuffed trash into a plastic garbage bag and tied the top. When she started toward the door, Ryan spotted a second bag of trash already sitting there. When she would have taken both, he seized one and went with her outside to the Dumpster. It was hidden behind an L-shaped redwood wall, obscuring the unsightly view from the guests.

"I'm not changing my plans," he said while holding open the Dumpster lid. "Just modifying them. Hopefully, accelerating them."

"Nothing wrong with that, I suppose."

She didn't sound excited, and Ryan's spirits sank.

They returned to the house. At the door to the kitchen, he delayed her from entering with a hand on her arm.

"Wait. Tell me. Why don't you think me selling the property is a good idea?"

"It's none of my business, Ryan."

"I'm asking you. I'd like your opinion."

"Okay. You told me you wanted to eventually buy a small ranch outright and not have a mortgage payment."

He had. That was true.

"Is it possible for you to clear enough money from selling your property now to buy a ranch? And please don't think you have to divulge your finances to me."

"I guess that would depend on the offer."

She gave him a smile that appeared forced. "I wish you luck."

Again, she attempted to go inside and, again, Ryan stopped her. "Nothing's happened yet. But…"

"What, Ryan?"

"Something could happen." He captured her hand and squeezed it. "Between us. Because, if I sold early, I'd be closer to my goal and more inclined to…"

"To…?" she prompted when he didn't continue.

"Give us a shot."

"At…?"

She was making this difficult. Well, nothing worthwhile came easy. Another of his grandfather's sayings.

"Seeing where this could go." And before she asked him what *this* was, he said, "I like you, Bridget. A lot. The only reason I haven't pursued you is because I couldn't offer you what you want. What you deserve. What I could offer if I sell my place for the right price."

"Please don't make any decisions because of me."

"I'm not changing my goal, just adjusting the time line."

"But you'd be doing that for me."

He moved closer, trapping her between the closed kitchen door and himself. When she didn't object, he took a breath and spoke from the heart.

"I'd sell the property tomorrow if it gave you and me a chance at a future. You heard the story your grandmother told about the bride and groom. They wouldn't be getting married today if they hadn't opened themselves up to possibilities."

"And if you don't sell?"

What Ryan heard in her voice was concern, and he understood why. There were risks. She could agree to move ahead with their relationship only to be disappointed six months or a year from now when he was no closer to settling down than he was today.

"Stop overthinking." He hooked a finger beneath her chin and tilted her face to his. "Tell me what you really feel."

"I like you, too," she confessed in a whisper.

"And?"

"And I'm open to possibilities."

"That's my girl."

He kissed her then. Hard and hungry. She twined her arms around his neck, pulling him close and moaning softly as she arched into him.

It was heaven. It was torture. It was more than he'd ever dreamed possible, and Ryan willingly lost himself in the soft feel of her skin and the sweet taste of her lips.

She liked him, she'd admitted it. They had a chance. More than a chance, a real possibility. He could make this happen. They could—together.

When she pulled back to smile up at him, Ryan's chest nearly exploded from the sudden surge of emotions. She was here. With him. Eager and willing.

"I want to see you," he insisted. "Tonight. Tomorrow. Soon."

"All right."

"No kids this time."

"No kids," she agreed with a throaty laugh.

He kissed her again, and it was like coming home. No longer tentative and no longer exploring, they moved their lips in the familiar pattern of two people who were deeply connected and fully committed.

Too soon, they heard Emily calling for Bridget on the other side of the door. She disengaged her arms from around Ryan. Reluctantly, he noted with some satisfaction.

"We'd better answer her," she said, "or she'll come looking for us."

Ryan wondered if that would be so bad. He suspected that, like Bridget's mother, Emily wouldn't object to him dating Bridget.

He let her go with his own share of reluctance. Reaching around her, he opened the door.

Emily stood on the other side. Her glance cut from Bridget to Ryan, and suspicion flared in her eyes. "I was just about to send a search party."

"We were taking out the trash," Bridget answered smoothly.

Ryan was impressed. He'd have tripped over his words.

"I see." Emily's tone implied she guessed a whole lot more than trash disposal had occurred. "Ryan, they're waiting for you out front. You'd best hurry."

"Yes, ma'am."

Nodding to Emily, he squeezed past Bridget while plucking his cell phone from his shirt pocket. Twenty seconds later, he was standing on the veranda and talking with Cheryl-Anne.

"I'm ready to sign the listing agreement. When can we meet?"

CHAPTER THIRTEEN

BRIDGET AND HER grandmother stood on the veranda, observing the carriage return with the newlyweds from their ride through town. Cheering well-wishers gathered just outside the front gate, packets of birdseed in their hands.

Ryan pulled the draft horses to a stop. Damp patches of sweat covered their hides. Ryan, too, must have been feeling the heat because his cowboy shirt, previously ironed to a crisp, hung limply in the places it didn't cling to his skin.

None of that detracted from his appeal, as was evidenced by the many female guests, including ones old enough to be his mother and young enough to have barely graduated high school, flashing pretty smiles in his direction.

Responding to a handsome man apparently had no age restrictions. Bridget wished her own heartbeat would slow to a speed resembling normal.

As the happy couple, a little wilted from the heat but no worse for the wear, climbed down from the carriage, guests showered them with birdseed. Hand in hand, they hurried toward the house, up the veranda steps and inside, passing Bridget and Grandma Em. The short-of-breath videographer trotted after them, filming.

Once the immediate area had cleared, Ryan skillfully directed the draft horses down the dirt road leading toward the stables. Bridget had been right. From what she'd seen, the videographer had taken only a few shots of Ryan and focused mostly on the happy couple.

The parents of the bride were next to climb the veranda steps, followed by the remainder of the wedding party. They and most of the guests had stuck around during the ride, chatting, gathering personal items and packing up the wedding gifts.

"Thanks again for everything," the bride's mother said when she reached the veranda. "The wedding was absolutely perfect. We couldn't be more pleased."

"We're so glad." Grandma Em smiled brightly. "It was our pleasure."

While her husband went inside, the mother of the bride remained. "Would you and your granddaughters like to join us for dinner? You're more than welcome."

The wedding party and guests were heading to an Italian restaurant in nearby Rio Verde for the reception, where they'd reserved the banquet room. The bride and groom would change clothes in their cabin before leaving with their families.

"That's very kind of you," Grandma Em said. "But I'm afraid we can't accept." She looked to Bridget, who nodded in agreement. "We have another big wedding tomorrow to prepare for."

"I don't know how you do it," the woman said on a long exhale. "Personally, I'm tuckered out. And we still have the dinner and drive home. I intend to spend the entire day tomorrow with my feet up and a cold beverage in my hand."

"Good for you." Grandma Em patted the woman's arm. "If you need anything else, just give a holler. One of us will be in the parlor or the kitchen."

"One of us" translated into Bridget and her grandmother. Molly had left shortly into the ceremony. She and Owen were taking his son to a soccer teammate's birthday party.

"I think we're in good shape," the woman said. "As soon as my daughter and her husband get back from changing clothes, we're leaving for the restaurant." She paused, her eyes misting and her voice growing thick. "Her *husband*. Guess I'm going to have to get used to saying that. My baby girl is married. Only yesterday she was three years old."

"They grow up awful fast." Grandma Em slung an arm around Bridget's waist.

A short time later, the house was empty and blissfully quiet. Bridget and her grandmother had retired to the kitchen. They'd accomplished everything that needed doing, other than a few preparations for tomorrow's continental breakfast.

Grandma Em sat at the table and rested her feet up on one of the empty chairs. "Whew! The mother of the bride had the right idea."

"She did." Bridget poured two glasses of leftover champagne and brought them to the table. "Here. I hate to see this go to waste."

"Me, too." Grandma Em clinked glasses with Bridget. "Cheers. And to another great wedding tomorrow." They sipped in companionable silence for a few minutes until Grandma Em dropped the not-unexpected bombshell question. "What was going on with you and Ryan earlier? And don't give me that line about taking out the trash."

Not quite ready to talk about the kiss, Bridget said, "Ryan listed his property for sale with a real-estate agent."

"Huh! That's out of the blue."

"Yes. It is." Bridget described Ryan meeting Cheryl-Anne a week ago at the engagement party.

"But why would he sell before the renovations are complete? He'll make less money."

"He hopes to get one step closer to buying a small ranch and one step closer to settling down."

"With you?"

"We've talked about dating." More than talked, but Bridget was gauging her grandmother's response before admitting to more.

"I must be more tired than I thought. I should have seen that coming given the way you both drool over each other whenever you're together."

"I suppose we have been obvious."

"I thought he didn't meet enough of your requirements."

"He does, actually. He's fun and kind and sweet and ambitious. Really good with children. A lot of things I'm looking for in a man. And now that he's selling his property…" She stopped short when her grandmother made a face. "What's wrong?"

"Look, I like Ryan. He's a decent guy, and I'm in favor of you two dating. For the right reasons. I'm a little concerned that he's making such a drastic decision like selling his property based entirely on you."

"I agree. I raised the same concerns with him myself."

"What did he say?"

"He's just listing the property," Bridget said, repeating Ryan's argument. "He may not accept any offers."

"What's the point of listing if he doesn't sell?"

"To see if there's an interest and get an idea of what the property's worth."

Grandma Em shook her head. "And if he doesn't sell, then he's no closer to buying a ranch. What happens to the two of you then?"

"He and his real-estate agent are very optimistic."

"All right. Let's say he does sell. What if three months from now you realize you're not right for each other? He's gone and changed his whole life for you and made less money on his property than if he'd finished the renovations. And he might well be without a roof over his head."

Bridget's smile dimmed. A moment ago, she'd been on cloud nine. Now, she was crashing back to earth. Had she gotten so completely caught up in Ryan's enthusiasm she failed to heed her common sense?

That wasn't like her. Bridget proceeded with caution.

"I'm sorry," Grandma Em said. "It wasn't

my intention to upset you. I just love you and like Ryan and would hate to see you both hurt."

"I know." Bridget pressed a hand to her chest, where a heavy weight resided. "I want the kind of relationship Mom and Dad had. Head over heels for each other. I think I could have that with Ryan. Eventually."

"Soon enough for you?"

"I can wait a little while. Better that than marrying the wrong man, like Doug."

"Your mother isn't unhappy, Bridget."

"She isn't ecstatic, either."

"You're wrong." Grandma Em drained the last of her champagne. "Doug has his faults, but he's good to your mom in other ways. Ways that matter to her now at this stage in her life, and that didn't matter as much when she married your dad."

"He's controlling."

"That's how you see him. Your mother sees him as a good provider who's devoted to her. The fact he may not be the man you'd choose for yourself doesn't automatically make him a bad choice for your mother."

Bridget considered that statement for a moment and had to admit maybe she and Molly hadn't given Doug a fair shot.

"I guess Mom has different requirements than me."

Grandma Em groaned. "You need to ditch that ridiculous list of yours. It has you so afraid of making the wrong decision, you're not making a decision at all."

"Not true. I'm going out with Ryan."

"Only because you pressured him into taking an action he wouldn't have otherwise."

Had she? The weight in her chest grew heavier.

"Oh, honey." Grandma Em reached for her hand. "I'm worried you've been using that list for years to protect yourself from being hurt."

"I'm not like Molly," Bridget insisted. "I don't have a history of men breaking my heart or leaving me at the altar like her."

"No, you had a father who adored you and then suddenly and tragically died."

"You think I have abandonment issues?"

"I think you haven't gotten over the hurt and pain of losing someone without any warning and who meant the world to you. When your grandfather passed, I had time to prepare. He'd been sick for almost a year. You, Molly and your mom had no warning whatsoever with your father. He went to work one day and never came home. No one walks away from a blow like that emotionally unscathed."

Bridget wanted to refute her grandmother. She wasn't afraid or hiding behind her list.

Only it made too much sense and explained a lot about her life up until now, including gaining weight after her dad died and putting her career first.

Self-realization was a difficult process and left Bridget drained. If not for having to deliver chilled champagne and chocolate-covered strawberries to the newlyweds' cabin, she'd go upstairs, crawl into bed and stay under the covers until morning.

She pushed away from the table.

"Where are you going?" Grandma Em asked.

Pointing to the ice bucket on the counter, she said, "Taking the champagne and strawberries to cabin five. I'm tired and would rather do it now than later."

"I didn't mean to upset you. If I spoke out of turn—"

"You didn't, Grandma."

The older woman stood. "All I want in this world is for you to be happy."

"I know that." She kissed her grandmother on the cheek. "I'll be fine. I promise."

She would, too, once she had time to process what her grandmother had said. It was a lot to think about.

While Bridget swirled chocolate sauce on a china plate in the design of a heart and topped it with the strawberries, her grandmother left to straighten the chapel and rearrange the altar for tomorrow's wedding. Carefully packing the delicacies in a soft-sided cooler, she carried it and the ice bucket to the golf cart outside. At the last second, she included scented candles and a bag of dried rose petals to sprinkle on the bed.

While setting out the goodies for the newlyweds in their cabin—they'd long since left for their dinner—she considered telling Ryan she'd changed her mind. Or, at the least, that they needed a little more time.

Grandma Em was right. His selling his property purely for her was a bad idea. If things didn't go well, Ryan could come to resent her. She'd hate that. They both would.

After locking the cabin door behind her, she dropped the cooler in the golf cart.

What now? Back to the house? Call Ryan?

As if in answer, she noticed his truck parked beside the stables. It hadn't been there before.

On impulse, she turned the wheel of the golf cart and pressed down on the pedal with her foot. The golf cart silently sped up the slight rise toward the stables as fast as its battery-powered motor would allow.

Ryan was just coming out of the stables when she braked to a stop. "Hey there."

He still wore his clothes from earlier, though

he'd rolled up the sleeves of his shirt to reveal tanned, muscular arms. He'd also unfastened the top two buttons, and the collar of his white undershirt peeked out.

She liked him this way best. Not that he hadn't looked yummy for the wedding earlier. But Ryan was at his most attractive when dressed casually and hard at work.

"You busy?" she asked.

"Not at the moment." His grin stretched wide. "Cheryl-Anne just left. You missed her by five minutes."

Bridget hopped out of the golf cart. She and Ryan met up near the hitching post. "She was here?"

"We signed the listing agreement. And, get this." His grin grew, if that was even possible. "The second I did, she presented me with an offer."

Bridget's jaw went slack. "You're kidding!"

"She's been in talks with that investor client of hers the past few days while waiting for me to make up my mind. He saw the property back before I bought it and didn't act fast enough."

"Can I ask if you got the price you wanted?"

"I did. There are a couple of items we're negotiating. But if the buyer agrees, Cheryl-Anne will bring the amended offer by tomorrow."

"On Sunday?"

"Real estate is a seven-day-a-week business."

Bridget had to ask. "Are you sure this is what you want?"

"I've never wanted anything more." Ryan reached for her and, wrapping his arms around her, lifted her high in the air and twirled her in a circle.

She protested with a half-hearted "Put me down."

He did. "Let's go out tonight and celebrate."

"It's too soon. The sale isn't finalized."

"Even if it falls through, there'll be another one."

"You can't be sure," she insisted.

"I'm more sure about this than I've been about anything in my life."

"All right." Like before, his enthusiasm was contagious. How could she refuse?

"Dinner at the Poco Dinero?"

She shook her head. "Because I refuse to jinx anything, let's go on a horseback ride instead."

"I'll saddle up."

She laughed, loving his exuberance. "Not today. How about Wednesday morning? Early. There's no wedding scheduled, and Molly can set out the continental breakfast for me."

"It's a date."

Date. Bridget took a moment to let the word

sink in. It'd been over two years since she'd last gone out with a man.

It felt good. Incredible. And absolutely right.

Whatever obstacles she and Ryan faced, she had faith they'd surmount them. Fate was clearly on their side. What other explanation could there be for such a quick offer on his property?

"HOW WAS YOUR DATE?" Molly asked the moment she answered Bridget's call.

"Gee, not even a hello?"

"Hello. How was your date?"

Bridget's gaze traveled across the paddock to the backyard, where Ryan alternately peered in the kitchen window and stared up at the roof. "It wasn't a date."

"I don't believe you."

"We went on a morning horseback ride. Not to dinner. Not to a movie. Not to a concert."

"You packed food, right?" Molly asked.

"Streusel and a thermos of coffee. We stopped for breakfast along the old camp trail."

"That's a picnic and, by your own definition, a date."

There was no arguing with her sister, not that Bridget was inclined. She still got tingles whenever she thought about her and Ryan as a couple.

"Did you have a good time?" Molly prodded.

"Very good. The scenery was great."

Who was she kidding? Bridget had barely noticed the spectacular views. She'd been too busy laughing at Ryan's jokes and going all soft inside at his smiles and drowning in his intense gaze while they walked the footpaths, leading their horses by the reins.

"I'm glad for you, sis. You deserve a nice guy."

"This is still very new," Bridget cautioned. "Don't go sending out engraved invitations just yet."

She was working hard at not making more of her and Ryan's relationship than there was: they were two people who clicked and enjoyed each other's company. But ask her again in a few months, and she might have an entirely different answer.

"What's next on the agenda for today?" Molly asked. "A continuation of the date-that-isn't-a-date, I hope."

"Well, I just put the horses away."

Bridget had unsaddled the horses and given them a good brushing down while Ryan met with the home inspectors. Not long after they'd returned from their ride, the two pair had pulled into the driveway, one right behind the other.

Bridget had sent off Ryan to greet them and assumed charge of the horses.

"After that," Bridget continued, "I guess I'll wait on Ryan and the inspectors."

"How's that going, by the way?"

"I can't really tell." She shielded her eyes from the bright sunlight and squinted at the house. "He's still pacing in front of the ladder."

"The inspector? Why?"

"No, Ryan. You'd think he hadn't been through this three times before."

Bridget's knowledge of real-estate sales was limited. But from what Ryan had told her, home inspections were routine. That way, the buyer was made aware of any problems before money changed hands, and the seller had the opportunity to make repairs or adjust the sales price accordingly.

The buyer for Ryan's property had insisted on both a general inspection and a more thorough plumbing inspection at the first available opportunity and at Ryan's expense. The Chandler place was old and had been poorly maintained these last several years. Despite the buyer's knowledge of the property's history and present midrenovation condition, Ryan still worried the inspection results would affect the sale.

Bridget worried, too, that they were counting too much on the outcome of this sale.

"There shouldn't be a problem," she said, reassuring herself as much as her sister. "Supposedly the buyer is an experienced investor. He's planning on completing the renovations himself." Surely he wouldn't balk at a few small problems.

"I'm still trying to wrap my head around Ryan flipping houses," Molly said. "It's kind of cool. Maybe he could be on one of those cable TV shows."

"Yeah." All joking aside, he was every bit as good-looking as that guy with the hit house-flipping series.

"Would Ryan then buy a new property?"

"That's the idea." Bridget reached into each horse's water trough and scooped out the dried leaves that had fallen in. "Though he has to find the right one first."

"Then what?" Molly persisted. "You two getting married?"

"One small step at a time."

Bridget liked daydreaming about walking down the aisle with Ryan and indulged frequently. She was also a realist.

The next instant, a movement at the house caught her attention. "Oh, it looks like the guy's climbing down from the roof."

"Call me later, okay?" Molly said. "Tell me how the inspection went."

They disconnected after saying goodbye. Bridget gave each horse a kiss on the nose that they didn't seem to mind, but didn't enjoy, either. She missed riding regularly and was glad she and Ryan shared the same interest. Perhaps one day she could have her own horse again. When she and Ryan—

Wait. Stop. Here she was getting ahead of herself and doing exactly what she'd warned her sister not to do.

By now, the inspector on the roof had collapsed his ladder and his associate had come outside. Ryan met up with them, and the three men walked around the side of the house to the front. Bridget noted there was a lot of talking on Ryan's part and expansive gesturing.

She'd watched from a distance as he tried his best to assist both inspectors when they first arrived, offering his own ladder and the use of his tools. They'd declined, citing something about policy mandating they use their own equipment. Bridget suspected that what Ryan had really wanted was to be directly involved with the men's inspections. Possibly read what the men were inputting into the electronic devices they carried or have a closer look at the images on the specialized cameras they used.

She took the same path as Ryan and the men, rounding the corner of the house and entering the front yard in time to see Ryan making payment to each man and receiving paperwork in return. Then, the two men got in their respective trucks and drove away. Bridget made her way over to where Ryan stood, staring after the men as if he could divine what they were thinking.

"Everything go okay?" she asked.

"I have no idea." His shoulders drooped. "They were as tight-lipped as they come. Said the buyer and I would each receive copies of the reports via email when they're finalized."

"When will that be?"

"Not for a couple of days from the home inspector. The plumbing report isn't as long or involved. I could have it by this afternoon."

"Is it me or did they take a lot of pictures?"

"That's par for the course." His frown increased. "But that one guy spent a lot of time on the roof. I know he's going to find some holes. Or recommend replacing the air-conditioning unit. It's old. He had a funny look on his face when he came down from the crawl space over the garage."

"What was that strange paddle thing the other guy had?"

"An infrared camera. For detecting plumbing leaks. With my luck, I'll have to tear out a wall to fix a faulty pipe"

"Don't drive yourself crazy, Ryan. It won't do any good and just keep you up at night."

"You're right."

He reached out and pulled her into a tender hug, their second of the day. He'd also kissed her this morning when she'd arrived at 7:00 a.m. sharp for their ride. They'd been doing that with increasing regularity the past three days. Not in plain sight and not when they were working.

"I just want this sale to go through." Releasing her, he skimmed his palm down her arm and claimed her hand.

"What if it doesn't?" she asked, taking measure of their linked fingers and thinking how very nicely they fit. "Would living here be so bad? Once you finish the renovations."

"I can't run a small herd on a single acre of land. And the house is small. There's no place for my folks to live if they decide to move, other than on top of me. I'd like a barn with sufficient space to build them an apartment and sufficient land for a construction office and storage yard. That's just not feasible here."

He was right. The property was small by Mustang Valley standards.

He was also right to be thinking ahead to owning his own construction business. His job at Sweetheart Ranch, while great for someone just starting out or was semiretired, like their former wrangler, wasn't enough pay-wise or benefit-wise or advancement-wise for a man planning on eventually getting married and having a family.

"I have an idea." Ryan lifted her hand to his mouth and pressed his lips to the sensitive skin behind her knuckles. "Let's have an early lunch at the café. I can't think of anything better to take my mind off the inspections."

He pulled her along after him, and Bridget went willingly. The time they spent together was quickly becoming magical as her feelings for him deepened. She wasn't ready for it to be over. Not yet and, at the rate they were going, maybe not ever.

CHAPTER FOURTEEN

THERE WEREN'T A lot of restaurants in Mustang Valley to choose from. Ryan would have taken Bridget someplace fancier than the Cowboy Up Café, but other than the coffee bar at the bookstore or the food truck selling street tacos that came to town on weekends, their only other choice for lunch was the local bar and grill.

Personally, he liked the fare at the Cowboy Up. Then again, Ryan didn't possess a refined palate. No one who subsided primarily on sandwiches and boxed meals did.

He hoped Bridget wasn't too disappointed. She'd acted upbeat on the drive from his place to the café. The reason might have been that they were together. Ryan was feeling rather upbeat himself.

Though it was just past eleven and not quite officially lunchtime, the café was surprisingly busy. The hostess greeting them requested they wait while a table for two was cleared and set up. A large party with reservations was expected, she explained. Hence, the wait.

"You want to sit?" Ryan nodded at a bench just inside the door.

"I'm fine. They're pretty quick here. We should be seated soon." Bridget's smile faltered. "Unless you want to sit."

Three days into their relationship, and they were already trying to second-guess the other.

"I like standing."

He did. Especially now. A small group leaving the café squeezed past them, forcing Ryan to press closer to Bridget in order to make room.

Behind them, the door whooshed open. Twenty or so people filed in and congregated to the left of the hostess podium, laughing and talking up a storm. Happily, Ryan was again required to cozy up to Bridget. He secretly wished the wait for their table took longer than promised.

The last two stragglers entering were no strangers: Emily and Homer.

"Grandma!" Bridget motioned them over and gave the older couple affectionate hugs. "I forgot you'd be here." She turned and looked up at Ryan, placing their faces inches apart. "Grandma and Homer belong to the church lunch bunch."

"Lunch bunch?" he asked.

"Some of the members meet here for lunch

on the last Wednesday of every month," Homer explained. "Would you like to join us?"

"Thank you," Bridget said. "That's very nice—"

"Homer!" Emily gave him an impatient ribbing with her elbow. "They don't want to sit with us old folks. I'm sure they'd much rather be alone."

"Oh." He looked momentarily chagrined, then realization dawned, and he smiled. "*Oh! I see. This is a—*" his index finger pinged back and forth between Ryan and Bridget "—a tête-à-tête."

"Who even uses that word anymore?" Emily rolled her eyes.

Ryan chuckled. "Can't say I'm sure what it means."

"They're obviously here on a date." Emily tugged on Homer's sleeve. "Now, let's leave them alone so they can get to know each other better without any interruptions."

"Maybe next month," Homer said before being dragged away.

"Sorry about that." Bridget offered Ryan an apologetic smile when they were once more alone. "Sometimes Grandmother has no filter."

He chuckled. "Not a problem."

And it wasn't. Not to him. He liked their relationship being public knowledge.

By then, the hostess had returned and escorted them to their booth. Ryan slid in opposite Bridget, picking up his menu as he did.

"What's good?" he asked.

"Pretty much everything. The food here is the home-cooking variety. Meat loaf, chicken-fried steak, chili. They do have some salad entrées. Well, two salad entrées. Chef and grilled-chicken Caesar."

He supposed there was little on the menu that appealed to her. She probably preferred something along the lines of poached trout or crepes. He, on the other hand, ate almost everything, even liver and onions. That was a favorite of his dad's.

"Have you decided?" Bridget closed her menu.

"I'm leaning toward the club sandwich."

"Good choice. The wedge fries are excellent."

"You?"

"A patty melt."

He drew back. "No fooling?"

"My guilty pleasure." Her green eyes flashed with mirth. "I let myself have one every now and then."

What Ryan wouldn't give to be her guilty pleasure, and a whole lot more often than every now and then.

They lingered over lunch, chatting about this and that. He avoided any discussion of the inspections and instead shared amusing childhood memories.

While simple, his meal was stick-to-his-ribs good. Bridget finished every last bite of her patty melt. When she voiced a concern about the enormous amount of calories she'd consumed, he let his gaze slide over her.

"You're gorgeous."

"And you're a flatterer," she chided him.

There was a lot more he could say about what he thought of her. This wasn't the time or place, however. Another day, like when he took her someplace fancier for dinner and they ate by candlelight.

The church lunch bunch was socializing over dessert and coffee when Ryan and Bridget left and returned to his truck. On the drive to his place, his phone beeped, signaling an email.

His glance cut from the road to Bridget. "I wonder if that could be the plumbing inspector's report."

"Do you think? It's awfully quick."

At the upcoming stop sign, he quickly checked his phone. Seeing the sender's name, his pulse quickened. "Mind if we pull over?"

Bridget shook her head. "Not at all."

In the bank parking lot, he let the engine idle

and the air-conditioning run while he accessed his email app.

"It's from the inspector." Downloading the report to his phone, Ryan tried to view it. "Too difficult to read on this small screen," he complained, his frustration mounting.

"Do you have a computer?" Bridget asked.

"Not anymore." His old laptop had died a terrible death a few months ago, and a new one was an expense he'd decided could wait. Now, he wished he'd been less frugal.

"You can use the computer at the ranch if you want to print out the report. No one will mind." She suddenly reached for her door handle. "Wait! If you want, you could email me the report. I'll open it on my tablet when we get back to the house. The screen is larger than your phone."

"You brought your tablet?"

"I *always* bring my tablet."

He should have figured as much. "What's your email address?"

She told him. Ryan forwarded her the report before pulling into traffic. He drove as fast as the speed limit allowed, his club sandwich wreaking havoc on his stomach and his hands choking the steering wheel. The moment they reached his house, Bridget hopped out of his truck and scurried to her SUV. Tablet in hand, she climbed back in beside him.

A minute later, she said, "I got it," and passed him her tablet with the inspector's report open.

He scrolled through all the mandatory legal mumbo jumbo until he reached the actual report. It was lengthy, but in his experience, these reports usually were. Especially with older properties like Ryan's.

At that point, the reading got more interesting. The inspector had included a slew of notes and comments along with photographs he'd taken with the regular and infrared cameras. There were also several short videos embedded in the report.

Ryan skimmed. At first, there was nothing he hadn't already anticipated in the way of recommended repairs. By the third page, the tone of the report changed, and he read more slowly and carefully. Here were findings he hadn't expected, and they weren't good.

By the time he reached the summary, a loud roar filled his ears, and his fingers fumbled as he scrolled up and clicked on the first video. The wavy, surreal images moving across the screen made no sense. Then, all at once, they did.

He must have been frowning, because Bridget asked, "What's wrong?"

"I need to take a look at something." He set down her tablet on the seat, turned off the truck and shoved open his door.

"Ryan!" She hurried after him.

Inside the house, he went directly to the laundry room.

"Hey, slow down and tell me what's the matter." Behind him, Bridget trotted to keep up.

"The inspector says the plumbing system is entirely shot and needs a complete overhaul. Every single pipe inside and outside replaced. Even those in the horse stalls. According to him, the system is a disaster waiting to happen."

"He said that?"

"Practically word for word."

"That sounds...like a lot."

"A lot of money," Ryan said. "And work and time." He didn't want to think about how much a complete plumbing overhaul would set him back.

In the laundry room, he studied the hookup for the washer. According to the inspector, this was a serious trouble spot. In Ryan's opinion, it looked okay. He didn't find much in the master bathroom, either, or the one in the hall.

Maybe the inspector had been exceedingly cautious and the whole report was exaggerated.

"Now where?" Bridget asked when he took off again.

"Outside."

Like the washer hookup in the laundry room, he didn't think the connection from the underground pipes into the house was in bad shape. Some rust, for sure. A little mold around the spigot. Also some corrosion on the pipes. Leaving Bridget there, he raced to the shed in search of a shovel.

Returning to the house, he dug around the base of the pipe, exposing it in order to get a better look. Infrared cameras were reliable. Even so, he wanted to see with his own eyes.

The tip of the shovel hit the pipe with a dull clank. Ryan ignored it and kept digging, though more carefully.

"Is that water?" Bridget leaned down and pointed.

"Yeah." He didn't like what he saw. The rusted pipe was sweating water at an alarming rate. Rivulets were disappearing into the dirt and turning it dark brown. "I'd better get some tape and patch that."

He no sooner spoke than the pipe shimmied as if alive and split with a sharp cracking sound. The tiny fissure that had allowed drops to leak suddenly ruptured, and water sprayed in a large fan shape, soaking Ryan and hitting Bridget in the face. She jumped back, giving a small shriek.

Squeezing his eyes shut against the water's assault, Ryan reached in and attempted to tighten the bracket above the rupture with his bare hand. His efforts only made matters worse. The weakened pipe separated completely, and water rushed out in a fast torrent, instantly flooding the hole.

Ryan muttered choice words under his breath that he didn't dare speak aloud. Tossing the shovel aside, he ran to the front of the house. He should have figured Bridget would be behind him.

"Where are you going?" she demanded.

"To shut off the water."

In the front yard near the street, Ryan located the in-ground box containing the main water valve. Prying off the lid, he reached inside the box and twisted the valve with all his might.

"Run back to the broken pipe and see if the water's stopped," he told Bridget.

She did, and a minute later he heard her shout, "It's off."

Ryan straightened, scrubbing his wet face and feeling his spirits sink to his knees. He was no expert at plumbing, but even he could tell this was a disaster of monumental proportions.

Bridget returned, her features etched with worry. "What are you going to do?"

He shook his head. "I don't know."

For her, the question was probably simple. How to fix the plumbing problem? For him, the questions were many and complex. They started with where would he find the money and ended with how might this affect the sale of his property and, ultimately, his plans for a future with Bridget?

He struggled to maintain focus. One step at a time, he told himself.

"What about the horses?" Bridget asked once they'd returned to the broken pipe. "Won't they be out of water now that you shut off the main valve?"

"Yeah." That was the least of his problems. With no running water, the house was practically uninhabitable and construction on it would come to a grinding halt.

"Want to move them to the ranch temporarily? I'm sure Grandma won't mind."

"Let's wait. See how long the repairs take. I'm sure Nora will let me fill a barrel of water at her house."

"What about you?" She touched his arm. "You can't stay here. Not for more than a day or two."

"I'll figure something out."

"I'm sorry, Ryan." Her voice cracked.

"Me, too." Not the romantic first-date ending he'd been envisioning.

"What can I do to help?"

"Nothing at the moment, but I appreciate the offer."

She accompanied him through the house and over the entire grounds as he investigated every problem listed in the plumbing inspector's report. Eventually, she had to leave.

He walked her to her SUV. There, they briefly kissed. Ryan would have liked for his attention to be entirely on her these last minutes together, but he was too distraught.

Before he could pull away, Bridget wrapped her arms around him, laid her head on his chest and held him tight. They remained that way for a full minute. Her silent show of support meant more to him than any words.

"Call me later," she said and climbed into her vehicle.

"I will."

He stayed and waved goodbye until she was on the road. Then, he turned and went to the shed, where he found an empty, heavy-duty plastic barrel. Ryan carried it to his truck and loaded it in the bed. He then drove next door to Nora's.

Luckily she was home and very concerned when he told her about the broken pipe and disheartening report from the plumbing inspector. They stood on her back porch, conversing.

"Of course you can have water," she said. "Take as much as you want."

"You're a good friend, Nora."

"Why don't you stay here? You can bunk in the spare room the grandkids use when they sleep over."

"Thanks, but I'm going to rough it. Been there, done that. I'll survive"

"Living without running water will get old fast."

"Shouldn't take more than a day or two for me to hire a plumber to fix the pipe. After that, I can turn the water back on."

For a while. If he made all the repairs the plumbing inspector recommended, the water would be off and on for weeks.

"What about the sale of the property?" Nora asked. "Will it still go through?"

"No idea. The buyer also gets a copy of the inspection reports. He'll learn soon enough the plumbing needs a complete overhaul. He may have already contacted the real-estate agent." Ryan exhaled a long breath. "Depending on what the buyer decides, either the sale will fall through, or I'll have to reduce my price by the cost of the repairs."

Neither choice appealed to him. Overhauls of this nature generally ran into the tens of thousands. There went the small percentage of profit he'd hoped to make on the sale.

"I have a good plumber I can recommend," Nora offered.

"I'll need one. I'd like to get two or three quotes on the work."

"Don't suppose you can do the work yourself."

"I might be able to jury-rig the broken pipe," he said. "Overhauling the entire plumbing is way beyond my abilities."

"Going to be expensive."

"You can count on that."

Ryan knew how these things went. There were almost always extra costs because more problems were discovered once the repairs were underway.

"I suppose telling you not to fret is pointless," Nora said.

"You suppose right."

He mentally berated himself as he filled the barrel with water from Nora's garden hose. The out-of-the-blue offer to buy the property had been too good to believe. Yet, he'd rushed ahead without exercising caution because selling the property made him more husband-worthy in Bridget's opinion.

Not that he blamed himself. Wanting her, wanting what they could have, was understandable. But if he'd waited just a little longer, he might not have pinned all his hopes and dreams on a nearly impossible outcome.

BRIDGET SLIPPED HER hand into her apron pocket. Angling her body, she pulled out her phone and discreetly checked the display while her client, Gregory's sister, had her nose buried in the binder of hors d'oeuvre and appetizer selections.

A quick glance confirmed what Bridget already knew. Ryan hadn't called. The phone dropped from her fingers, bumping against her hip as it landed in the pocket.

There were no carriage or trail rides scheduled today. After feeding the horses and completing an assortment of chores around the stables, Ryan had gone home to await the two different plumbers coming out to review the work and provide him with quotes.

He and Bridget had talked for a mere five minutes when he'd come inside that morning for breakfast and his regular meeting with Grandma Em. He'd informed Bridget about the two plumbers and that he'd yet to hear from the buyer regarding the sale. As of this moment, it was still pending. Bridget prayed that status didn't change.

Yesterday, Ryan had taken her up on her offer to print out the inspection reports on the ranch computer. Most of what the dozens of pages contained made no sense to her.

But Ryan had deciphered them and given her the *Reader's Digest* version. He'd left the house after that with his shoulders slumped and a dejected look on his face.

As much as she longed to help, there was little she could do for him other than be a sounding board and a cheering section.

"Do the wontons have crab in them?"

Bridget was yanked from her reverie by Kinsey, Gregory's sister. "They do," she answered, infusing a smile in her voice.

"What if people have a shellfish allergy?"

"I can substitute whitefish."

"Will it taste the same?"

"To anyone without a discriminating palate, yes. But whether we use crab or a substitute, I guarantee you, the wontons will be delicious." Bridget turned a page in the binder, revealing a striking color photo of a fluted crystal bowl filled with dip and wreathed by crackers. "You can always go with smoked salmon."

"I'm not sure what to do." Kinsey cradled her cheek in her palm. "Can I think about it?"

"Take your time."

She'd flown in from Vermont for a long weekend of second-wedding organizing—the first one would take place in Vermont for her fiancé's family. She'd already met with Molly and Grandma Em. All that remained was selecting food items for the reception.

She was very nice if a bit particular. Bridget cut her some slack. She had only a small window of time in which to finalize a huge number of details for a big event. And it was her special day, after all. Neither was it her fault that Bridget couldn't stop thinking about Ryan and his house problems.

Poor guy. She hadn't raised the subject of how this recent setback might impact their future, though she'd been considering the ramifications for hours on end. How could she not? She'd been the one to make the conditions. No dating unless he was further along in his life plan.

She could tell herself she'd expressed her concerns repeatedly and given him every chance to say no. That didn't relieve her guilt or sense of responsibility. If not for her, he wouldn't have listed the house for sale or had the inspections conducted.

Bridget held on to the hope that things could change for the better with the plumbing quotes. The problems may not be as bad as they first appeared or as costly to fix. She just had to be patient and think positive. At least the general inspection had gone reasonably well. Ryan's concerns about possible roof leaks and the air-conditioning unit needing replacing hadn't materialized.

"Let's go with the pepperoni *caprese* bites," Kinsey said.

"Good choice."

Fifteen minutes later the menu was finalized. Choosing the cake was a whole separate matter and required an additional forty-five minutes. When they were at last done, Bridget walked Kinsey to the foyer, where they met Molly.

"Thanks so much for all your help," Kinsey gushed.

"Thank you for choosing Sweetheart Ranch," Molly said. "Don't hesitate to call, whatever the reason."

"It still seems a little unreal to me," Kinsey gushed. "My family was starting to believe I'd never get married. And here I am having two ceremonies, two weeks and two thousand miles apart."

Bridget was surprised to learn that Kinsey hadn't been previously wed. She pegged the other woman to be several years her senior, late thirties at least. It was wrong, she supposed, to assume that just because she herself didn't want to wait for a husband and children, neither did anyone else.

Were Kinsey and her fiancé planning on having a family? She hadn't mentioned stepchildren.

Bridget was curious but refrained from asking. That would be rude and none of her business.

As her biological clock liked to remind her, should she wait to marry and then experience difficulties getting pregnant, she'd have less childbearing years ahead to explore various options.

While it wasn't romantic or spontaneous to consider the mechanics of having a family, Bridget was a realist.

"He was worth holding out for," Kinsey continued, her attractive features aglow. "Everything I ever could want in a husband. Handsome. Great job. Financially secure. Established. Owns a beautiful home in the hills."

It sounded as if Kinsey had a dating list, too.

Molly asked about where they'd met. Bridget only half listened as Kinsey relayed the story of a wine-tasting party at a mutual friend's house.

"I'm so glad I didn't say yes to the first few men who proposed," Kinsey said. "If I'd married one of them, we'd probably still be scraping by, up to our ears in debt, driving clunkers and working at menial jobs. I don't regret for one second putting my career first and waiting for my soul mate."

Technically, Ryan's pickup could be called a clunker. And, in its present condition, his house was far from beautiful. It may even qualify as a disaster site. Neither was he what one could call established.

Bridget found herself wondering if Kinsey's fiancé knew how to square dance or if he appreciated the beauty of a sunset. Did he make the world disappear when he kissed her and cause her heart to leap with excitement when he entered the room?

"You know when you've met the right one." Molly smiled at Kinsey as if they shared the secret to happiness—which, in a way, they did. They'd both found their soul mates.

Was Ryan Bridget's soul mate? Sometimes, she thought yes. Other times, she was less sure.

"I'm so glad my brother told me about this place." Kinsey glanced around. "It's exactly what I was looking for."

"We're glad, too. He was here recently and went on the hayride with his children and friend. What was her name?" Molly swiveled to face Bridget, her expression expectant.

"Celeste," Bridget answered drily.

"That's right." Molly returned her attention to Kinsey. "She seemed very sweet. We chatted a bit during the square dancing."

"Not sweet at all." Kinsey leaned in, her tone changing to a conspiratorial one. "They aren't seeing each other anymore."

"Really?"

"She has a boyfriend. They were apparently on the outs briefly. Long enough for her to make a play for my brother and then drop him cold when the boyfriend suggested a reconciliation. Poor Gregory. He feels like a fool."

"That's a shame," Molly sympathized.

Bridget did, too. Gregory had seemed quite taken with Celeste. He'd deserved better treatment than what he'd gotten.

The three women exchanged polite hugs, after which Kinsey left to meet her mother and matron of honor for lunch and dress shopping.

Closing the front door, Molly wiped pretend sweat from her forehead. "I hate to say it, but I'm glad that's over. She had a lot of requests."

"She did." As a result, Bridget was behind on work. "There's leftover pasta for lunch if you want some."

Molly blocked her escape. "Wow, can you believe it? Gregory's girlfriend dumped him."

"Is there some reason you want to talk about this?"

"I'm just shocked. Aren't you?"

"Doesn't sound like they were together very long," Bridget said. "Calling her his girlfriend might be a stretch."

"Still, he's taking the breakup hard according to his sister."

"I'm sure he'll bounce back."

The town doctor had a flock of female fans. He wouldn't be alone for very long, or if he was, it would be by choice.

"Are you going to pursue him now that he's available?"

Bridget grimaced. "Why would I do that?"

Molly burst out laughing. "You should see yourself."

"Very funny."

Bridget tamped down her irritation. She and her sister had teased each other mercilessly when they were young. It was a practice that occasionally continued as adults.

"I just wanted to see how much you like Ryan." Molly grinned. "And now I have my answer."

"Of course I like him. We're dating, for crying out loud."

"Does that mean you've decided to wait for him?"

"I may not have to wait long if the sale of his house goes through." *Please, please, please.*

"And if it doesn't?" Molly asked.

He was worth holding out for.

Kinsey's words came back to Bridget. The bride-to-be did seem deliriously happy. And wouldn't it be better to wait and spend the rest of one's life with a wonderful and loving spouse than to marry the wrong person in haste only to be miserable?

Yes. Emphatically. Unequivocally.

Bridget's entire list of dating nonnegotiables had been created because she'd seen firsthand a marriage made in heaven. Her parents'. Why quit wanting the same for herself just because it was taking longer to achieve that for herself than expected?

She was about to say that no matter what happened with Ryan's house, she would wait until he was ready and for however long it took. But in the next moment she bit her tongue. She hadn't yet told Ryan how she felt and wanted him to be the first to know.

She shouldered past her sister, suddenly in a hurry to call Ryan. "One day at a time."

Breezing into the kitchen, she came to an abrupt halt. Ryan stood with his back against the counter and his hands stuffed in the front pockets of his jeans.

"Hi." The word stuck in her suddenly dry throat.

He looked good. Amazingly so. He must have been going hatless, for the slight breeze cutting through the valley today had left his dark hair in an attractive state of dishevelment. His somber expression lent him a sexy, brooding appearance that made her think of Heathcliff in *Wuthering Heights*. She found herself falling a little harder for him and was eager to share her recent revelation.

"Did the plumbers show?" she asked when her voice returned.

He ignored her question. "When I first got here, I went into the parlor looking for you."

"Okay."

"You were with Molly and the doctor's sister."

"Yeah. She was making arrangements for her wedding. Second wedding, technically. They're getting married in Vermont, then—"

"I heard her say that her brother and his girl-friend broke up."

"Apparently so."

"I also heard Molly ask if you were going after him."

Ah. That explained the Heathcliff imperson-ation. "Then you must have heard my response."

"Actually no. I didn't want to and left."

She started walking toward him, her steps slow and deliberate. "Then let me repeat my-self, and I believe this is an exact quote." She cleared her throat. "No. Why would I do that?"

He watched her every move as she advanced, his gaze intense and his mouth set in an im-placable line. "You're not interested in him?" It was less a question and more a statement.

When she reached him, she looped her arms around his neck. Every synapse in her body fired at the same moment, triggering a response like a dozen fireworks launched in succession. She saw the same sparks igniting in his blue-grey eyes. Standing on her tiptoes, she brought her lips to within a hairbreadth of his and waited, loving the anticipation almost as much as she knew she would love his kiss.

"The only man I'm interested in is standing right in front of me." She pressed herself against him.

He groaned, the sound emanating from deep in his chest.

"I couldn't care less about Dr. What's-His-Name."

She expected him to devour her mouth and her bones to turn to liquid.

He didn't. He just stood there motionless with his big, rough hands that she liked so much resting on her waist and his chest rising and falling.

"Ryan?"

Something was obviously wrong. She knew it for certain when he removed his hands from her waist and unclasped her arms from around his neck, placing them at her sides.

"We have to talk," he said.

"About the house?"

"About us."

He stepped away from her then, leaving an ever-widening gap between them.

CHAPTER FIFTEEN

FOR THE LAST two hours, Ryan had been struggling with what to tell Bridget. Actually, that wasn't entirely accurate. He'd been struggling with what to tell her ever since reading the plumbing inspector's report and the pipe behind his house bursting. He just hadn't been ready to address the future of their relationship until this morning, when he'd received the phone call from Cheryl-Anne, his real-estate agent, shortly after the second plumber left.

Ryan's stomach churned at the thought of the two quotes he'd received and all the numbers on them. So many *big* numbers. They swam around on the pages in a murky blur each time he looked at them.

He'd tentatively scheduled a third plumber to come out on Monday but was reconsidering. He doubted that man's estimate would be significantly different or his price any lower. And if it was, that raised the possibility that the man could have missed something important or cut corners. Two dangerous possibilities Ryan couldn't risk. His property simply *had* to pass any future plumbing inspection, regardless of when he finally sold it. Neither could he afford a recurrence of the problem at a later date.

Cheryl-Anne hadn't been much help. Not that Ryan had expected any. She wasn't a miracle worker any more than he was, or the two plumbers who'd provided quotes today.

"What about us?" Bridget asked, her features knit with worry.

Like that, Ryan returned to the present and the dreaded conversation they needed to have. How he wished he could reassure her that everything would be okay, but the news wasn't good, and she deserved to be told.

Cutting to the chase, he said, "The buyer backed out of the sale."

"Oh, no!" Her hands flew to her mouth.

"I'm not surprised."

"Did you just find out?"

"He apparently gave the real-estate agent a heads-up yesterday. She waited to tell me until this morning after she received the official paperwork."

"I'm sorry." Bridget hugged him tightly but unlike earlier, there was no move to kiss him.

Ryan's arms were slow to go around her. This was the kind of heartfelt response he'd wanted from her almost from the moment they'd met. The kind of response he'd expect from someone who cared deeply for him and whom he cared deeply for in return.

It made what he had to tell her all the more gut-wrenching. For that, he couldn't cut to the chase, so he chose his words carefully.

"I've gotten quotes from two plumbers so far," he said and named the amounts.

She stared at him in shock. "I figured the repairs would be expensive, but not that expensive."

"Yeah, well, the first price doesn't include repairing the broken pipe in back. The second guy told me if I went with him, he'd throw that work in for free. Then again, his price is marginally higher than the first guy, so there's really no difference when you get right down to it."

"Have you made a decision?"

"Yes and no. The plumbing overhaul has to be done. I have no choice. And by overhaul, we're talking the entire plumbing system inside and outside." He expelled a weary breath. "It's going to take a huge chunk of my remodeling funds."

Huge chunk was no understatement. The work would cost roughly half of what Ryan had sitting in his bank account. Money he'd designated for other renovations, like the master bathroom and kitchen cabinets and landscaping.

"With luck," he said, "I'll make the money back and more when I sell the property. A whole new plumbing system is a big selling point, especially with a house as old as mine. The downside is that I won't be selling for a while."

"How long?" Bridget asked.

"A year or two."

"That's not bad."

"In addition to the year or two I was already planning." He shut his eyes rather than see the disappointment reflected in hers. "It's a big setback."

She nodded. Swallowed. Tucked a loose strand of hair behind her ear. "What if you were to sell now at a lower price? You were talking about that, anyway."

"That was before I'd have to reduce the price by substantially more. With what I could get for the property in its as-is condition, I wouldn't realize any profit and would likely lose money once all the commissions and fees were paid."

"Lose money? Really?"

"That's assuming I could even sell. There aren't many buyers interested in a property needing the amount of work mine does. Not unless they can get it for a steal. My fault. That's what I get for buying a fixer-upper."

"Buying fixer-uppers worked well for you in the past. You had every reason to think it would again."

It had worked well, though on a smaller scale. And as a result, he'd grown complacent and overconfident.

"I'm in a catch-22." He leaned his back against the counter and braced his palms at his sides. "I either get out now, hopefully walking away with an amount near what I've invested to date, and end up where I started before coming to Mustang Valley. Or, I keep the property and continue with the repairs and renovations as best I can with a new timetable."

"You don't sound enthusiastic about either choice."

"Trust me, I'm not. I'm less enthusiastic about my third choice—minimizing my losses and getting out of the house-flipping business altogether. I could probably acquire a decent starter house with the money I'd have left over. A small ranch and running a herd of cattle one day is out of the question. For the foreseeable future, anyway."

Bridget nestled in the crook of his arm. "Would that be so terrible?"

"I know you're right—it shouldn't be terrible.

Except it feels like I'm quitting at the first sign of trouble, and that's not how I operate. There's also my parents and eventually bringing them out here. I can kiss that idea goodbye."

Sensibly, Ryan knew the care of his parents postretirement wasn't entirely his burden to bear. He was simply in the best position to help. Or, he had been in the best position until this morning.

"They've lived their whole lives with just enough money to scrape by. I wanted more for them in their so-called golden years."

"I understand."

She did. She sympathized, at least. Ryan could hear it in her voice.

"Cheryl-Anne said she has a couple of clients she's going to reach out to but not to get my hopes up." He chuckled mirthlessly. "Maybe I'll win the lottery. I have better odds at that than finding a buyer willing to spend the kind of money I need to climb out of this hole I'm in."

"What can I do to help?"

Bridget's plea was delivered with such tenderness and compassion, it tore Ryan's heart in two. Especially in light of what he'd come here to tell her.

"I'm mad at myself most of all," he admitted.

"Why? You've done nothing wrong."

"I beg to differ. I've made a bunch of mistakes, starting with when I bought the property."

"You couldn't have anticipated plumbing problems of this magnitude."

"Actually, I could have. I *should* have. There was an inspection done at the time. Granted, the report didn't go into as much detail as this one, but issues with the plumbing were mentioned. I didn't pay enough attention. I was so eager to acquire the property and beat out the other potential buyers, I glossed over the report."

"That's a mistake anyone could have made."

"Not anyone. I'm no rookie. This is my fourth property. And what kind of construction contractor would I make if I can't pay attention to an inspection report? A lousy one, that's what kind." He cut her off when she was going to respond. "I don't know what made me think I could have my own construction company. I'm obviously underqualified."

"You're being too hard on yourself."

"I'm not. You're being too easy on me."

"This is my fault. Not yours." Tears choked her voice. "If I hadn't pressured you to sell, none of this would have happened."

"You didn't pressure me. I chose to sell."

"Because of me."

"Because I wanted to."

She sniffed. "You're just trying to make me feel better."

"Look, the plumbing was a disaster waiting to happen. Sooner or later I'd have woken up one day with the entire kitchen flooded or had a thousand-dollar water bill from an underground leak I wasn't aware of."

"I suppose it's better you found out now than later."

"Yeah."

Say, three months down the road when he and Bridget were further along in their relationship, wildly in love and had a lot more at stake. She still might sympathize with him then, but she'd also be angry at him for building her hopes only to dash them.

Ryan took her hand in his, hoping the gesture would soften the blow he was about to deliver. "I can't…" He tried again. "We can't get involved right now. Not when I'm in over my head with the property. It wouldn't be fair to you."

She stared at their joined hands, and he imagined she was processing the information.

"You must hate me," he said.

"I don't." Her answer was soft, barely above a whisper.

"You should. I pursued you. Hard. And when

you finally said yes, the first thing I do is let you down by making promises I can't keep."

"The circumstances are out of your control."

"No, they're not. That's what I've been trying to say. I plowed ahead without doing proper due diligence. Never a good thing."

The sob she'd been visibly holding at bay broke free.

Ryan waited until she'd quieted. "You've said all along you didn't want to start something and then become angry or resentful when the other person wasn't on the same timetable. Bridget, honey." He drew her into the circle of his arms. "I can guarantee you from this day on, our timetables won't match."

"Can't we wait and see? For a little while?"

She amazed him. Here she was, willing to put her wants and desires on hold for him. And what did he do in return? Rip the rug out from under her.

Ryan wasn't just a jerk. He was a heel.

"I need to find a second job. That's the only way I can fund the remaining renovations. Between that and my job at the ranch and working on the house, I won't have any spare time to date."

She said nothing, merely sighed heavily.

Ryan squeezed his eyes shut. For years, his goal had been to be in a better position financially than his parents when he found the love of his life. And here he was, in the exact same boat as them and pushing away Bridget. Could things get any worse?

Better watch what he said. Things could get worse. He might find himself living out of his truck or going back to Texas and moving in with his parents like his sister. That'd be a laugh. Instead of helping his parents live a more comfortable life, Ryan would be relying on them for a roof over his head.

"Are you sure you don't blame me?" Bridget asked softly. "I couldn't live with that."

"Never. Not in a million years."

"You said I was a distraction."

"No, you were a motivation." He reached up and stroked her hair, marveling at the silky texture and saddened that this might well be the last time he touched it. "I need to concentrate on the house. If I don't, I'll go broke."

She must have started crying because he felt a damp spot on the front of his shirt.

"The thing is," he said, "you're not the only one who refuses to settle."

She groaned. "I'm sorry I ever told you that."

"I'm not." He waited until she looked up and met his gaze. "You're an incredible catch. You deserve a man worthy of you. At the moment,

I'm not him, and I won't be for a few more years."

"Ryan…"

"Shh."

They stood there for several minutes, neither of them speaking. Eventually, he released her. One of them had to take the first step and officially call whatever it was they had together quits.

"You can't possibly know how much I wish things were different," he said.

"Oh, I think I do know." She wiped at her damp cheeks.

"I'd better go."

She didn't call him back. Closing the kitchen door behind him felt like he was closing the door on his entire future.

Ryan was doing the right thing. He didn't have to convince himself of that. Bridget would be sad and hurt for a while, but she'd recover. It wasn't as if they'd had more than a few mind-blowing kisses and a few semi-dates.

Who was he kidding? They'd had way more than that. A chance at a lifetime of love and happiness. The spouse and family they'd always wanted. The world by the tail.

Until he lost it for them.

The invisible fist gripping Ryan's chest squeezed until no air remained in his lungs and the ground beneath his feet disappeared. He eventually found himself at the stables without having any idea how he arrived there.

SWEAT DRIPPED DOWN the sides of Ryan's face and neck and into his shirt, soaking it. He'd traded his usual cowboy hat for a baseball cap after the former kept sliding down his forehead and obscuring his vision.

This was what he got for toiling away on a sweltering Monday morning. *Morning*, he reminded himself. Ten thirty-eight in the a.m. to be exact. Yet, it was already unbearable outside. Then again, Mustang Valley had yet to reach its renowned 115-degree days that would arrive come July. For now, May was content to be unseasonably warm and torture poor humans like Ryan, who were stupid enough to work intensely outdoors.

He paused from digging in the dirt to take another long swig of ice water from the beverage jug he'd brought with him. Holding the jug high, he drank from the spout, letting the cold liquid bathe his throat. When he was finished, he removed his ball cap and, depressing the lever, moved the thermos back and forth over his head. Water splattered onto his hair and scalp. The relief was instantaneous—and vanished the moment he slipped his ball cap back on and adjusted the fit.

Rather than return to digging, Ryan jammed the shovel into the loose dirt and then leaned an elbow on the handle, assessing the progress he'd made with the trench. Off to the right, his gelding snorted.

"Yeah, partner. I agree. There's a lot more work here than I anticipated."

The phrase was beginning to sound like a mantra to Ryan, starting from when he'd first bought the place. Every project he tackled was taking longer and costing more money than he had in his budget.

"What was I thinking?"

He could answer that; he hadn't needed to ask the horse for advice. To begin with, he'd assumed flipping this property would go as easily as his previous three. Also that his prior successes had nothing to do with luck when, in fact, luck had *everything* to do with them. He'd also believed that just wanting something was enough to make it happen. Like, for instance, a relationship with Bridget. Lastly, he'd been thinking he was indestructible when, in reality, he was fallible.

Confidence had never been one of Ryan's problems. Overconfidence? Apparently yes. Big-time.

Just look where it had landed him. On shaky financial ground, back to square one, working his you-know-what off and with zero romantic prospects with the only woman who interested him.

That last thought gave him pause. Bridget *was* the only woman who'd seriously interested Ryan in…he couldn't remember when. Ever? She was special, no question about it. And unattainable. Not because she was out of his reach but because he'd fallen so incredibly low.

The mare wandered over to sniff at the exposed waterline leading to a spigot mounted between the stalls. Abruptly, she lifted her head and shook it, only to glance away, her nose raised in disdain.

Ryan let out a groan. "Everyone's a critic."

During the last week and a half, following what he now referred to as the plumbing fiasco, he'd hired the second plumber and had the broken pipe behind the house repaired. The bulk of the work was scheduled to start next month, giving Ryan time to find a second job and set aside some money.

Speaking of money, in order to knock a few thousand dollars off the plumbing price, he'd opted to complete a portion of the plumbing repairs himself—that portion being replacing the sprinkler and bubbler systems for the landscaping in the front and backyards as well as the waterline leading to the horse stalls.

The current warm spell had him reconsidering his decision.

At least he was no longer making daily trips to Nora's. For a while there, he'd filled and driven home five-gallon buckets of water, heating what he needed for bathing and washing dishes and cleaning. He'd put additional five-gallon buckets in the horses' stalls, refilling them two to three times a day because of the warm weather. With Emily's permission, he'd used the guest washer and dryer in the clubhouse for his laundry.

Having running water again was a godsend. That would change intermittently while the plumbing system was overhauled, with periodic hours—or even days at a stretch—when the water would need shutting off.

Hardly the best time of year for this, he thought while wiping his damp brow with the back of his hand. Perhaps fate had a dark sense of humor and was giving him what he deserved.

Ryan didn't dismiss that notion. In his opinion, he'd screwed up about as badly as one could, and there were few people he hadn't disappointed, including himself, his parents and Bridget, most of all.

He missed her and was desolate without her. Seeing her every day at the ranch was akin to torture. When they spoke, they were always friendly. Gone, however, was the easy banter and subtle flirting. The acute awareness remained, on his part, anyway. But instead of searching for signs that their attraction was mutual, he searched for signs she wasn't hurting too badly from the pain he'd inflicted. Tears in her eyes. A catch in her voice. A dejected slump to her shoulders. Calculated efforts to steer clear of him.

Saturday night at the campfire had been particularly difficult for him. She'd skipped the hayride and, as far as he knew, they'd both skipped the square dancing. Had it really been a whole month since their first kiss?

Their last one was permanently etched into his memory. It was the day in the kitchen when he'd told her they couldn't continue to see each other and he'd pressed his lips to her forehead. He hadn't dared kiss her on the lips; his resolve would have crumbled.

Thankfully, Emily hadn't asked him and Bridget to demonstrate the square dancing Saturday night. Ryan assumed Bridget had told Emily about them and she'd recruited another couple. Molly and Owen, perhaps? At the end of the hayride, and after unharnessing the horses and returning the wagon to the carriage house, he'd gone directly home.

Here he was, two days later, constantly bemoaning what might have been and what could never be.

"Better get your act together," he scolded himself and reached for the shovel. The trench wasn't going to dig itself.

At that moment, the horses whinnied and trotted off toward the fence separating the paddock from the backyard. Ryan squinted in the direction of the house, curious as to what had excited them. He saw a female figure approaching, her features shadowed by the bright sunlight.

Bridget! She was here.

Even as his heart raced at the unlikely possibility, his brain recognized the approaching woman as Emily. She stopped at the fence and called to him.

"You busy?"

"Perfect timing." Leaving his tools, he headed toward the fence. "I was just taking a short break."

The horses crowded together in front of her, demanding equal attention, which she willingly gave by patting their noses and scratching them between the ears.

"Scram, you troublemakers." Ryan squeezed

324 THE COWBOY'S PERFECT MATCH

in between the unruly pair, and they grudgingly made room.

"I don't mind." Emily smiled fondly and gave each horse an extra pat. "Been a critter person my whole life. I missed having house pets, but a wedding ranch wasn't the place. Now that I'm married to Homer, I get to share his little terrier. And I mean share. She's very possessive of him. Plants herself between us whether on the couch or in bed."

"You don't sound like you object."

"She's a sweetie, and I understand." Emily broke into a wide smile. "I'm possessive of him, too."

"What brings you by?" Ryan asked. "Did we forget to go over something this morning at breakfast?"

There had been only one short trail ride scheduled that morning. Ryan and the honeymooners had left the ranch at seven thirty and returned before nine. He'd be heading back to the ranch at three o'clock this afternoon for a sunset trail ride and to attend his regular chores.

"I was in the neighborhood," Emily answered. "Figured I'd let you show me around the place. I haven't been here since before the Chandlers moved."

In the neighborhood? Not visiting her best friend, Nora? That would seem the likely explanation. But Ryan had a clear view of Nora's house from his paddock, and she hadn't received any visitors today.

"Bridget bragged about the work you've done."

"Not a whole lot to see now." Ryan strode toward the gate, shutting it quickly behind him before his mare and gelding snuck out. "But you're welcome to have a look around."

Before the plumbing fiasco, Ryan would have been pleased and proud to show off his accomplishments. Now, everything felt like a review of his failures.

Emily was complimentary as they toured the grounds and house, making statements like "It looks a lot better than before," and "You did this yourself? I'm impressed." He experienced no pleasure, however, at her remarks.

They ended the tour in the kitchen, which was in the same disastrous condition as when he'd first shown it to Bridget. Faded paint, bare concrete floor, old appliances propped against the wall like battle-scarred soldiers standing at attention, the rickety table and chairs literally on their last legs.

"You, by chance, need any help?" she said.

"How good are you at running PVC?" That was next on his list when he finished digging the trench.

"Not very." She chuckled. "I was talking more along the lines of recommending vendors and maybe using my influence to get you a friend discount. I've been living in this town for more than thirty years. Ran the local inn for most of those. Oversaw the construction of the guest cabins on my ranch. I'm not without connections and construction experience."

"I appreciate the offer, Emily, and will likely take you up on it at some point."

"Who did you wind up using for the plumbing, if you don't mind saying."

"Horizon Statewide. They seemed the easiest to work with, and their estimator had a few cost-saving ideas I liked."

"They're a decent outfit. We used them for a big project at the inn five or six years ago. Make sure you get lien waivers from all their suppliers. If memory serves me, Horizon was a little slow cutting their checks. But the quality of their work is above standard."

"That's good to know. Thanks."

"Don't take this wrong." Emily paused. "And if I offend you, I'm sorry, but have you ever considered taking on a partner for your house flipping?"

"A partner? Like someone to share the work?"

She shrugged. "That. Or investing money in exchange for a percentage of the profits."

He shook his head. "I don't want to borrow money."

The added pressure of having a loan to repay wasn't anything Ryan wanted or needed. He'd managed to purchase and fund all his house-flipping projects with the money he earned, either through work or when he sold at a profit.

That was another valuable lesson his father had taught him: paying interest was like throwing money away. Despite always scrimping and saving, his parents had refused to borrow money. The only exception had been medical emergencies.

"Not a loan in the strictest sense," Emily clarified. "There'd be no regular payments. The money would be paid back when the property was sold. Along with a percentage of the profits."

No regular payments? That sounded too good to be true to Ryan. His father had words of wisdom on that subject, too.

"I've always worked alone," he said.

"You haven't had a major setback before."

He resisted. "I don't like the idea of being indebted. It makes me feel like I'm a loser who can't pay his own way."

"You should feel like a smart businessman. Successful people borrow money all the time for all kinds of reasons when the circumstances benefit them."

"If I were smart, I wouldn't be in the position I am."

She ignored his self-deprecating remark. "Just think, with a surplus of cash, you could continue with the rest of the renovations rather than having to wait because you depleted your entire bankroll on the plumbing overhaul. And the sooner you finish, the sooner you can sell and pay back the investor."

"That would be great in a perfect world. In reality, things go wrong." All he had to do was look at his current situation.

"That's the risk the investor takes. But if it pays off, both parties win."

"Who in their right mind would want to partner on a place that needs as much work as this one?"

A twinkle lit Emily's eyes. "You'd be surprised."

Ryan studied his boss, intrigued despite his better judgment. "What are you getting at?"

She motioned toward the table and chairs. "Have a seat, and I'll tell you."

CHAPTER SIXTEEN

Ryan poured himself and Emily glasses of cold water before joining her at the table. She thanked him and took a long swallow.

He couldn't help but harken back to the day he'd sat in these same chairs with Cheryl-Anne and discussed listing his house. He'd been optimistic then, convinced he would have a quick sale and see a decent return on his money. The sharp stab of regret still wounded him. Ryan wasn't getting his hopes up again, regardless of how promising Emily's suggestion sounded.

"You know someone with a pile of cash lying around they have no good use for?" He took off his ball cap and hung it on the chair back, then used his fingers to comb his damp hair into a semblance of order.

"As it happens, I do," Emily said. "Me."

He barked a laugh. "Oh, I am not taking your money. Rest assured."

"Hear me out first."

"I don't need charity."

Her eyebrows rose, and she seemed mildly offended. "I'm not offering any. I fully expect my investment to be repaid and then some. This is strictly a business proposition."

"Is it? Can you honestly say your offer has nothing to do with Bridget?"

"I can say it, and I will. I love my granddaughter. I also know that she's fully capable of landing a man on her own. She doesn't need me *buying* one for her. And she'd be insulted you thought that of her. I'm insulted on her behalf."

"I didn't mean to imply she can't land a man. She could have any one she wants."

Emily nodded. "That's more like it."

"But I'm sure you can see how I might jump to the conclusion you were attempting to get us back together."

"Possibly. If I had a vivid imagination, which I don't."

Ryan remained unconvinced.

"Think about it," Emily said, apparently able to read his mind. "You see her every day at work. A reconciliation will either happen or it won't. Nothing I do is going to have an impact one way or the other." She gave an impatient huff. "You two are grown-ups. You need to work out your problems on your own."

"I was under the opinion we had. We agreed not to see each other." Actually, he'd decided for them, and Bridget had gone along. Was that the same as agreeing?

"Care to hear my opinion?" Emily asked.

"Do I have a choice?"

Ryan stretched his legs out in front of him. In addition to swapping his cowboy hat for a baseball cap, he'd traded his usual boots for athletic shoes more suitable for digging trenches.

"Deep down, Bridget's afraid to take a risk. Comes from her dad being killed in that automobile accident when she was fourteen." Emily took another swallow of water. "That's a lot for a teenaged girl to cope with. She's built various shields around herself, such as pouring herself into her career and that infuriating list of hers. Much as she wants to get married and have a family, she's still afraid."

"I don't know what I can do to change that."

"Only solution I know of is to make her fall so deeply in love with you her desire for a life together is stronger than her fear of losing that life."

"I would if I could, trust me."

"Which brings us to your problem. You lack faith in yourself, Ryan."

He laughed again, this time with genuine mirth. "Me? You've got to be kidding. My middle name is risk-taker."

"When the odds are in your favor, yes. When they aren't, the very first thing you do is turn tail and run."

"I'm here. I'm dealing with the plumbing problem. I'm not running."

"I was referring to you and Bridget." Emily released a long breath. "Just as well, I suppose. I wouldn't want her to wind up with a man unwilling to fight for her."

He grimaced. "Yikes, lady. You don't pull any punches."

"Not when it comes to the people I care about."

"You're not entirely wrong about me," he admitted, manning up.

"Oh, I think I pretty much hit the nail on the head."

"Guess I'm going to have to think on that, too."

"While you are, let's get back to our partnership."

He evaluated her carefully. "You're assuming an awful lot."

"Forget that I'm your boss and grandmother to the woman you're crazy about."

She'd hit a second nail on the head. Ryan was crazy about Bridget.

"I'm talking to you about a partnership only because I'm an astute business person and I think this property has a lot of potential."

Ryan had always thought that, too. Until he didn't.

"You invested all your money in Sweetheart Ranch. Bridget told me."

"Did she now?" Emily's tone conveyed her amusement. "I wasn't aware she had such intimate knowledge of my personal finances."

"I assumed you told her."

"I did no such thing. The fact is—and neither of my granddaughters are aware of this—I set aside a sizeable reserve of money before we opened last fall. I wanted to have a cushion should we fail or grow at a slower rate than hoped for. As it turns out, we're doing well. Better than I dreamed of. I don't need the reserve anymore."

"That could change. The economy is a mean, tricky beast who shows no mercy."

Ryan paid close attention, particularly how it related to the real-estate market and property values. He was no expert, but neither was he a novice.

"I hope you'll have long sold this place and repaid me before the next economic upheaval."

"It's too chancy," Ryan said. "Even if I was inclined to borrow money from my boss."

"Not borrowing money. Entering into a partnership. There's a big difference." She grabbed a piece of scrap paper from the table and a pen. "Let's assume money isn't an object and the plumbing overhaul is finished in a month. Is that doable?"

"It'll take a month, once the work's started."

She scribbled down notes and numbers. "How long after that until the remaining renovations are complete? Again, assuming money isn't an object."

"Minimum a year, if I hustle and all goes well. But I may not need to do the renovations. The buyer said he'd reconsider his offer to purchase if the plumbing was overhauled."

"Even better." Emily's smile grew. "Best case, you can sell the property in a month. Worst case, a year. What price do you think you can get for each different scenario?"

Ryan told her. Emily made three columns on the paper. When she was done, she tilted it toward him.

"This is how much I'm prepared to invest in our partnership. This is what I'd expect in return when you sell, in a month, a year and eighteen months."

"What if the sale takes longer?"

"We can put a schedule in the agreement, which I'll secure with a deed of trust. I'll also have the attorney we use for the ranch draw up an agreement. Make everything legal."

Emily was clearly experienced and nobody's fool.

Ryan's gut tightened at the prospect of owing a substantial sum to someone, especially his boss and Bridget's grandmother.

"I don't know…"

"It can be a good deal for both of us," she said. "I wouldn't risk my money at this stage in my life if I wasn't confident of a return."

"I still need to think about it."

"Of course. Take your time. Get back to me in, say, three days?"

Definitely nobody's fool. She was savvy enough to put a time limit on her offer, and a short one at that.

"Fair enough." He stood and picked up the scrap of paper. "Can I keep this?"

"Please do. And don't hesitate to call me with any questions."

Even her farewell had a decidedly business ring to it.

"I won't."

Ryan walked her outside to her car. She chatted about the new guests arriving this afternoon and the weddings scheduled for the weekend, as if they hadn't just been discussing a business proposition that could potentially change the course of his life.

"Can I ask a favor?" he said before she got in her car.

"What's that?"

"More of a question, I guess. Are you going to tell Bridget about our conversation?"

"I'm not. I will tell Homer—he's my husband. But for the time being, this will remain between us. I'd also like you to keep it that way until, and unless, I say otherwise."

"Not a problem." He wasn't ready to advertise that Emily had offered to lend him money. *Invest in a partnership with him*, he amended, trying the idea on for size.

Once she'd pulled onto the road, Ryan went back inside and hunted down his cell phone. Finding it on the table, he dialed Cheryl-Anne's number and waited for the call to go through.

She answered promptly. "Hi, Ryan."

He didn't beat around the bush and told her about Emily's proposition. She was silent the entire time, listening.

"What do you think?" he asked when he was done.

"It almost sounds too good to be true."

"My feelings exactly."

"But it's well worth considering." A beat of silence passed. "I'd worry a bit about the personal-relationship aspect. She is your employer. If things went south," she continued, "you might lose your job and even the property."

That wouldn't happen. Ryan would go into debt first.

"Is there a balloon payment?" Cheryl-Anne asked.

"It wasn't mentioned."

"I'd find out." She raised a few more good points, then said, "Investment partnerships aren't uncommon. I have a number of clients involved in them, including our buyer."

"Interesting."

Ryan still wasn't sure what he was going to do when he hung up from the real-estate agent. But doing nothing wasn't the answer, either.

He placed two calls while fixing himself a quick lunch—first to an old team-roping buddy who worked as a financial advisor for a bank and next to his older brother, whose advice he trusted. Neither person answered, and Ryan left messages.

It was a long afternoon of waiting until they got back to him, and he took to heart what they each had to say.

THE SHELVES WILL work well for displaying products." Grandma Em stood back and rubbed her chin, evaluating the library's built-in book-cases.

"I agree." Bridget made a note in her tablet.

"We can put the checkout here." Molly drew an invisible circle to the right of the doorway.

"I think we should use that antique desk in the guest bedroom upstairs."

"Good idea." Grandma Em retrieved a tape measure from the small stand beside the wingback reading chair. Giving one end of the tape measure to Molly, she motioned for her to walk it to the other end of the room. "We'll need a table and chairs for customers to sit and view catalogs and samples. I think the one we're storing in the carriage-house loft will fit."

When Molly reached her designated spot, Grandma Em looked at the tape measure and called out the number of feet and inches to Bridget, who recorded them in her tablet.

The three of them had spent the last twenty minutes inspecting the library from top to bottom and brainstorming ideas for converting it into a small wedding boutique. They weren't ready to proceed until after the June wedding rush, which started in just three days. The ranch had a record number of ceremonies scheduled, beating out their previous record from Valentine's Day. They had eight weddings on one Saturday alone, including a midnight ceremony taking place outside on the veranda and two sunrise ceremonies with mimosas being served at the reception.

Grandma Em was having trouble saying no to anyone who asked. She felt that a June wedding was the dream of many brides, and she was determined to make that dream a reality if at all possible.

The money rolling in wasn't bad, either. Molly had reported the ranch's second-quarter earnings to date were far exceeding projections.

Which made affording expansions like the wedding boutique and the additional staff necessary to operate it possible. Especially if they used as many items on hand as possible to furnish and decorate the boutique.

A record number of weddings also meant a record number of catered receptions. Personally speaking, Bridget was grateful. Being swamped every waking moment helped her to not dwell at length on Ryan and how much she missed him.

She supposed that sounded silly; she saw him and talked to him multiple times a day. But they both went out of their way to keep those interactions pleasant and professional. Nothing personal or intimate or that hinted at the fact they'd once contemplated a future together.

What else did she expect? That he'd suddenly reverse his thinking? That she would? Not likely. His circumstances had yet to change and wouldn't for a year or more.

For weeks now, Ryan had been consumed with the property renovations. She'd heard this from Nora, not him. He'd green-lighted the plumbing overhaul and work had recently begun. Bridget assumed he'd used the bulk of his available funds to finance it. She'd seen his truck one afternoon in the bank parking lot on her way through town.

Also according to Nora, he was continuing with the interior renovations. He'd hired Nora's oldest grandson to help him install the ceiling beams in the living room and master bedroom.

She wondered how they looked. Really nice, she supposed. She supposed, too, that he must be living very frugally as he'd yet to land a second job. Bridget had frequently witnessed him and Grandma Em in quiet conversation, after which she'd slip him some food. He'd always refuse but then ultimately accept the paper sack or plastic container.

Bridget swallowed a painful lump in her throat. Missing what she and Ryan had previously shared topped a long, sad list.

List. How she hated the word. If not for her nonnegotiable dating one, she and Ryan wouldn't be nursing broken hearts. More than once these past few weeks she'd considered deleting the list from her tablet. She'd gone so far as to hold her finger over the delete button, only to chicken out at the last second.

Was she really wrong to want to find the love of her life? A man like her late father?

Too late now—she and Ryan were over.

Bridget went momentarily still. He wasn't the love of her life, was he?

"Hey, sis, did you get that?"

She startled at Molly's question. "What did you say?"

"We were talking about that silver-framed wall mirror Homer has. The one belonging to his mother."

"It's just sitting in the back of a closet," Grandma Em said. "I'm going to ask him if we can hang it in here for the boutique. It'll make a nice mirror for customers to try on hair ornaments or jewelry. I'm sure he'll say yes."

"Okay." Bridget made a note in her tablet.

"Did you hear what we said about painting the walls versus new wallpaper?"

"Nope. Missed that."

"What's wrong with you?" Molly stared at Bridget, her mouth turned down at the corners. "You've been off on another planet all day. For weeks, actually."

Bridget produced a wan smile. "We're busy. I have a lot on my plate. No catering pun intended."

"You aren't still moping about Ryan."

"Leave her alone," Grandma Em chided, as if Molly was still a child and the sisters were squabbling.

"Sorry." She rolled her eyes in annoyance. "It's just that what happened with you two is all your fault. Which frustrates me to no end."

"Frustrates you?" Bridget scoffed. "Typical Molly. Always making everything about her."

"Enough!" Grandma Em leveled a finger at them both. "This is a place of business. You will behave."

They both promptly shut up.

"Things change," Molly said a minute later while they were measuring the bookcase shelves. "You shouldn't give up hope of getting back with Ryan."

"I'm not," Bridget answered.

"Good."

"I'm not hoping." She let her arms fall to her sides, the tablet clutched in her hand. "He was perfectly clear, and the door wasn't left open."

Bridget was still grappling with that fact. She was the one with the long list of dating requirements—anyone would expect ending a relationship with a person lacking sufficient prospects to be her choice. Yet, it had been Ryan's.

Molly came over and patted Bridget's back. "You're mad he didn't fight harder for you. For what you two could have."

She didn't like that her sister was right.

"I have no one to be mad at but myself," she

admitted. "I was too picky. My standards too high." She sighed. "I'm been thinking of lowering them."

"Don't. I'm serious," Molly insisted when Bridget sent her an arch look. "Lowering your standards isn't the answer and, in the end, you'd just be unhappy. What you need to do is revise them."

Her sister's statement intrigued Bridget, but before she could respond the bell over the front door jangled, announcing a visitor.

Molly turned around. "Are we expecting anyone?"

"No." Grandma Em set down the tape measure and swiped her hands together. "I'll go see who it is. You two straighten up in here."

While she was gone, Bridget and Molly pushed the furniture they'd previously moved around back into place. The sound of Grandma Em and a man talking carried from the parlor. Bridget didn't give it much thought, assuming a delivery had arrived. With all the June weddings, they were receiving packages on a daily basis.

Grandma Em returned and poked her head into the library. "Bridget, do you have a few minutes?"

"What's up?"

"Dr. Hall is here. His sister has requested

some catering menu changes, and asked him to stop by."

"Of course."

Bridget followed her grandmother to the parlor, where Gregory waited. Upon seeing him, she realized something significant. At least, she thought it was significant. He stirred absolutely no response in her whatsoever. Neither excitement at seeing him, nor regret or even embarrassment. He was just another customer.

"Hi, how are you doing?" she greeted him.

"Great." He offered her a big smile. "Nice to see you again."

The three of them exchanged a few pleasantries. Celeste's name wasn't mentioned. After that, they got down to business. Gregory's sister had returned to Vermont earlier in the month and her wedding there was taking place this coming weekend. Her second wedding at Sweetheart Ranch was in mid-June.

Gregory pulled a sheet of paper from his shirt pocket and put it on the table, then dialed his sister. The four of them, his sister on speakerphone, handled each item on the paper.

Eventually, everything was resolved to the bride's satisfaction. Gregory disconnected the call and thanked Bridget and her grandmother for their help.

"Delighted to oblige," Grandma Em said. "Looking forward to the wedding."

"Bridget, are you by chance free to talk?" he asked.

"Um…" His request took her by surprise. "Yes. Of course."

"Is on the veranda okay?"

"Absolutely."

After exchanging glances with her grandmother, she accompanied Gregory outside. They stood by the railing in the shade. She couldn't help recalling the last time they'd been out here, when she'd awkwardly flirted in a desperate attempt to get his attention. What a fool she'd been.

When he shifted uncomfortably, she asked, "Is something the matter?"

"No." He laughed. Nervously, Bridget noted. That wasn't like him. "I was wondering if you might like to have dinner with me Saturday evening."

"Dinner?" Not at all what she'd been anticipating.

"I thought we could drive into Fountain Hills and try that new French restaurant."

She'd been dying to go there; the sous-chef was a former classmate of hers from Le Cordon Bleu. She opened her mouth to accept Gregory's invitation, only that wasn't what came out.

"Thank you. I'm flattered. But I can't."

"Why not? Are you seeing someone?"

"I…no. It's not that."

"I see. My mistake," he added contritely. "I thought you…liked me."

"I do. You're a terrific guy. And I clearly gave you the wrong impression, which is entirely my fault. I can't apologize enough and hope there are no hard feelings."

Bridget's insane plan had come back to bite her in the butt.

"None at all," he assured her, giving her a pass when he had every right to be angry. "If you ever change your mind, let me know."

With a grin and a mock salute, he jogged down the veranda steps toward the parking area and his BMW. Bridget stood for a moment watching him and thinking he'd forget about her soon enough. The dinner invitation was, in all probability, a response to being dumped by Celeste. He didn't really like Bridget, not the way she wanted a man to like her.

Not the way Ryan liked her. *Had*, she reminded herself. Possibly still did, but was resisting it with every ounce of willpower he possessed.

She went back inside. Stopping in the parlor first for her tablet, she then headed to the kitchen. Grandma Em was waiting, her foot tapping impatiently.

"Well, what was that all about?" she demanded.

"He invited me to dinner."

"I hope you had the good sense to tell him no."

"I did. Though good sense had nothing to do with it." Bridget swiped her tablet screen, waking up the device. There was a new scone recipe she was thinking of trying for the continental breakfast tomorrow.

"You weren't ever interested in him," Grandma Em said. "You'd have realized that quickly enough if you two went out."

Bridget wasn't listening. Instead, she stared at her tablet. As always, the icon for her list of dating nonnegotiables sat in the upper corner. She was reminded of Molly's statement about revising her standards.

"What are you thinking of?" Grandma Em asked.

"About deleting this list."

"Which one?"

"Which one do you think?" With a tap, Bridget highlighted the icon.

"Are you serious?" Grandma Em came over to peer at the tablet.

"I was wrong." The realization wasn't sudden. Bridget only just now was able to admit it.

"About what?"

"I have twelve nonnegotiable requirements." She turned her head to look at her grandmother. "Twelve. Did you know that?"

"No." She shook her head.

"I should have one. The only one that matters. And it's not even on this stupid list."

"What's that?" Grandma Em asked gently.

"A spark. Chemistry. Instant attraction. Whatever name you want to give it. I want a man who makes my heart sing the first and every time I look at him."

"Like Ryan?"

Bridget nodded solemnly. "Like him."

"So, tell him."

"What difference would it make? He'd just tell me again he's overwhelmed with repairs to the house and can't date."

Grandma Em tsked.

"What?"

"You said earlier that he gave up too quickly on the two of you. Here you are doing the same."

Bridget considered that for a moment. "Maybe."

"Oh, honey. You have to stop being afraid. Look at your sister. Look at me. We opened ourselves to possibilities and, low and behold, we found love."

She hesitated. Long-held fears didn't vanish in an instant.

"You could always drop by his house," Grandma Em suggested. "Fabricate an excuse. Then, once you're there, you can test the waters a little. He could be having second thoughts, too, but is afraid to tell you or doesn't know how."

Could he? Bridget wondered. She did sometimes find him gazing at her with regret and yearning in his eyes.

"I bet he's hungry. Take him some lunch," Grandma Em urged.

"Isn't that what you've been doing? Giving him food?"

"Don't argue with me."

A chance. Even if Ryan didn't want a second one with her, Bridget had been stuck in one place long enough.

"I'll go. But first, this."

She hit the delete button, and her list of dating nonnegotiables disappeared. For good or bad, she felt as if the ropes binding her these many years had suddenly been severed.

What she did with her newfound emotional freedom was entirely up to her.

CHAPTER SEVENTEEN

RYAN READJUSTED THE face mask he wore over his mouth and nose. It kept the thick cloud of dust and particles floating in the air from being sucked into his lungs. Barely. The earplugs muffled the sound of the jackhammer demolishing his concrete kitchen floor, reducing the level from eardrum-splitting to migraine headache.

He was in the master bedroom of his house. Two rooms and a hallway away from the kitchen. He couldn't imagine what it was like for the man operating the jackhammer and his helper, coping with the dust and the noise. Their face masks must be made of thicker material than Ryan's and their headphones were probably the kind that airport tarmac workers used to block the noise of jet planes at takeoff.

He was going to have to get used to it. Demolishing concrete floors was a slow, tedious and meticulous process. But it was the only way to gain access to the faulty water pipes beneath the floors.

Ryan had retreated to the bedroom after getting home from the ranch a few hours ago. He'd been joined shortly after that by Scott, Nora's grandson and Gianna's younger brother. Ryan had hired the college student to help him install the ceiling beams in the living room and master bedroom. He'd been coming back since then to help Ryan with various other manual jobs.

They were just finishing up the items on today's agenda. Ryan stood on a stepladder in the middle of the empty master bedroom, applying a final coat of sealer to the beams he'd previously stained and distressed before installing. It was backbreaking work, requiring him to hold a raised paintbrush over his head for long stretches at a time.

Scott was in the hall bathroom, on his hands and knees, removing the old linoleum with a scraper. He'd done the same in the master bathroom yesterday. It was also backbreaking work, though, in Scott's case, more like knee-breaking.

Like the kitchen, the concrete floors in the bathrooms would be demolished with a jackhammer in order to replace the faulty water pipes. There were also large holes in the kitchen, both bathrooms, laundry room and garage walls. Eventually, the pipes there would be replaced.

When that stage was completed, new concrete would be poured, new flooring installed over the concrete, and the holes in the walls re-paired and repainted. Ryan had been thinking of upgrading to ceramic tile in the bathrooms, matching what he'd laid in the living room.

Extracting a handkerchief from his jeans pocket, he wiped his eyes and his forehead and, lifting the face mask, blew his nose. He swore he had concrete dust clear up into the top of his brain and all the way down his throat to his stomach. At this rate, he'd be smelling and tasting it for four weeks—about how long the plumbing repairs were going to take.

On the plus side, the commotion drowned out the voice inside his head that kept remind-ing him of his many mistakes with Bridget and calling him an idiot.

Unfortunately, it was all too quiet at night when he tried to sleep on the cot in the second bedroom and mostly tossed and turned.

Seeing her at work, talking with her, remem-bering what it was like to hold her in his arms and slowly move his lips over hers until she moaned in response—it was all excruciating. Given the choice, he'd rather listen to the jack-hammering all day *without* earplugs.

What if he'd agreed when she told him she was willing to wait for him? How different might things be? But instead of making his own vow of commitment to her in return, he'd insisted they couldn't date.

Ryan's determination not to end up like his parents, existing hand-to-mouth and struggling to support a large family, was definitely succeeding. It was succeeding so well, he'd likely end up alone for the rest of his life. He certainly wasn't going to have a future with Bridget.

Pride. Misplaced pride at that. He had too much of it. And fear of failure. Emily had been right on that point. Painfully right. If he could just muster the courage to tell Bridget how wrong he'd been, they might have a chance of reconciling.

Except she wasn't interested in getting back together with him. He'd hurt her too badly. Reiterated repeatedly that he wasn't ready for marriage and a family. She wouldn't believe him now if he went to her and begged. Moreover, he wouldn't blame her.

Ryan lowered his arms, rolled his aching shoulders and tipped his head from side to side. His stiff joints barely loosened. What he'd give to quit for the day. But he couldn't. Not yet.

He'd practically cheered when Cheryl-Anne called earlier and informed him the buyer was still interested, once the plumbing overhaul was completed, the floors fully restored and the holes in the walls repaired. She'd also said if the man did buy the house, he'd complete the remaining renovations with his own construction crew. Ryan could simply walk away.

Best of all, the price Ryan quoted the buyer had been well-received. No new formal offer had been made yet. The buyer had said they'd move to the next step when the plumbing was done to his satisfaction. A reasonable request in Ryan's opinion.

He couldn't believe his luck. A sale in the near future appeared promising. Even likely.

Nothing could please him more. Well, short of going back in time and telling Bridget that he was crazy about her and would do whatever it took for them to be together.

Also lifting his spirits was the possibility of repaying Emily the money she'd invested along with about a six-percent return. Not a fortune. Also not bad for the current economy and in what would amount to roughly three months' time. Emily could do a lot worse.

Neither would Ryan walk away empty-handed. He'd get his original investment, the cost of the renovations he'd personally funded to date and roughly a two-percent return. He, too, could do a lot worse, considering how close he'd come to losing his you-know-what.

He had to remind himself this would happen only if all went well. There were plenty of obstacles still ahead. Ryan needed to pay strict attention and work his tail off if he wanted out of this house.

And did he ever. He couldn't wait for the day. There were far too many memories haunting him here, good and bad. Taking Bridget on a tour and watching the nuances of her changing expressions. Trimming the rosebushes and selecting the best blooms for her. The hours he'd spent dreaming of this being his last step before buying the mini ranch. The desolation he'd experienced when the pipe broke, and he realized the full extent of the plumbing problems.

If the sale went through, he'd pack his few possessions and get the heck out. No looking back.

And do what? Stay in Mustang Valley? Go home to Texas? Look for another property? Take off for parts unknown and get his head together, not to mention heal his wounded heart?

There was also Emily to consider. Ryan wouldn't feel right about leaving her and the ranch high and dry after all she'd done for him. He'd have managed the plumbing overhaul by draining his bank account but not been able to sell the house this quickly. He owed her more than a return on her investment, even a decent one.

Plus, he liked his job at the ranch, the difficulty of seeing Bridget every day aside. It really was a great fit for him in all ways but that one.

He dipped his paintbrush in the can of sealer and, after scraping off the excess on the side of the can, reached up and applied the sealer to the beam. After this, he'd have to climb down and move the ladder five feet to the next section. And the next. There were two more beams to do after this one.

An invisible knife abruptly stabbed him in between his shoulder blades. The motion caused Ryan to drop his arm, which hit the side of the can resting on the ladder's shelf. The can jiggled, and a small amount of sealer spilled. When he went to grab the rag he'd been using, it slipped through his fingers and fell onto the floor.

His grunt of frustration was muffled by the face mask. What he'd give for a hot, relaxing shower. But, sadly, that was out of the question. Water to the house was turned off for the next several days. Fortunately, the water outside was still on, which meant he took showers with a garden hose near the horse stalls. At least he didn't have to haul barrels of water from Nora's house.

With his back to the door, and the din of the jackhammer still audible even with the earplugs, he sensed more than saw a movement behind him. Scott must be finished in the hall bathroom and was coming to check in with Ryan.

He pulled down his mask and hollered over his shoulder to the young man, "Hey, can you grab that rag for me?"

A moment later, the rag appeared from behind Ryan. It was attached to a hand.

"Thanks, pal." He plucked the rag and started blotting up the spilled liquid from the ladder shelf.

"You're welcome."

Huh. Either Scott's voice had changed drastically, becoming an octave higher, or the hand didn't belong to him.

Ryan twisted sideways and looked down, nearly losing his balance. He grabbed the top of the ladder, holding tight.

Staring up at him were a pair of green eyes, a nose and cheeks covered with a smattering of freckles and a face framed by strawberry blond curls.

Bridget!

"Hi…uh, wait," he murmured.

Realizing she probably couldn't hear him, he whipped off the face mask and set it on the top of the ladder. He also took out his earplugs and dropped them beside the face mask. The hands he used to grip the sides of the ladder as he descended were shaking slightly.

Once on the floor, he reached out to touch her. No, she wasn't an apparition.

"What are you doing here?" He had to shout to be heard above the jackhammering. "Something happen at work?"

She shook her head and smiled tentatively. "Can we talk? It's important," she added.

His stomach clenched even as his excitement grew, and he motioned for her to follow him. "Let's go outside. It's too noisy and dusty in here to carry on a conversation."

Particularly this one.

Ryan cautioned himself as they walked through the living room and out the front door. There'd been no indication things had changed between them when he'd seen her this morning at the ranch.

But his heart pounded harder than the jackhammer in the kitchen. Bridget had come to see him. Her reasons must have something to do with them, and he couldn't stop the surge of hope rising inside him.

ONCE THEY WERE outside and able to hear each other, Ryan made straight for the water spigot.

"Give me a second. I'm a mess."

Twisting the handle, he proceeded to wash

his face, neck and hands with a wet handkerchief. He was reminded of that night after the hayride, when she'd brought him dinner and he freshened up before the square dance. Then, he'd been attempting to woo Bridget. Today, he had no idea what was going to happen.

"I'm surprised you have running water." She waited for him by the back door.

"I don't. Not inside."

"How are you managing?"

"Microwave meals and plastic forks." He straightened. "Showers with the garden hose."

Her tentative smile from earlier widened. Ryan stared. She hadn't smiled at him like that in weeks. He tried not to read more into it than there was…and failed.

"You must be tired of roughing it," she said.

He cleared his throat in an attempt to keep his voice level. "Trust me, I'm willing to put up with a lot worse as long as this plumbing overhaul gets done."

It was hot standing in the direct sunlight. Ryan suggested they sit at the rickety kitchen table he'd moved outside and placed beneath the tall ash tree. His ice chests and crates were stacked nearby.

At her puzzled expression, he explained, "I needed to empty the kitchen for the demolition," and offered her a seat.

Bridget accepted. "Kind of cozy. Gives new meaning to the term *outdoor dining*."

"Sorry. The place is still a mess." He sat in the chair adjacent to hers.

"I'm serious. I love eating outside. The cookouts after the monthly hayrides were my idea."

He could have guessed that.

She glanced around. "The place is going to be nice when you're done. The ceiling beams look fantastic."

"They do," he agreed, wondering when she'd arrive at the purpose of her visit.

"Have you decided on a design for the kitchen? I can offer some input. If you're interested."

"With luck, that'll be up to the new owner."

She gasped. "You sold the place?"

"Not yet. But I'm renegotiating with the previous buyer." He summarized his call with Cheryl-Anne. "Nothing official yet, but it appears promising. If the sale does go through, he'll be finishing the renovations with his own construction crew."

"How do you feel about that? Is it hard walking away from something you started?"

"Normally, I'd say yes. Not in this case, however."

He didn't mention him wanting a quick sale in order to repay her grandmother. Until Emily said otherwise, he'd honor her request to keep their agreement private.

Neither did he mention the memories of Bridget associated with the house and his eagerness to put those behind him. If such a thing was even possible.

"Where do you plan to live?"

He thought he detected a hitch in her voice. "I'm not sure."

"Are you leaving Mustang Valley?"

He leaned toward her, eliminating half the distance between them. They hadn't been this close since the day of their first, and last, date.

"I like my job at Sweetheart Ranch, and I don't want to leave your grandmother in a bind. She's been good to me."

"Okay." A flash of emotion danced across her face, only to vanish.

"I have to admit," he said, "it isn't always easy for me to be around you."

She glanced down at her lap. "It isn't easy for me, either."

Enough stalling, Ryan thought. "Why are you here, Bridget?"

"Whew." She blew out a breath and smiled weakly at him. "I'm not as brave as I'd like people to think I am."

"Tell me."

She started out slow. "I've spent a lot of years

using food and lists and even my career to hide behind and avoid being hurt."

Ryan was guilty of the same thing. "It's human nature."

"I'm going to take a leap. A scary one." She pressed a hand to her chest as if to calm her racing heart. "I could land on my face or the other, more padded, part of my anatomy. But if I don't at least try, I'm afraid I might lose something precious to me. Something precious to *us*."

Ryan went still, afraid to assume. This leap could simply be her way of unloading and clearing the air between them in order that she could move on to someone new. He'd seen the doctor's BMW at the ranch earlier. Maybe the business the doctor was there to conduct had to do with Bridget and not his sister's upcoming wedding.

She swallowed. Fidgeted. Brushed at an errant lock of hair. Ryan gritted his teeth. When he didn't think he could wait a second longer, she finally spoke.

"I had a bit of an epiphany earlier. It had to do with my list. The dating nonnegotiable one."

"Okay."

"I realized only one item matters, and it wasn't even on my list." She paused. "Sparks. I want sparks."

"Doesn't everyone?"

"Yes. I suppose most people do…" She faltered again. "This is really, really hard."

Inside the house, the noise suddenly stopped. The workmen must be taking a break or had finished demolishing the kitchen floor. Ryan was only vaguely aware; his concentration remained focused on Bridget.

"What are you afraid of?" he asked. "Besides falling on your face?"

"Losing what I love. The person I love. The life I love."

He wanted to ask more about the person she loved. Instead, he remained silent and let her continue.

"Here I am claiming I want nothing more than to be a wife and mother. But the reality is I've done my dead level best to prevent it. You know what the really sad part is?" She didn't give him a chance to respond. "If I continue hiding behind my list and refusing to date a man who doesn't meet every one of my requirements, I'm going to wind up alone and miserable. The very opposite of what I swore I wanted."

It was a big, courageous confession. Ryan had one of his own to share.

"I think I'm the same when it comes to flipping properties. That's been my excuse for not settling down. I tell myself I need to wait until I'm ready. But my parents didn't wait, and they've been as happy and in love as two people can be."

"We're a pair, aren't we?"

He happened to think they were a perfect pair. "What are you going to do, Bridget, now that you've tossed your list?"

"That depends on you."

"Does it?"

Her hand rested on the table. He could reach for it, but she might reject him, and he didn't think he could take a second one. Except she was here, and that had to mean something.

One way to find out. Ryan gathered her hand in his. She didn't snatch it away, and he took that as a good sign.

"I told you once I admired you for having a goal and working toward it."

He nodded. "I remember."

"What if…" She paused again. "What if we…worked toward that goal together?"

He grinned. "I like the sound of that word. Tell me more."

She squeezed his fingers, and he swore he felt a jolt travel up his arm and straight to his heart.

"I want to be a part of you realizing your dreams, Ryan. Not just standing by, watching and waiting impatiently for you to achieve them. I don't care how many years it takes, as long as we're together."

That word again. Ryan replayed the last minute in his head, making sure he hadn't misunderstood her.

She met his gaze and this time when she spoke there was no hesitation. "I think I might be falling in love with you. It was the sparks. I felt them the first time I saw you in the parlor, and I kept feeling them again and again. When we talked. When we kissed. When you made me laugh. At the park when you brought me the roses." She moved fractionally nearer. "Once you have sparks, the rest will fall into place. Right?"

Ryan stood so fast, the chair he'd been sitting on tumbled backward and fell onto the ground with a clatter. He didn't care. He was too busy scrambling around the table and dragging Bridget out of her seat.

"I'm going to kiss you now," he said. "After that, we'll talk because there's a whole lot I need to say to you. But I can't wait any longer for this."

"Neither can I—"

He didn't let her finish and covered her mouth with his. The next instant, she was locked in his embrace.

And, like that, Ryan was home, in the place he'd been searching for all these years.

They kissed and kissed. On and on. He eventually broke away only because if he didn't stop now, he never would.

"I'm falling in love with you, too." He searched her face. "I think it was that scowl you wore the first time we met. I knew I had to make you smile. Every day, for the rest of our lives."

Her expression melted into one of pure joy.

"Which makes what I have to say especially difficult."

A small furrow creased her brow. "Ryan?"

"I've got to be completely honest with you before this goes any further. It wouldn't be right otherwise."

The furrow deepened.

He held her arms, refusing to let her go. "Your grandmother asked me not to tell you. I hope she isn't too angry at me."

"My grandmother?"

"I'm in a hurry to sell because it means a quick payoff to her." He closed his eyes and prayed Bridget wouldn't tear free and leave when she heard the news. "She's my business partner."

"In what?"

"This place. She funded me the money for the plumbing overhaul."

Bridget retreated a step, forcing him to release his hold on her arms. Ryan's hopes sank. He'd reconciled with Bridget only to lose her again.

"Wow. I'm stunned."

"In return, she gets a percentage of the profits when I sell. If all goes well, that'll be soon."

"I don't know what to think." Bridget shook her head in disbelief. "Grandma's making money off your misfortune?"

"It's not like that at all, I swear," Ryan quickly assured her. "The arrangement is mutually beneficial. With luck, we'll both walk away with a few more dollars than when we started."

"Then why didn't she tell me?"

"I think, and this is only my opinion, she didn't want our business partnership to affect your and my personal relationship."

After a moment, Bridget lifted her shoulder. "I can see that, I suppose."

"Please don't be mad at her. She quite literally saved me from the poorhouse."

"I'm not mad." Her lovely features softened. "At either of you."

Ryan's relief was so intense, he had to grip the edge of the table in order to steady himself.

"Let me qualify that statement." She narrowed her gaze. "I'm not mad as long as she sees a return on her investment. If she doesn't, I'll be furious with you."

A laugh broke free, and it felt good. "Yes, ma'am," he said. "I'll do my best."

"Grandma has always been pretty savvy when it comes to investments."

"I can learn a lot from her."

"Does that mean you're going to stick around?"

In response, Ryan hauled Bridget up against him. "Try and get rid of me."

He kissed her again, and for a while, the world disappeared, leaving only the two of them.

Too soon, however, the jackhammer started up again inside the house. Anchoring her to him with one arm, Ryan stroked her cheek with the knuckles of his free hand.

"I promise not to make you wait too long for me to become everything on your list."

"You already are." She snuggled closer, her body flush with his. "Can't you feel the spark?"

Sparks? He was feeling fireworks. He swore he could see them exploding all around him and Bridget as they ran to the edge and took their leap of faith, hand in hand.

CHAPTER EIGHTEEN

Six weeks later

BRIDGET CLOSED HER eyes and counted to ten, a technique she used to help herself relax. Her agitated nerves didn't listen and insisted on humming with a combination of anticipation and trepidation.

What if Ryan said "no way, never happening"? He might think her idea harebrained and tell her to forget the whole thing. Then, she'd not only have embarrassed herself, but she could also have potentially sidetracked their relationship, if not ended it altogether.

Which would surely devastate her. They'd come so far these past weeks. A minor miracle considering their rocky start.

Bridget couldn't remember ever being happier. Love did that to a person, she decided. The constant infusion of endorphins had her walking around with a grin on her face, acting all manner of silly and floating from room to room.

People were noticing and commenting. In a

good way. Saying things like "What's gotten into you lately?" and "Have you done something different with your hair?"

Finally, she understood what her grandmother and sister had been trying to tell her all along and why they'd pushed her into giving Ryan a chance. Holding so much joy and love inside was simply impossible. She had to let it out with smiles and sighs of contentment, and by singing to herself and busting out a dance move every now and then.

"How about we go to lunch and celebrate?" Ryan asked.

"You have a place in mind?" Bridget did but food wasn't involved.

"The Cowboy Up Café, unless you're in the mood for somewhere fancier."

"I like the café."

Maybe later, after she'd shown him her surprise, they could have lunch. That was, if she ever worked up the nerve and he didn't end up hating her.

She sat beside him in the front seat of his pickup truck while they drove through the center of town. They'd just left the bank, where Ryan had gotten a cashier's check made out to her grandmother. Repayment for her investment in the old Chandler place plus interest.

They'd started calling Ryan's property by

its former name, seeing as of yesterday he no longer owned it. The sale had gone through with only a few glitches, all of them eventually resolved.

Ryan and the buyer had agreed on a price that, when all was said and done and the various fees paid, left him in a marginally better place financially than before and her grandmother with a respectable profit. Nowhere close to the amount of money he'd originally planned to make, but he wasn't complaining.

He'd moved out of the house earlier that week in preparation of the sale, and she'd helped him pack. Three trips with the bed of his truck and his horse trailer crammed full—the last trip hauling his two horses—and he was officially ensconced in his temporary quarters at Sweetheart Ranch.

The horses were currently residing in the small corral behind the stables while Ryan had set up his bed and a few pieces of furniture in the loft above the carriage house, once the items stored there had been relocated to Homer's shed. Bridget had convinced him to haul the old kitchen table and chairs to the dump and replace them with a cute breakfast set they purchased at the local thrift shop.

Ryan insisted he didn't mind the sparse conditions or having to use the bathroom in the clubhouse. According to him, the accommodations were luxurious compared to some places he'd lived. As long as he had his microwave, he'd be fine. Besides, the arrangement would hopefully only last a month. Two at the most. He was already working with Cheryl-Anne on finding a new property to flip.

Naturally, Bridget made sure he didn't go hungry. After three days, sharing dinner with the family every evening, along with breakfast, had become a routine.

Grandma Em didn't mind. If fact, she seemed to accept Ryan's constant presence in the ranch house as normal. Their morning meetings continued, with Molly and Bridget often joining them.

Business had slowed this month, a nice change after their whirlwind of weddings during June. Summers, it seemed, weren't the most popular time of year to get married. Too hot, for one. People on vacation, for another. The cabins remained occupied, but with more tourists and less honeymooners.

The monthly hayrides and square dances continued to be a hit and well attended. Bridget was using the slight lull in weddings to expand her catering efforts, and her hard work was paying off. She'd even recruited Ryan's help, teaching him the proper way to serve.

He'd delighted the Literary Ladies at their last luncheon with his charm and humor.

Bridget was also now hosting monthly dinner meetings for the local business owners' association. The same one her grandmother, Owen and Cheryl-Anne were members of.

To her incredible surprise, she was in talks with Gregory about an annual employee function for the clinic staff. She'd heard from his sister at her wedding a few weeks ago that, as Bridget had predicted, he was already seeing someone new.

She and Ryan slowed to a stop at the light in front of the library. The café was one block up the road. It was now or never.

Gathering her courage, she asked, "Do you mind if we make a detour first?"

"No." Ryan turned to look at her, the sexy grin she so adored lighting his face. "Where to?"

"Keep heading through town. Stay on the main road. For now," she added.

He laughed. "You aren't going to tell me?"

"Not yet."

"Ah. A woman of mystery. I'm intrigued." He pulled forward when the light turned green. A mile outside of town, he asked, "How far?"

"Gold Dust Lane. It's just before the cutoff to Rio Verde."

Five minutes later, Ryan was taking a right onto a dirt road. If not for the street sign, most people would pass by.

The truck bumped over ruts and potholes, and the tires left a long plume of dust in their wake. Bridget held on to the door handle when Ryan slowed to navigate a bone-dry wash cutting diagonally across the fence-lined road.

To the south, the McDowell Mountains rose majestically, their tips swallowed by the clouds. To the east, glorious desert terrain stretched as far as the eye could see. Every half mile or so, they passed a house, often with barns and horses. To their left, a scattered herd of grazing cattle could be seen in the distance.

"It's pretty here," Ryan commented. "I've never driven this far off the main road."

"This is actually the oldest part of Mustang Valley. The cattle ranch over there belongs to the Peralta family, one of the first families to settle here back in the 1800s."

"No kidding!"

Bridget pointed, her stomach a ball of nervous energy. "See the turnoff ahead?"

Ryan swung the steering wheel, and they ambled along the poorly maintained dirt drive. A moment later, a ramshackle two-story house came into view that looked like the only inhabitants were ghosts.

Ryan pulled into the semicircle driveway and parked. "Where are we?"

"This belongs to the Ruiz brothers. They inherited it from their dad, who passed away last year. It's been empty almost four years, which is when he had a stroke and they moved him to a nursing home. He let the property go long before then, obviously, and no one's done anything with it since. The brothers couldn't agree. Until now. They've decided to unload it. That's the term the family's attorney used when I spoke to him."

Ryan climbed out of the truck and started walking toward the house.

Bridget hurried to keep pace. "There's acreage. Not much, but enough to run twenty or thirty head. The attorney says the brothers are very eager to sell and are getting ready to list it."

"Did he happened to mention the price?"

She told him.

Ryan whistled. "Not cheap."

"There aren't many places for sale in Mustang Valley with this kind of acreage."

"The house is no more than a pile of timbers. It needs to be leveled and a new one built."

"But look at the barn!" Bridget grabbed his hand and pulled him with her around the side of the house. "It could have come off the pages of a calendar. With a little work, it'll be spectacular."

"It is nice." He slung an arm around her shoulders. "Let me guess. You think I should buy the place."

"Well…" She smiled.

"It needs a ton of work. We're talking years."

She curled into him and rested her head on his shoulder. "Wouldn't that be fun? Building a house from the ground up?"

"Honey, I can't afford it. The asking price is three times what I have in my account. And there'd be nothing left over for remodeling, much less building a new house. I'd have to take out a mortgage."

"But a ranch like this is your dream."

"Still out of reach."

She extracted herself to face him. This was the moment of truth. The reason she'd brought him here. "Not if we did this together. Pooled our resources. We could build an apartment in the barn and live there until the house was finished. Then, your parents could move here and have the apartment, if they wanted."

"Thought about this some, have you?"

"A little."

Their gazes met. His was intense and unwavering. "That would require a big commitment from you."

"You, too." She held her breath. Waiting, hoping, praying.

He looked around, saying nothing, his features contemplative.

Bridget immediately worried she'd gone too far. He'd barely sold one property, and she was suggesting he buy a new one that was well beyond his price range. And she was throwing herself in as part of the deal. For someone supposedly willing to wait until he was ready to settle down, she was sure rushing him.

"Forget it." She started to walk away. "I was wrong."

He hooked her arm, preventing her escape. "I didn't say no."

"It's too much. I overstepped."

"What if I said I was willing to talk to the attorney?"

Excitement bubbled inside her. "Really?"

"On one condition. And it's a big one. Huge."

"What?"

Ryan let go of her and dug in his jeans pocket, withdrawing a small black velvet box. "If we do this together, and believe me, I want that more than anything, we do it as man and wife."

Bridget's heart lurched. "When did you…?" She couldn't finish. Her jumbled emotions were interfering with her brain's ability to form coherent speech.

"This morning. Before I picked you up."

"Ryan! You shouldn't have spent your money on a ring."

He thumbed open the box lid. A stunning half-carat diamond solitaire caught the sun's rays and reflected them back in a hundred shimmering slivers of light.

"Are you saying no?" he teased. "Because I can return the ring."

"What! Absolutely not." She squealed with delight. "Yes, I'll marry you."

Laughing, he removed the solitaire from the box and reached for her left hand. "Technically, I haven't proposed yet."

"You were taking too long." She gasped when he slipped the ring on her finger and, after admiring it, threw her arms around his neck. "It's gorgeous."

"I love you, Bridget. I want to make a life with you. In this house, or another one. Anywhere. As long as we're together."

"I love you, too."

They kissed, sealing their vows with a language known only to people in love. Bridget had to admit, Ryan was rather proficient at it.

When they finally separated, she reached into her pocket. She had something for him, too.

"Want to look inside the house?" She held up a key. "I drove into Scottsdale yesterday and picked this up from the attorney."

He grinned. "Let's go."

Racing for the front door, they unlocked it and stepped across the threshold.

"Wait," Bridget exclaimed. "I forgot my tablet in the truck. We might want to start a list."

"Leave it," Ryan said. "No lists. Not today."

He was right. Besides, she had a feeling they'd be returning very soon.

* * * * *

Look for the next book in Cathy McDavid's
The Sweetheart Ranch miniseries,
The Cowboy's Christmas Baby,
coming November 2019,
only from Harlequin Heartwarming!

Get 4 FREE REWARDS!

We'll send you 2 FREE Books plus 2 FREE Mystery Gifts.

Love Inspired® books feature contemporary inspirational romances with Christian characters facing the challenges of life and love.

FREE Value Over **$20**

YES! Please send me 2 FREE Love Inspired® Romance novels and my 2 FREE mystery gifts (gifts are worth about $10 retail). After receiving them, if I don't wish to receive any more books, I can return the shipping statement marked "cancel." If I don't cancel, I will receive 6 brand-new novels every month and be billed just $5.24 for the regular-print edition or $5.74 each for the larger-print edition in the U.S., or $5.74 each for the regular-print edition or $6.24 each for the larger-print edition in Canada. That's a savings of at least 13% off the cover price. It's quite a bargain! Shipping and handling is just 50¢ per book in the U.S. and 75¢ per book in Canada.* I understand that accepting the 2 free books and gifts places me under no obligation to buy anything. I can always return a shipment and cancel at any time. The free books and gifts are mine to keep no matter what I decide.

Choose one: ☐ **Love Inspired® Romance Regular-Print** (105/305 IDN GMY4)   ☐ **Love Inspired® Romance Larger-Print** (122/322 IDN GMY4)

Name (please print)

Address   Apt. #

City   State/Province   Zip/Postal Code

Mail to the **Reader Service:**
IN U.S.A.: P.O. Box 1341, Buffalo, NY 14240-8531
IN CANADA: P.O. Box 603, Fort Erie, Ontario L2A 5X3

Want to try 2 free books from another series? Call 1-800-873-8635 or visit www.ReaderService.com.

---

*Terms and prices subject to change without notice. Prices do not include sales taxes, which will be charged (if applicable) based on your state or country of residence. Canadian residents will be charged applicable taxes. Offer not valid in Quebec. This offer is limited to one order per household. Books received may not be as shown. Not valid for current subscribers to Love Inspired Romance books. All orders subject to approval. Credit or debit balances in a customer's account(s) may be offset by any other outstanding balance owed by or to the customer. Please allow 4 to 6 weeks for delivery. Offer available while quantities last.

Your Privacy—The Reader Service is committed to protecting your privacy. Our Privacy Policy is available online at www.ReaderService.com or upon request from the Reader Service. We make a portion of our mailing list available to reputable third parties that offer products we believe may interest you. If you prefer that we not exchange your name with third parties, or if you wish to clarify or modify your communication preferences, please visit us at www.ReaderService.com/consumerschoice or write to us at Reader Service Preference Service, P.O. Box 9062, Buffalo, NY 14240-9062. Include your complete name and address.

LI19R

Get 4 FREE REWARDS!

We'll send you 2 FREE Books plus 2 FREE Mystery Gifts.

UNDERCOVER MEMORIES
NEW YORK TIMES BESTSELLING AUTHOR
LENORA WORTH
LARGER PRINT

VALIANT DEFENDER
SHARLEE McCOY
MILITARY K-9 UNIT

Love Inspired® Suspense books feature Christian characters facing challenges to their faith... and lives.

FREE
Value Over $20

THE FORTUNES OF TEXAS COLLECTION!

18 FREE BOOKS in all!

Treat yourself to the rich legacy of the Fortune and Mendoza clans in this remarkable 50-book collection. This collection is packed with cowboys, tycoons and Texas-sized romances!

YES! Please send me **The Fortunes of Texas Collection** in Larger Print. This collection begins with 3 FREE books and 2 FREE gifts in the first shipment. Along with my 3 free books, I'll also get the next 4 books from The Fortunes of Texas Collection, in LARGER PRINT, which I may either return and owe nothing, or keep for the low price of $5.24 U.S./$5.89 CDN each plus $2.99 for shipping and handling per shipment*. If I decide to continue, about once a month for 8 months I will get 6 or 7 more books but will only need to pay for 4. That means 2 or 3 books in every shipment will be FREE! If I decide to keep the entire collection, I'll have paid for only 32 books because 18 books are FREE! I understand that accepting the 3 free books and gifts places me under no obligation to buy anything. I can always return a shipment and cancel at any time. My free books and gifts are mine to keep no matter what I decide.

☐ 269 HCN 4622   ☐ 469 HCN 4622

Name (please print)

Address   Apt. #

City   State/Province   Zip/Postal Code

Mail to the **Reader Service:**
IN U.S.A.: P.O. Box 1341, Buffalo, N.Y. 14240-8531
IN CANADA: P.O. Box 603, Fort Erie, Ontario L2A 5X3